IV

The Girl Who Ran Off with Daddy

Kiddo
Boss
The Man Who Died Laughing
The Man Who Lived by Night
The Man Who Would Be F. Scott Fitzgerald
The Woman Who Fell from Grace
The Boy Who Never Grew Up
The Man Who Cancelled Himself

The Girl Who Ran Off with Daddy

David Handler

A Stewart Hoag Novel

DOUBLEDAY

New York
London
Toronto
Sydney
Auckland

PUBLISHED BY DOUBLEDAY
a division of Bantam Doubleday Dell Publishing Group, Inc.
1540 Broadway, New York, New York 10036

DOUBLEDAY and the portrayal of an anchor with a dolphin are
trademarks of Doubleday, a division of Bantam Doubleday Dell
Publishing Group, Inc.

Library of Congress Cataloging-in-Publication Data

Handler, David, 1952–
The girl who ran off with daddy: a Stewart Hoag mystery/David Handler.
  p. cm.
1. Hoag, Stewart (Fictitious character)—Fiction. I. Title.
PS3558.A4637G57 1996
813'.54—dc20 95-21938
CIP

ISBN 0-385-47528-4
Copyright © 1996 by David Handler
All Rights Reserved
Printed in the United States of America
April 1996
First Edition

10 9 8 7 6 5 4 3 2 1

For Laura Felice,
my favorite sister

The Girl Who Ran Off with Daddy

One

Sometimes as I sleep I hear a creak on the stairs. For a moment I think it is my father on his way down to the kitchen for a glass of milk in the night, and that I am in my old room, snug in my narrow bed. Briefly, this comforts me. But then I awaken, and realize that it is my own house that is creaking, from the wind, and that I am in the master bedroom. She sleeps next to me, secure in the belief that I know what I'm doing. I don't know what I'm doing.

I wonder if he did. I wonder why he was awake in the night. I wish I could ask him. But it is too late for that. It is too late for a lot of things.

I WAS CHANGING Tracy's diapers at four o'clock in the morning when Thor Gibbs showed up. Not the height of glamorous living, I'll give you that one. And definitely not something I thought I'd ever be caught doing for any midget human life form, particularly my own. But, hey, you want the whole story, you're going to get the whole story—poopy and all.

It was his bad black '68 Norton Commando I heard first. I heard its roar from miles away in the still of the country night. Heard it grow closer and closer, then pause. Then came the crunching of gravel as he eased it up the long, private drive that led from Joshua Town Road to the farmhouse. Silence followed. This didn't last long. Silence was always brief when Thor Gibbs was around.

"How the hell are you, boy?" he asked me, standing out there on the porch. He was not alone. *She* was with him, sitting on the bike untangling her mane of windblown hair with her fingers.

I stood in the doorway holding the baby, a towel thrown over the shoulder of my Turnbull and Asser silk dressing gown to guard against the seven different categories of discharges Tracy was capable of producing—the standard six plus one more for which there was still no known scientific classification. "About as well as can be expected," I replied.

He threw back his head and roared like a lion. "Same old Hoagy."

"Quality, you'll find, never goes out of style." I glanced up at our bedroom window, which overlooked the herb garden and was open. "Better hold it down or we'll wake Merilee."

"And we don't want to do that, do we?" Thor boomed, grinning at me mischievously.

"Not if we know what's good for us."

"Never have, Hoagy. Never have and never will." He stuck his finger in Tracy's tiny palm. She gripped it tightly, giggling and cooing at him. A born flirt. Then again, as David Letterman was so fond of pointing out, Thor Gibbs had a way with small children. "Christ, she has Merilee's eyes."

"And you, Thor?"

"Me, boy?"

"How are you?"

"Still kicking."

That he was. Thor was seventy-one that year, but it was hard to imagine it, looking at him. The man still possessed such remarkable vigor, such charisma, such *power*. Always, it seemed, he had drawn on an energy source that the rest of us could only wonder about. He was a big man, burly and weatherbeaten, with scarred, knuckly hands and a bushy gray beard and that trademark gleaming dome of his. It was Thor who had made the clean-head look all the rage among fifty-something white-collar professionals in quest of their lost hormones. He had a huge neck and chest, dock ropes for wrists and a mouthful of strong white teeth, one of the front ones still missing from a bar fight in Key West with Hemingway, which made him look even more ornery and disreputable than he. He wore a fringed buckskin vest over an old Irish fisherman's sweater, jeans and cowboy boots, a bracelet of hammered silver and turquoise. His posture was erect, his stomach flat, his electric-blue eyes clear and bright. The man didn't even seem the least bit tired.

She did. Clethra sure did. Little Clethra, Thor's eighteen-year-old stepdaughter—and lover. She was making her way slowly toward us now, yawning and shivering and looking rather miserable. Or maybe she was just a little bit overwhelmed by it all. After all, she had just stolen her own mother's celebrated husband and dropped out of Barnard so as to run off with him who knows where. And Thor had just destroyed his marriage to her celebrated mother, Ruth Feingold—that's right, the feminist—so as to run off with her, this girl he'd raised as his own since she was three, this girl who was fifty-three years younger than he. Face it, at that particular moment in American history, Thor Gibbs and Clethra Feingold were right up there among the oddest, the sleaziest, the most notorious couples of all time. Bigger than Woody and Soon-Yi. Bigger than Joey and Amy. Bigger than Jacko and Lisa Marie. *Big.* And here they were, standing on Merilee's porch by the light of a silvery moon. Harvest moon, as it happened.

"Where are you headed, Thor?"

"Here," he replied simply.

"Here?" I cleared my throat and tried it over again, minus the surprise. "Here?"

"Rode all night. We have to talk, boy. But first . . ." He put his big arm around Clethra. She snuggled into him, her teeth chattering. "I want you to say hello to my . . ."

"Yes, what is it you call her now?"

Thor's blue eyes twinkled. "My woman."

"It's nice to see you again, Clethra."

She stared at me blankly. One of her more common facial expressions, I was to discover. She said, "Like, do we know each other?"

"It's been a while. You had just graduated to big-girl pants the time I saw you."

She rolled her eyes at me, unimpressed. Another common expression.

I shifted Tracy, cradling her into me. "I sure wish I could make up my mind, Thor."

He frowned. "About what?"

"Whether to hug you or hit you."

Thor raised his massive chin at me. "How about giving me a glass of sour mash and some eggs? And maybe just a little understanding, for old times' sake."

"I can do that. Come on in."

We went on in. Clethra made right for the glowing embers in the front parlor fireplace and warmed her chubby white hands. I threw another hickory log on, poked at it and got a good look at her. The most sensational homewrecker since Amy Fisher was a small, moonfaced girl, rather pretty, with big brown eyes and a plump, heart-shaped mouth that she painted blue. Or maybe that was from the cold. She wore a gold ring in her right nostril. Her tangled black ringlets cascaded all the way down to her butt. It was a nice, ripe butt. In fact, Clethra Feingold was nice and ripe all over. Possibly she would end up shaped like her mother when she got older. Right now she was as luscious as a basket of fresh fruit, desirable in the old sense of the word, before spavined waifs like Kate Moss became our feminine ideal. An aged black leather motorcycle jacket fell carelessly from her shoulders, rather like a shawl. She wore a gray sweatshirt under it, a pair of baggy jeans torn at the knees and heavy, steel-toed Doc Martens. The look was part punk, part hip-hop and all fake. She was a product of the Dalton School and the Ivy League, not the street. But street was all the buzz that season. As for the sulky expression on her face, that went with being eighteen and always had. Same with the upper lip, which she kept curling at me in distaste, much the way Ricky Nelson used to when he sang. I didn't know if Clethra sang. I didn't want to know.

Lulu, my basset hound, marched right over and showed the little vixen her teeth. Lulu doesn't care for homewreckers. Never has.

Clethra widened her eyes. "Like, does she bite?"

"Only people she knows real well," I assured her. "Total strangers she's just fine with."

She shrugged at this and looked around at the parlor. She did not seem impressed. I didn't expect her to be. It wasn't huge or flashy. Center chimney colonials tended not to be in 1736, which was when the place had been built by Josiah Whitcomb, a shipbuilder by trade. The recessed cupboards and drawers flanking the stone fireplace, all of them of butternut, were Josiah's doing. So was the chestnut paneling and the wide planks of cherry on the floor. The rest we had brought with us. The Shaker tall clock made and signed by Ben Youngs in Watervliet, New York, in 1806. The Shaker meeting room bench and ladder-back rockers, the baskets filled with Merilee's newly harvested lavender and artemisia. The muzzle loader over the fireplace, which had belonged to her great-great-grandfather, Elihu, and was five feet long and weighed over forty pounds. The paintings of dead pilgrims, all of them Merilee's ancestors. The worn leather sofa that was our only concession to modern comfort and my bony backside.

Clethra took it all in, slowly, as if she were computing its resale value piece by piece. "I'm, like, you don't have a TV," she noted with some dismay.

"It's in the corner cupboard."

"How come?"

"So we don't have to look at it when we're not looking at it."

"Whoa, that makes, like, zero sense, homes," she informed me with an insolent toss of her head. Bashful with her opinions she wasn't. This, too, went with being eighteen. "Like, you *know* it's in there, right? So isn't *hiding* it just, like, totally bogus or what?"

"Or what," I suggested. This was me being pleasant. Or what passes for pleasant from me at four A.M.

She fished a Camel out of her jacket pocket and stuck it between her teeth, reaching for a match on the mantel.

"Please don't light that," I said.

"Oh, God. It's the green planet pigs."

"No, it's Tracy."

"Huh?"

"The baby, Clethra," Thor explained patiently. "You mustn't smoke that in front of the baby."

She sighed hugely and stuffed the cigarette back in her pocket. She twirled her hair around one finger. She turned her inattention back to me. "Is there a bathroom?"

"Down the hall, first door on your right. Don't mind the changing table—or the smell."

"Or the *what?*"

"Never mind."

She went flouncing off.

I turned and looked at Thor. "Nice girl."

He looked away, unable to meet my gaze. "Damned place is like a museum, boy," he said, running his hand over his slick dome.

"I'll take that as a compliment."

"I gave it as one. Damned hard to find, though."

"That," I explained, "is kind of the whole idea."

Tracy began wriggling in my arms. And then she launched into her mow-girl cry, the one where she sputtered three times, caught and started wailing very much like one of the larger Toro power models. She did this one whenever she wanted to be fed. Not my department. I excused us and carried her upstairs to the buffet table. Merilee was already starting to stir there under her aunt Patience's diamond-pattern quilt.

"One of us," I whispered, "is hungry."

Merilee grumbled something about having to leave an extra jar of Bosco in the trailer. She often mutters incoherently when awakened in the night. Me, I'm at my best. Slowly, she sat up, yawning and blinking from the hall light, long golden hair tousled, eyes puffy. She fumbled with her flannel nightshirt, half asleep, and then held her arms out to me, her hands clad in the white cotton gloves she wore to bed every night over a generous coating of Bag Balm, the old farmer's unguent she applied to her paws after a long day in the garden. It was a little like going to bed with Minnie Mouse. Actually, I should warn you: This was not the same Merilee Nash. She was not the woman she'd been when we met. In those days, our sunshine days, Merilee was about diamonds and pearls and Bobby Short's midnight show at the Cafe Carlyle. Now she was about beneficial nematodes and compost worms—and Tracy, who spent her days out there in the garden with her, swaddled in her old-fashioned Silver Cross buggy, gurgling happily.

I handed her over. Dinner was served.

"I could have sworn I heard voices," she murmured in that feathery teenaged girl's voice that is hers and hers alone.

"You must have been dreaming," I said quickly. Too quickly.

She raised an eyebrow at me. "At this time of night? Who is it?"

"You don't want to know." I hesitated, tugging at my ear. "It's Thor."

She made a face. She'd backed Ruth's mayoral campaign to the limit, and had been crushed by her narrow defeat. Ruth she adored. Thor—well, you can guess how she felt about Thor. "What does *he* want?"

"So far, he wants some eggs. I don't know what else he wants."

"Is *she* with him?"

"*She* is."

Merilee gazed up at me, her green eyes shimmering. "Hoagy . . ."

"Don't say it, Merilee. And don't worry. They'll be gone by morning."

I took the narrow back stairs down to the big, old farm kitchen, which was probably my favorite room in the house. We'd left it pretty much as we'd found it. The gallantly hideous yellow and red linoleum on the floor. The deep double worksink of scarred white porcelain. The tin-paneled pie safe that someone long ago had painted a color not unlike belly lox. The butcher block, a massive two-foot-thick section of maple set atop short, stubby legs. We'd added the drying racks, from which Merilee's cooking herbs hung in huge bunches, and the stove, a massive four-oven AGA cast-iron that Merilee imported from Great Britain. Martha Stewart has one. Happily, that's the only thing Merilee and Martha Stewart have in common. Our kitchen table was a washhouse table from the Shaker colony in Mount Lebanon, New York, where the tongue and groove machine was first invented in 1828. Thor sat there with his elbows resting on it, waiting for me.

I put two skillets on the AGA and started them heating. There was a supply of single malt in the cupboard. I poured us each two fingers of the Macallan and handed him one. He added some well water to his and drank it right down, gripping it tightly. He suddenly looked tired and old and shaken. I'd never seen him look any of those things before.

He made himself another and sat with it, knuckling his deep-set blue eyes. "Clethra's curled up before the fire. All fagged out, poor child."

"Will she be hungry?"

"She doesn't eat. Not meals, anyway."

I got the slab bacon out of the refrigerator and cut four thick slices for him and put them in the skillet. As soon as I got a whiff of them sizzling I cut four more for myself and laid those in alongside his. There were some boiled new potatoes left over. I sliced them up and got them going in the other skillet with a clove of Merilee's elephant garlic. By now Lulu was standing on my foot. She wanted an anchovy and she wanted it now. She likes them cold from the fridge. The oil clings better. I gave her one. I got the eggs out. I put on water for coffee. Like many men who had spent years at sea, Thor drank it strong and by the gallon, even right before he went to bed.

I sat, sipping my scotch. Lulu curled up at my feet under the table. "Why did you do it, Thor?"

"I'm in love, boy. It's that simple."

"Nothing's that simple."

"A man's heart is," he lectured, carefully stroking his luxuriant beard. He always did this when he was holding forth, whether his audience was one or one thousand. "A resolved man's heart, that is. Man is by nature a conqueror, Hoagy. A warrior. If he sees someone he wants, he must grab hold of her. Take her and be proud."

"You're proud?"

"Why not?" he shot back indignantly. "Clethra's someone very, very special. A woman worth having. And, trust me, a woman worth having almost always belongs to someone else."

"Yes. Your wife, in this case."

He narrowed his eyes at me, stung. "You're not seeing my side, are you?"

I got up and turned the bacon. "I'm trying, Thor."

"This is the child's physical and spiritual awakening," he explained. "Christ, better me to guide her into mature womanhood than some clumsy premature ejaculator who'll be out the door as soon as he empties his carbine into her, some pimply hit-and-run artist who'll make her feel shitty about herself and hateful toward the male of the species. With me she's getting an enriching, life-affirming experience. Something beautiful." He sighed contentedly. "Besides which, she's a splendid young animal, eager and insatiable and—"

"I don't need to hear this part."

"You can't suppress the wild man, boy," Thor intoned. "You must celebrate him. The spirit must live."

"And where, may I ask, is yours living?"

He sat there in heavy silence a moment, his big chest rising and falling. "Nowhere. All we have is the clothes on our backs. Not so much as a suitcase between us. We've been persecuted, pilloried and reviled. I am not a criminal, Hoagy. I've broken no laws. But the thought police have tried, convicted and sentenced me—for being incorrect. As if correctness were some sort of goal. Correctness isn't a goal, it's a disease that's sapping us, depleting us, killing us all one by one by one!" His fists were clenched now, his bald dome agleam with sweat. The man did like to go on. As always, half of what he said was stimulating and challenging, and half was bullshit. As always, the trick was figuring out which half. "These are dangerous times we live in, boy. Dangerous times. Irrationality is one of man's greatest gifts. It's what sets us apart from machines. We should be down on our knees paying homage to it, not trying to suppress it. The single most important thing a man can do in this world is go a little bit crazy from time to time."

"Then I guess that makes you and me a couple of pretty important guys."

He let out a short, harsh laugh. "They're killing me, boy. *She's* killing me."

"Ruth?"

He nodded. "She's put a stop on my credit cards, frozen my assets. She's even gotten a court order barring me from seeing my own son."

"Surely you're not surprised."

"Not surprised," he admitted. "Disappointed. I miss him. Arvin's the very best part of me. And this is all so hard on him." Thor folded his big scarred hands on the table, staring down at them. "She's a stubborn woman, Ruth. A proud woman. She won't let us be—not without a fight."

"And to the victor goes the spoiled?"

He grinned at me, the aw-shucks, gap-toothed country boy grin. "You'll like that girl once you break through her crust. This whole experience has made her hard on the outside. Can't blame her. But inside she's got a lot of Ruth in her. Helluva woman, Ruth."

"I always thought so."

"She always thought you were a delight."

"She doesn't know me very well."

He drained his whiskey and reached for the bottle. "Is there a novel?"

I poked at the potatoes in the skillet. "I'm working every day."

"Is it good work?"

"Only if you consider crap good."

"I'd like to read it."

"No, you wouldn't."

He frowned at me, considering this. "What else are you doing with yourself?"

"Doing with myself?"

"Out here, I mean. Do you hunt?"

"Don't own a gun."

"Why not?"

"Guns go off."

"We should camp out, you and me. Like the old days. Howl at the moon. Talk trash. Drink mash. We should do that."

The bacon and potatoes were done. I cracked the eggs into the pan. And said, "What are you doing here, Thor?"

He leveled his gaze at me. "They think Clethra's a star waiting to happen."

"Who does?"

"Her publisher."

"Clethra has a publisher?"

"They want her to tell her story, Hoagy. Why our love happened. How it happened. Her side. Her words. They're giving her two million dollars to tell it. More goddamned *dinero* than I've made in my entire career. We sure can use it, too." He took a gulp of his drink. "You don't seem surprised."

"Nothing about the publishing business surprises me anymore." I got out plates and forks. "All that matters to them is that you two are hot right now."

"Oh, no, they're thinking beyond right now."

"Okay, that does surprise me."

"They're going to make her into the next major new voice in American feminism," he proclaimed loftily. "She'll be as big as Ruth ever was—if not bigger." Thor, you should know, had never gone in for understatement. "They think her words will mean something to those millions of college girls out there who are searching for answers and for truths and for . . . what's that word they use now? *Empowerment.* Which, if you ask me, is just a politically correct way of saying a good, hard dick."

At my feet, Lulu let out a low moan of dissent.

"Will you supply those words for her, boy?" Thor asked, turning bashful. Bashful was a new one. "Will you write it with her?"

I put his food in front of him, along with a bottle of Tabasco sauce, which Thor ate on pretty much everything, including Grape-Nuts. "Why me?"

"Because a woman writer will turn it into some ballbusting feminista manifesto, that's why," he replied, ignoring his food.

"So why don't *you* write it with her?"

"I'm no good at that kind of thing. Not like you are."

"I'll take that as a compliment, too."

"I gave it as one. It's a genuine gift you have, boy."

"Don't remind me." I sat with my own food and dug in. "I'm sorry, Thor, but I'm all grown-up now. I've quit the circus."

"No one has to know you're involved," he persisted. "Not even Clethra's publisher. We can pay you right out of her end."

"I don't want her money."

"And this place is ideal." He gazed out the window at the purplish pre-dawn. "Not a soul will be able to find us here."

"Here?" I cleared my throat and tried it again, minus the surprise. "Here?"

"Why not? It's the perfect hideout for a few weeks. And, wait, I know exactly what you're thinking . . ."

"No, Thor, I don't believe you do."

"I'll work hard for my keep while you two are busy writing. I'll chop wood. I'll clear brush. There's no job I won't do. And there's nothing I can't build or repair." This was true. Thor had been just about everything in his time —merchant seaman, forest ranger, railroad brakeman, even an ordained minister. "How about it, boy?"

I shook my head. "Thor, it's out of the question. That chapter of my career is over. Besides which, there's Merilee to consider. There's the baby . . ." At my feet, Lulu grunted. ". . . There's Little Miss Short Legs."

"Will you at least think about it?"

"I'll think about it. But I'm not doing it."

"Good man," he exclaimed, grinning at me. "Knew I could count on you."

"I said I'd think about it, period," I snapped. "Now shut up and eat your eggs."

But he kept right on grinning at me. Because I was going to say yes—and he and I both knew it. Because he was my friend. Because he needed me. And because once, twenty years ago, when I was standing at the crossroads, not sure whether to shit or go blind, Thor Gibbs had come along and changed *my* diapers.

. . . . .

Thorvin Alston Gibbs. Ah, me. Where to begin? He was, perhaps more than anything else, a grizzled son of the Big Sky Country. Part cowboy, part wilderness advocate, part champion hell-raiser—a bard of the barroom, through and through. And the last of the literary he-men. His autobiographical first novel, *A Montana Boyhood,* published in 1949, squared him right up against Mailer as the most gifted novelist of the post-war era. Critics even labeled him the heir apparent to Hemingway himself. Thor was, in fact, the last man to interview Papa. And the first to champion the Beat era. It was Thor Gibbs who coined the expression "beat generation." He was a pallbearer at Kerouac's funeral. He held Cassady's head when the legendary hipster died by the side of the railroad tracks in Mexico. He rode the bus with Kesey's Merry Pranksters. And he inspired a generation of young writers to dream.

Chief among them—me. Thor Gibbs was writer-in-residence for a year at that overrated Ivy League breeding ground where I received my so-called education. He was my teacher, my drinking companion, my mentor. It was Thor Gibbs who gave me the courage to take those first faltering steps down my own road. It was Thor Gibbs who pushed me, goaded me, dared me to transform my raw, feverish ramblings into a novel—*the* novel. It was Thor Gibbs who pronounced me a writer and proudly passed my manuscript on to his agent. I dedicated the first one to him. So did other writers of my generation. Thor Gibbs was our hero, our guru, our shaman. I suppose he was the only man I'd ever looked up to and, possibly, even loved.

Which is not to say that everyone was crazy about Thor Gibbs. A great number of women, for example, had hated his guts ever since the 1980 publication of *The Dickless Decade,* his bestselling male-backlash treatise which dared to link the decline of America in the post-Vietnam era to the rise of modern feminism. "Seemingly overnight, we have gone from the America of Tricky Dicky to the America of limp dicks," Thor wrote in his trademark incendiary prose. "In the name of women's rights we have created a generation of tame, passive, spiritually detumescent little whiners. Men who are afraid to lead, afraid to create, afraid to dream. These are the new lost boys, and they are dragging this once mighty nation down with them." Seemingly overnight, *The Dickless Decade* transformed Thor Gibbs into the high priest of the hairy-chested men's movement—and possibly the most famous chauvinist pig in America. To feminists, he was a loudmouthed troglodyte, a misogynistic boob. He was Rush Limbaugh in faded blue jeans and Native American jewelry.

Not that he hated women. He had loved and been loved by many women through the years, including a number of rather famous men's wives. But no woman had he loved quite so passionately, so publicly and so improbably as Ruth Feingold. Baby Ruth, the self-described loudmouthed New York broad, the crusading public defender and U.S. congresswoman, and one of the driving forces of the women's movement in America for the past thirty years. A co-founder of the National Organization for Women as well as a major ERA and abortion rights activist, Ruth Feingold was one of the movement's founding four. Betty Friedan was its architect. Gloria Steinem was its face. Bella Abzug was its engine. And Ruth Feingold was its mouth. She'd debate anyone, anywhere, anytime. She was a windup sound bite, a feisty pit bull, impatient, prickly and razor sharp. It was a few months after her unsuccessful 1978 bid for mayor of New York that her marriage to millionaire real estate scion Barry Feingold went belly up. He left her for a man (or another man, as numerous wags quipped), the young fashion designer Marco Paolo, who went on to popularize the Hasidic look in leisure wear. Barry Feingold left Ruth with their little girl, Clethra, and some serious ill will. She met Thor Gibbs not long after that on *MacNeil Lehrer*. The two of them had been brought in to debate the ERA. Their heavyweight confrontation was such a whopping success that a lecture agency decided to pit them against each other on the college campus circuit, much as they had Timothy Leary and G. Gordon Liddy. To everyone's shock, they fell madly in love (Thor and Baby Ruth, not Timothy Leary and G. Gordon Liddy—at least not as far as I know). They got married. They had a son, Arvin, presently aged fourteen, for whom Thor had penned *The Thinking Man's Diet,* his slim little guidebook of pithy thoughts on modern maleness ("Every man should own at least one dog and one motorcycle in his lifetime, and learn how to take good care of both"), which enjoyed a robust 173 consecutive weeks on the *New York Times* bestseller list. And, inevitably, led to *The Thinking Man's Diet for Mind and Body,* a he-guy celebration of beans, nuts and wild greens. Low on cholesterol. High on flatulence. It, too, became a bestseller.

And then it blew up big time. Mega-big time.

Thor had just left Ruth for little Clethra. The pair claimed to be madly, passionately, blindly in love—and Ruth be damned. Devastated, outraged and humiliated, Ruth first tried to take her own life with sleeping pills. When that failed, this noted champion of battered spouses then tried to take Thor's life with an eight-inch boning knife, an attack for which she was widely applauded by sympathetic women on a number of television talk shows. When *that* failed she went to court—suing for sole custody of Arvin. According to Ruth, Thor was perverted, evil and totally unfit to be a father. According to Ruth, this was a man who had actually been having sexual relations with his own stepdaughter in their own home while Clethra was only sixteen, which in New York State constituted statutory rape. And which opened the door to criminal proceedings. Thor had countersued, branding Ruth as not only desperately insane but as a physically abusive parent. Clethra was claiming that her famous mom routinely beat both her daughter and Arvin about the head and neck with her fists, her open hands and sometimes a rolled-up newspaper. *The Village Voice,* if you must know. Frequently, Clethra charged, she even drew blood. For the time being, a judge had sided with Ruth, barring Thor from seeing Arvin. But the bitter custody case was still working its way through the courts.

And, mostly, through the media. It was a first-class tabloid whopper, an egonomic calamity of global proportions, the loudest, tawdriest, horniest real-life soap opera of the year.

Everyone, it seemed, had dirt to spill. Arvin's onetime nanny, a Colombian woman whom Thor said he'd fired years before for stealing, claimed she found the macho author and his stepdaughter together on the girl's bed when Clethra was only fourteen. His finger, the nanny revealed, was where it shouldn't have been. And Clethra was moaning with pure animal pleasure. *And* little Arvin was watching . . . A would-be poetess who had once been a college classmate of mine and was now a high-ranking official of the Home Shopping Network claimed Thor had routinely forced her and other attractive young students to perform oral sex on him in his office while he talked dirty to them. She said he smelled like a goat.

Everyone, it seemed, had a joke. Did you hear? Thor Gibbs is writing his life story. He's going to call it *Honey, I Fucked the Kids.*

Everyone, it seemed, had an opinion. "I'm sorry, but decent men do not mess around with the siblings of their children," wrote one outraged *Daily News* columnist. "I don't care if she was fourteen at the time or sixteen or seventeen. It's still de facto incest." Many of his followers felt betrayed by him. "Thor Gibbs showed me the way," wrote a Fortune 500 CEO in a letter to *The Wall Street Journal.* "He taught me how to live my own life when I thought I had forgotten how. Now who do I turn to?"

Opinion about Clethra was quite divided. Some thought she was a dirty, conniving little nympho. Others felt she was merely the sexual prey of a sick, cruel older man. Her mother's stand remained unequivocal. "Clethra is not to blame," Ruth stated flatly. "I want her to know I love her. I want her to know she can come home anytime she wants." Possibly the most poignant opinion of all came from the youngest member of the family. "Dear Dad," young Arvin wrote in an open letter that was widely reprinted. "Why can't we be a family again? Why can't we just love each other?"

Why, indeed. No one had a very good answer to that one. Except that it was way too late. All of them had become the human bait in that season's media feeding frenzy. Trashed for cash and burned. And once that happens there is no going back. And there are no longer any heroes and there are no longer any villains. There are just victims.

With the possible exception of little Clethra, who wasn't making out too shabbily. After all, she was getting the man she loved, two million dollars and a career—her publisher wanted to morph her into a feminist star like her mother before her. Shrewd thinking on their part. The women's movement needed stars, needed leaders, needed an agenda. Since its heyday of twenty years before, it had become splintered and somewhat besieged. Personalities had clashed. Feuds had erupted. And the center had given way. There were no vanilla feminists anymore. There were eco-feminists, deconstructed feminists and post-feminists. There were neo-feminists, New Age feminists and egalitarian feminists. There were victim feminists and there were power feminists. There were radical feminists like Andrea Dworkin and Catharine MacKinnon and there were anti-feminists like Hurricane Camille Paglia. True, abortion remained a powerful issue. True, a galvanizing event like the Clarence Thomas hearings emerged from time to time to unite everyone. But for many women, such as the millions of single working mothers who were just trying to survive month to month, there really was no women's movement anymore. Just a shelf marked Self Help at the nearest chain bookstore, where women ran with wolves or from wolves, where women loved too much or too little, where their genuine fears and fantasies were reduced to so much touchy-feely grist for the psychobabble mill. More than anything, the movement needed new blood. There were a few young stars, like lite feminist Naomi Wolf, author of *The Beauty Myth,* and Katie Roiphe, who had written *The Morning After* when she was barely out of college. But no one who'd been able to grab center stage and hold it. So why not she of the royal blood? Why not Ruth Feingold's own daughter, Clethra? She already had one leg up, so to speak. She was a famous bad girl, a rebel. Lots of young women would be anxious to hear what she had to say. No question there.

The only problem was I didn't feel like helping her say it. And about this there was no question either.

Me, I'd been living the sweet life on the farm for the past several months. Merilee's farm, technically. The one she'd bought after we split up the first time. Or maybe it was after we split up the second time. Who the hell can remember anymore? The farm was in Lyme, Connecticut, that relentlessly bucolic little Yankee eden situated at the mouth of the Connecticut River on Long Island Sound, halfway between New York City and Boston. Lyme, for all of you history buffs, was established in 1665 by whalers and shipbuilders. These days it was known mostly for ticks, as in Lyme disease. Also for its gentlemen's farms, its historic homes, its rich WASPs and its very rich WASPs. There was a town hall, a Congregational church, general store, boatyard, and not much else, unless you count cows. Modern civilization was seriously frowned upon in Lyme. No condos. No cinema multiplexes. No Golden Arches. Not much in the way of crime. Unless you count bad taste, and in Lyme they do. Lyme did pride itself on being open-minded. Minorities, eccentrics, even politicians were welcome, provided they didn't try too hard to impress—showiness of any kind was seriously frowned on. Good manners were considered important. Privacy was prized above all. Only a couple of thousand people lived there. Happily, very few were celebrities.

Actually, Merilee was probably the biggest one, but this tends to be true no matter where my ex-wife finds herself. Merilee Nash is a beautiful and glamorous star of stage and screen, winner of an Oscar and two Tonys. She doesn't exactly blend in. Lately, though, she'd been keeping a pretty low profile. We both had been. Call it a taste of early retirement. Call it an escape from the prying eyes of the so-called real world. Call it what you will. The simple truth was we wanted to be left the hell alone for a while. The farm was our safe haven. Eighteen acres in all. There was the main house with its seven working fireplaces. There was the post-and-beam carriage barn of hand-hewn chestnut, the chapel with its stained glass windows, the duck pond, the brook that babbled. There were the vegetable gardens and herb gardens and flower gardens, all of them Merilee's doing. There were the apple and pear orchards and the open pasturage that tumbled down to Whalebone Cove, where there were six acres of freshwater tidal marsh that held one of the state's largest remaining stands of wild rice, not to mention several rare marsh plants. Also birds, if you like birds. There were bald eagles, great blue herons, long-billed marsh wrens. In the fall, osprey hunted the shallows. For a while, Merilee had kept animals—until she developed an unfortunate attachment to Elliot, her late pig. So lately we'd shared our safe haven only with Lulu, my faithful, neurotic basset hound, and Sadie, the gray and white barn cat.

Oh, and there was the baby.

I suppose you want to hear my horrifying tales of the crib. All about it . . . her . . . *Tracy.* Everyone does. She was six months old that fall, blonde and beautiful, possessor of Merilee's bewitching emerald eyes and her full attention. As I'm sure you must know if you read a newspaper or watch *Hard Copy, A Current Affair, Inside Edition* or *Entertainment Tonight,* Merilee had decided to go have herself a love child. Much fuss was made over the identity of the father, since she told the world it wasn't me. Hey, she told *me* it wasn't me—until several weeks after the blessed event. She did this because she knew I wasn't big on midget human life-forms and because she didn't want to pressure me and because she is an actress, and therefore incapable of doing anything in a quiet, rational way. It was an ugly experience. I know I found it ugly. I can only imagine how it was for Merilee. The two of us weren't speaking at the time. This often happens when you throw together two highly gifted, highly sensitive semi-adults who are not completely sane. That fall, when Thor Gibbs showed up, we were. Speaking, that is. I had decided to forgive Merilee. And she had decided to let me.

Mostly, Merilee and Tracy were in their own little world. Tracy was *hers,* hooked up to her day and night. Me, I had my own full-time responsibility—Lulu, who deeply resented this new little throw pillow that drooled and spit up and cried and sometimes smelled really bad. We're talking serious sibling jealousy. I tried to convince her we loved her as much as we ever had. I got a videotape called *What About Me?* for the two of us to watch together. We read a story, Ezra Jack Keats's *Peter's Chair.* We even did a coloring book, *My Book About Our New Baby.* But it was no use. Lulu was inconsolable. Periodically, she'd even taken to wading morosely out into the middle of the duck pond with the intention of drowning herself. She can't swim, you see. I didn't know what to do about her. I only knew Merilee and I both had our hands full. It was just as well we'd both decided to retire for a while.

Not that I had walked away from my first career. Not me. Not Stewart Stafford Hoag, that tall, dashing author of that smashingly successful first novel *Our Family Enterprise,* the one that led *The New York Times* to label me "the first major new literary voice of the Eighties." I'm referring to my second career. I'm a pen for hire, a ghostwriter of celebrity memoirs. Not just any ghost, mind you. I am *the* ghost—the best money can't buy—with five, count 'em, five no. 1 bestselling memoirs to my non-credit, as well as somebody else's bestselling novel. I am not one of the lunchpail ghosts. I cost a helluva lot more, for one thing—generally a third of the action, including royalties. The usual As Told To kids don't command nearly so much. But they also don't know how to treat celebrities. They handle them with kid gloves. I wear steel mesh ones. I also carry a whip and a stool. And when I'm in the cage with them I never, ever let them know I'm afraid. If I did they'd eat me alive. There's something else that sets me apart from the others—and I'm not referring here to my wardrobe or to my uncommonly short, four-footed partner with the doofus ears and the unwholesome eating habits. It's simply that, well, some rather ugly things have this way of happening when I'm around. That's because memoirs, good ones at least, are about dirty secrets past and present. Generally, there's someone around who wants those secrets to stay safely buried. And will go to any length to make sure that they do. Just one of the many reasons why my days and nights doing the Claude Rains thing were behind me. Or so I had hoped and prayed.

I had given that all up so as to concentrate on novel number three. Yes, there was a novel number two, *Such Sweet Sorrow,* about the stormy marriage between a famous novelist and famous actress. Doesn't ring a bell? I'm not surprised. It hardly even got reviewed, unless you count that snotty capsule in *The New Yorker,* which called it "an appalling waste of trees." That one really hurt, because only God can make a tree. I don't know who or what makes critics. Possibly some form of virulent fungus. As for novel number three . . . it had been in progress for nearly four years now. Frankly, it was going a little slowly. Frankly, all I had to show for it was one paragraph. More of an image, really. A creak on the stairs. Not that this was all that I'd written. Hell, no. I'd written hundreds and hundreds of pages more. Whole plots, subplots, characters . . . You name it, I'd written it. And scrapped it. When you're young, writing is about the most fun you can have with your clothes on. You plunge recklessly ahead, utterly fearless, utterly convinced that no one has ever before done what you're doing. That gets harder as you get older. Because you realize that everything's already been said before—by better writers than you, by lesser writers than you and by you. Not that I was giving in to it. I rose early every morning and retreated to the chapel. It was a small chapel, one narrow room with no electricity and not much in it—one Franklin stove, one harvest table, one chair, one oil lamp, one typewriter, one former genius. There I sat, day after day, waiting for the damned thing to bubble to the surface. And waiting. But it wouldn't come. I was even beginning to wonder if it was there at all. This was me facing a cold, hard reality—that I simply didn't have anything more to say. Possibly I was even through.

Fortunately, there was plenty to keep me occupied outside. Autumn's your busy season in the country. Apples and pears to pick, firewood to lay in for winter, gardens to turn under, storm windows to repair, downed leaves to be gathered and shredded into mulch. The garden shed needed re-roofing. The battered old Land Rover needed its winter oil and its plow blade. There were rotten foundation sills to be replaced in the old carriage barn, one corner of which I was in the process of jacking up with the aid of a young local named Dwayne Gobble, who had come into our lives a few weeks back.

Know how every once in a while you'll be inching your way along a narrow, treacherous country road in the middle of a violent storm—trying desperately not to wrap your car and yourself around a tree—and some heavy metal testosterone case in a mondo pickup truck comes roaring up on your tail with all sixteen of his brights on, honking at you to speed up or move over or simply die? Meet Dwayne Gobble. That's how I did. I hit the brakes right there in the middle of the road, got out of the car and suggested the pinhead might want to step out of his truck so he wouldn't bleed all over his nice dashboard when I hit him. I've been known to get a little butch after I've been in the country for a while. Dwayne ended up coming to work for us. Autumn's a busy time, like I said. Plus our usual caretaker, Vic Early, Hollywood bodyguard extraordinaire, was on location in Maui guarding the body of Cindy Crawford. Poor Vic never could catch a break.

Yeah, I was living the sweet life, all right. But then again, I wasn't. I almost always awoke in the night, bathed in sweat, Merilee sprawled there next to me in deep, exhausted slumber. If Tracy needed changing, and she always did, I'd change her. Afterward, I'd sit up with her in the front parlor, staring gloomily at the glowing embers of the fire and sipping eighteen-year-old Macallan while she gurgled in my lap, studying me intently, waiting for me to explain myself. I'd study her right back. She was a calm baby, sunny and hopeful and not at all inclined to be irritable, which meant she took after Merilee more than she did me. Her head seemed abnormally large to me but I was assured that this was normal for a midget human life-form her age. I'd think about what lay ahead for her. In two years she'd be singing along with Barney. In three she'd be parked in front of her own Mac playing *Putt-Putt Joins the Parade*. In four she'd be calling me a butthead. I didn't know what I'd be calling her. I still hadn't made up my mind about her. I didn't love her. I didn't dislike her. I didn't feel anything toward her. I wondered if I ever would. Maybe when she got older and starting asking me questions, like where do duckies go when they die, Daddy, and why is there greed and is it okay to give a boy a hand job on the first date? Maybe then.

I'd sit there sipping single malt and staring at the fire and brooding a lot about life, death and fatherhood—three things I knew nothing about. I knew I'd never had it so good. Christ, I knew that. But I also knew I'd never felt so frustrated and unfulfilled and lost. Part of it was the novel, no question. But not all of it. I didn't know what it was, the rest. I only knew there seemed to be an absence of joy in my life.

That's what I was thinking about the night Thor Gibbs showed up, begging me to help Clethra pen her Tale of Whoa. Like I said, I didn't want to. And not just because I'd had it with ghosting. As far as I was concerned, Thor had behaved like a swine. A seventy-one-year-old man doesn't run off with his eighteen-year-old stepdaughter. Not if he's thinking straight. But therein lay my dilemma— the man *wasn't* thinking straight. Couldn't be. Something had to be wrong. Terribly wrong. And part of me felt that Thor knew it. That's why he'd shown up. Not because *she* needed a ghost but because *he* needed *me*. My old friend was crying out for help. So was poor Arvin, an innocent boy who was being ripped apart by his parents' battle— not to mention his half-sister's rather queer taste in boy-friends.

Face it, this was a family in desperate need of a healer. John Lee Hooker calls the blues our great healer. I don't disagree with the old master. It's just that most of the people who come to me for help are tone-deaf. And they don't see things too clearly either. They need someone to set them straight. Someone who'll tell them what they don't want to hear. Someone who'll whomp them upside the head if need be.

They need me.

And sometimes, if I get real lucky, I need them, too.

Two

I PICKED some white mums from the garden to put on Merilee's breakfast tray. Breakfast in bed may be Merilee's favorite thing in life, other than watching *Regis & Kathie Lee,* and she won't watch them anymore. Doesn't want to expose Tracy to crap. She'd heard that just as you are what you eat you are what you absorb—in other words, if you watch crap, if you listen to crap, if you read crap, you *become* crap. I don't know who told her that. It may have been me.

I'd been up for hours. Never went back to bed, actually. After I'd gotten Thor and Clethra settled in I'd stropped Grandfather's straight-edge razor and shaved. I dressed in an old, soft Italian wool shirt, thorn-proof moleskin trousers, ankle boots of kid leather and the eight-ply oyster gray cashmere cardigan I got at the Burlington Arcade in London. At dawn I'd grabbed my old hickory walking stick and went hiking off through the

woods with Lulu to Reynolds' general store for the *Times,*
the maple leaves turning a million different glorious shades
of orange and red, the geese flying over in formation, heading south. It was a bright, clear morning, the air crisp and
cold. Lulu had on her hand-knitted Fair Isle vest to ward
off the chill. She picks up sinus infections easily, and she
snores when she has them. I know this because she likes to
sleep on my head. After her most recent bout, her vet had
raised the idea of having her deviated septum repaired. I'd
never heard of a basset hound getting a nose job. The vet
assured me it was quite common and would not alter her
appearance in the least. Right away this cooled me on the
whole idea.

She came scrambling up the stairs with me when I took
Merilee's tray up, nails clacketing on the wood floor, desperate to jump up on her mommy's bed for a snuggle. But
this was a no-no. Not with Tracy there. She was on her
belly next to Merilee in her Babar the Elephant footed
rompers, arms waving, legs kicking. Looked like she was
break-dancing, actually. Merilee cooing at her with delight. Lulu had to settle for the rocker in front of the fireplace, grunting peevishly while I threw open the curtains
and let in the morning sun.

One entire wall of the master bedroom was a row of tall
mahogany casement windows that afforded a not terrible
view of the cove. The bedroom was not large. We kept it
rather sparely furnished. The rocker, washstand and lamp
tables were Shaker. The bed, of gently battered brass, was
not. Shaker beds, as you may know, tend to be, well, really
narrow.

"They're still here, aren't they?" Merilee demanded
when I presented her with her tray.

I stood there gazing at her. She looked weary. She always did now. But she also looked extremely delectable. It
was hard to believe she was past forty. Even harder to

believe she was mine. Not that Merilee Nash is a conventional beauty. Her nose and chin are too patrician, her forehead too high. Plus she is no delicate flower. She is just a hair under six feet tall, with broad sloping shoulders and huge hands and feet. What used to be called a big-boned gal, and is now called a Merilee Nash type.

"Can't I do something nice without you immediately being suspicious?" I said lightly.

"Hmphht." She reached for the paper and glanced at the headlines. Or I should say squinted. She won't read with her glasses on in front of the baby for fear Tracy will grow up wanting to wear glasses whether she needs them or not. This particular belief she cooked up all on her own. She took a sip of her hot milk. The milk was from a dairy in nearby Salem and came in glass bottles with the cream floating on top. She took another sip. She said it again. "They're still here, aren't they?"

"As a matter of fact, they're asleep in the chapel."

Without warning, Tracy tried sitting up. I gave her an 8.5 on form and a 9 on degree of difficulty—before she abruptly plopped over onto her side with a quizzical yelp.

Delighted, Merilee reached over and tickled her foot, producing a gale of giggles. I watched the two of them, wondering just how much longer Merilee would be content here on the farm with her, especially now that the summer gardening season was ending and the fall theater season beginning. How much longer before she'd need to hear that applause again?

She furrowed her brow at me. "Darling?"

"Yes, Merilee?"

"There's no bed in the chapel."

"He prefers the floor. Some back injury from his rodeo days."

"And she?"

"Not to worry. She's generously padded on both sides."

"Why, Mr. Hoagy, are you being meowish?"

"Who, me? Never."

"So what's she like?" Merilee inquired, trying to sound casual about it. And failing.

"I gave them the down comforter from the guest room."

"Is she awful?"

"And Sadie to fend off the mice."

"You don't like her, do you?" She seemed mildly amused by this.

"Thor asked me to give her a chance."

"You *detest* her." She seemed greatly amused by this.

"Possibly," I offered, "she's just in need of a positive female role model. After all, she and Ruth aren't exactly on good terms anymore."

"And I wonder why." Merilee took a bite of her toast, which was topped with her very own apple butter. She shook her head. "He's a dirty old man, Hoagy. And she's cruel and stupid."

"I guess that means you don't want them staying here for the winter."

Her eyes widened. "Staying here? Explain yourself this instant, sir."

I did. And to her credit, Merilee listened patiently and calmly before she responded, "I want peace and quiet right now, not *Hard Copy* camped out at the foot of our drive. That's exactly what I don't want."

"I don't want that either, Merilee. Nor do they."

She studied me over her mug. "You want to do this book with her, Hoagy? Is that what you're saying?"

"Not even maybe." I sat down at the foot of the bed. "But I do owe the man. And he is in trouble."

She sipped her milk, considering it long and hard. "Okay," she concluded, much to my surprise. "But only because of a certain person who I happen to care deeply for."

"Ruth?"

She shook her head.

"Arvin?"

"You."

"Me?"

"You haven't been very good company lately, darling. You've been pointy and distant and about as much fun as a dose of poison ivy in one's pink places."

"I know that, Merilee. Just one of those phases a guy goes through. Shouldn't last for more than another decade."

"Is this you being new-fatherish?"

"This is me being I-don't-knowish."

Tracy watched me intently from the bed. I watched her back.

Merilee watched us watching each other. "I wish you two would make up your minds about one another."

"How do you mean?"

"I mean you keep measuring each other like potential enemies."

"We're just getting ready for when she's a teenager."

Merilee hesitated, biting her lower lip. "Know what I keep thinking you ought to do, darling?"

"Oh, God, Merilee. You're not going to send me off in search of my smile, are you?"

"Hoagy, you never had a smile."

"Did so. It so happens I was a buoyant, fun-loving child."

Lulu started coughing. It's what she does instead of laughing.

Merilee's eyes were on the windows. "I keep thinking . . . What I mean is, if only you'd sit down with your father and—"

"I don't want to talk about him, Merilee," I said gruffly. "You know I don't want to talk about him."

"I know, I know," she conceded, coloring. "It's just that your mother and I were—"

"My mother and you were what?" I snapped.

"Don't yell at me!"

I stood and went over to the windows, gazing out at the cove. A hawk was circling over the marsh, slowly, in search of breakfast. "Merilee, I don't know what it is."

"Then maybe Thor can help you find out. He's always had some mysterious power over you, God knows why. And God knows why I'm agreeing to this. The two of you will probably end up facedown together in a brothel somewhere in Mexicali." She sighed grandly, tragically. "All right, they may stay—for your sake. And because I care about Ruth. Although if she ever finds out I'm harboring those two moral fugitives—"

"Let's try not to judge them, okay?"

"I'm trying," she insisted. "I'm just not having much success."

"Neither am I." I took her gloved hand, getting lost in her green eyes. "That's a rather agreeable mouth you have on, Miss Nash."

"Why, thank you, sir."

"Any reason I shouldn't kiss it?"

"None that I can think of."

So I did. She kissed me back, gently. And then not so gently. I reached inside her nightshirt for whatever I might find in there.

"Careful," she whispered. "They're sensitive."

"Nice and warm, too." I know I was certainly overheating. It had been quite a while since we'd been joined together in atomic passion. Longer than I cared to admit. "I could get back in there with you, you know."

Her eyes widened in mock horror. "Merciful heavens, Hoagy. Tracy could be permanently scarred."

"Or permanently impressed."

"I should have had her when I was twenty-two," she said ruefully. She said this a lot. Practically every day. "I would have had energy for the both of you then. I just don't now." She tugged primly at her nightshirt, buttoning it. "And I certainly don't feel sexy. More like some form of large, slow farm animal."

"You don't look like one, Merilee."

Her eyes softened. "Really?"

"Really," I said, reaching for her.

Only now we could hear Dwayne's truck turning in at the foot of the drive, stereo thumping, engine rack-racketing—the kid had little or nothing in the way of a muffler. He pulled up outside the carriage barn in a splattering of gravel and hopped out. I heard voices. Thor was up. The two of them were getting acquainted.

Merilee pushed me away, reluctantly but firmly. "I'll be down to say hello as soon as I do my post-natal exercises."

"I can suggest some terribly interesting new exercises."

"Those, mister, are very old ones. Now off with you. Go on. Scoot."

It was my turn to sigh grandly and tragically. I climbed to my feet and started for the door.

"The thing of it is," she pointed out, "I wasn't ready to be a mother when I was that age. I wasn't a grown-up, not like I am . . ." She stopped short, her brow creasing with concern. "Are you all right, darling? You look terribly pale all of a sudden."

"I'm fine. Still can't get used to the idea that I'm living with a grown-up, that's all."

"Hoagy?"

"Yes, Merilee?"

"Hello."

"Hello, yourself."

. . . . .

Dwayne was busy showing Thor the sill work he was doing. Thor was busy making all sorts of enthusiastic noises. The man always did have a gift for drawing people out. Making them see themselves and their work, whatever it was, as something to be proud of.

Proud made for a nice break in the day for Dwayne Gobble. He was a tall, grungy beanpole of a kid with veiny red hands and a scraggly goatee and dirty blond hair he wore in that style favored by heavy metal musicians and minor league hockey players—short on top, long and stringy in back. A strikingly ugly purple scar slanted across his forehead and halfway down his nose—this from when he'd gone headfirst through his windshield a while back. They hadn't done a very good job of sewing him back together. One eyebrow was higher than the other, one eye slightly atilt. It was as if two different people's faces had been stitched together. Dwayne had worn the same flannel shirt and torn jeans every day since he started working for us, his jeans stained and filthy and so loose they practically fell from his bony hips. He favored tattoos. Had any number of them on his arms. None said loser. He didn't need that one. Already had it written all over him. Chiefly it was his eyes, which never looked directly at you. Down at your feet or over your shoulder or up in the air—anywhere but at you. Dwayne was a troubled kid. The village outcast, actually. But nice enough, once you got to know him. And it really wasn't his fault no one in town besides us would hire him.

Thor knelt in the damp earth beside the twin hydraulic jacks that presently held up that corner of the barn, scrutinizing one of the pressure-treated two-by-fours Dwayne had sistered in. "Lay a transit on her, boy?"

"You bet I did, sir." Dwayne shook a Camel out of the crumpled pack in his shirt and lit it, using his calloused palm as an ashtray. "She's dead nuts, all right."

"Good work, boy. You're a born craftsman. And, believe me, there's no more valuable a man on God's green earth."

Dwayne pawed at the ground with his unlaced work boot, more than a little flattered by Thor's approval. "This is just a real honor, Mr. Gibbs," he said shyly. "Meeting you, I mean. I've read all your books backwards and forwards. Especially *Dickless Decade*."

This didn't completely surprise me. Young Dwayne was making a serious effort to improve his mind. One day on his lunch break I'd found him with his nose buried in *On the Road*. When I offered to loan him one of my own novels he allowed as how that would be righteous. I could tell when he'd started reading it—a look that approached awe crossed his lopsided face. Either it was awe or the hot sausage and peppers hero he brought for his lunch that day.

But it was nothing like the look he had on his face now, meeting Thor Gibbs. This bordered on the religious. It was positively Jordanesque. "Man, I just never imagined I'd actually be standing here talking to you."

Thor waved him off modestly. "You give me way too much credit, boy. All I do is connect words. Bunch of bullshit. Not like this . . ." He gazed admiringly at the post-and-beam structure overhead. "This is real art."

"No way, man," Dwayne disagreed heatedly. "All that stuff you said about how a man shouldn't accept being unhappy, how it's in his nature to go after what he wants . . . It wasn't until I read that that I even dared to think such stuff. I mean, everyone's always told me what I *can't* have, *can't* be . . ."

"Man is an animal of strength and force and purpose," Thor intoned, stroking his beard. "You have the power, Dwayne. It's in *here*." Thor thumped his chest. "And in *here*." He gripped his balls. His own, not Dwayne's.

Dwayne hanging on the man's every word. "Believe in yourself, boy. Be a man, damn it! And be proud." Thor brushed off his knees, smiling at the kid warmly. He loved nothing better than a new disciple. Hadn't had many lately. "How do you and your father get along?"

Dwayne looked down at the ground uncomfortably. "We don't," he replied, stubbing out his cigarette in his palm and pocketing it. "He's away."

Away in Carl Robinson State Prison, to be precise. For burning down the first selectman's house in a small dispute over a borrowed Weed Whacker. Dwayne and his mom lived in a shack out by Rogers Lake. She was a schoolteacher, or had been. Got herself fired from the local elementary school for tying an unruly eight-year-old to a chair. These days the two of them lived on whatever Dwayne was able to earn, which wasn't much—the child she'd tied to the chair happened to be the son of the biggest building contractor in the area.

Thor shook his huge, gleaming head at him, his electric-blue eyes moistening. "And so you're growing up with no male adult figure who you respect. You and a million other boys out there. In tribal times, you'd have been taken off in the woods for an initiation ceremony. A respected elder would let you in on what it means to be a man. Now, you sit and watch your football on TV, bombarded by beer commercials on the one hand and feminista bullshit on the other. It's killing mankind. Killing us, I tell you." He ran a hand over his weather-beaten face, disgusted, then heaved his chest and went strutting back out into the sunshine, where it was warmer.

Our fleet was parked out there, safely out of harm's way. Not that we doubted Dwayne or his hydraulic jacks. It was he who'd insisted we clear out the barn. Said it would be stupid not to. There was the '62 Land Rover, which was battered and bruised and either tan or olive drab, depending on the light and how clean it was. Lulu's favorite. There was the Jag, the sinewy red '58 XK 150 drophead, every inch of it original, right down to the sixty-spoke wire wheels. My favorite. And there was our latest addition, which we'd bought for carting Tracy around: a powder-blue 1950 Ford Woody wagon that had belonged to our dear, departed neighbor, Margaret, an aviatrix who'd been a test pilot during World War I. Solid as a tank, heavy and quiet. And the Woody wasn't bad either. Had 42,000 miles on it, no rust, its original wood and five brand-new wide whites. The clock even worked.

Lulu was curled up next to it, eyeballing the barn warily. She won't go in there if she can avoid it. It has bats and, from time to time, raccoons. Sadie was stretched out next to her in the sun chewing on a foot. She likes the barn just fine. But she likes being warm even more.

The chapel door opened and young Clethra came padding out, her eyes puffy and her hair uncombed. She was barefoot, and wasn't wearing any pants. Just a T-shirt and her black leather jacket, which just did cover her butt. Her legs were somewhat chubby, and blotchy from the cold. She painted her toenails black.

"Clethra, dear child!" Thor called out to her. "Come over here and say hello to my friend, Dwayne Gobble."

She came scuffling over, most grudgingly. Until she realized Dwayne was her own age. Then her manner changed completely. We're talking major thaw. "Whassup, cuz?" she asked him, all friendly and interested. Smiling even. All of a sudden, I felt very old. "You, like, work here?"

"Sometimes," he replied, gawking at her dumbly. Poor guy was utterly entranced. If this had been a cartoon he would have been hearing tweety birds. "For a while, anyway."

"Dwayne's an artisan," Thor informed her. "He works

where he wants, when he wants. A man with his gifts is always a free man."

"Cool," exclaimed Clethra, tossing her wild mane of black hair at him, her dark eyes flashing and playful. "Hey, can I bum one of those?"

He was fumbling for another Camel. "Uh, sure. You bet." He shook another one out of the pack and lit it for her. "I like your ring," he said, meaning the one in her nose.

"Check, I got this new one last week . . ." She pulled up her T-shirt so he could see it. It was in her belly button. "Jamaican dude in the East Village did it for me."

"Cool!" exclaimed Dwayne, very impressed. "Did it hurt?"

"Duh, yeah," she said most casually, dragging on her cigarette. "Like, I mean, if you want total excellence you have to do the time, know what I'm saying?"

"You got that right," agreed Dwayne, slipping her five and getting five back.

Thor stood there beaming at the two of them like a proud parent. Me, I was starting to feel like David Niven in *Prudence and the Pill.*

"Whoa, your truck is a piss," she observed, scuffling over to it.

Dwayne drove a jacked-up Dodge Power Ram, gunmetal gray, and bedecked with the usual he-guy bells and whistles—the mondo Trail Buster tires, the roll bar, the fog lamps. As well as some individual flourishes of his own. Homemade front and rear bumpers of pressure-treated lumber. And a rear window plastered with clever bumper stickers like "Red, Hot and Rolling" and "Lick My Meat" and "Perot for President."

"Awesome stereo," she raved, getting up on her tippy toes so she could see in the window.

"She's got eight-inch woofers," he informed her, his

eyes firmly fastened on her own eight-inch woofers. "You into death metal?"

"I used to be into Metallica, but then they got so commercial, y'know?"

He nodded vigorously. "They're totally bogus. I'm into Deicide now. They're the truth, man."

Dwayne had played me a sample one day when we were working on the barn. To me, the truth sounded like a garbage disposal eating up a live rodent, and I told him so. He thought maybe it was a generational thing. I preferred to think of it as a taste thing.

Dwayne tugged nervously at his goatee. "I'll . . . uh . . . play 'em for you sometime. If you're gonna be around, I mean."

"Cool!"

Dwayne grabbed his tools from the back of the truck and headed into the barn, work to do.

"Yo, is there like a shower, homes?" Clethra asked me, reverting instantly to her brattier self.

"I suppose we can arrange something," I said stiffly. I didn't mean to be inhospitable. I would have been plenty warm if she'd at least said good morning.

"And, like, maybe some coffee?"

"Of course, how cloddish of me. I'll get right on it."

"Wait, I can make the coffee, boy," Thor offered hurriedly.

Fortunately, Merilee picked this moment to emerge, wheeling Tracy toward us in her buggy. At least I think Tracy was in there somewhere, interred under several blankets, the little cap Merilee's sister, Gretchen, had knit for her planted firmly on her abnormally large head. Merilee was dressed for the mud in her denim bib overalls and green rubber wellies. Her waist-length golden hair was in a ponytail. She wore no makeup.

"By God, woman," Thor exclaimed, his voice booming. "You get prettier every time I see you!"

"And you, Mr. Gibbs," she said airily, "get more and more full of baked beans."

He gave her a big bear hug, lifting her off her feet.

"Careful, you'll get a hernia."

He laughed his lion's roar of a laugh. "Nonsense. You're light as a feather. Come meet my Clethra," he commanded, dragging Merilee toward her.

Merilee, still one of Miss Porter's girls, treated her young guest to a dazzling smile. "Hello, Clethra. And welcome."

Clethra treated her to a bored shrug. And said nothing.

"She needs a shower," I said, between clenched teeth.

Thor added, "I was just about to make a pot of coffee."

"Nonsense, I'll do it," Merilee assured him.

"Like, I don't even have a change of clothes," Clethra complained to her. "But I guess *you* wouldn't have anything that would fit me."

"Why, of course I would," Merilee assured her cheerfully. Not so much as a nostril flared. "I hope you don't mind spit-up stains."

"She's a fine, strong baby, Merilee," Thor observed, gazing down at Tracy in her buggy. "You must be very proud."

"Well, maybe a little," Merilee admitted, glowing radiantly. The two of them stood there making a fuss over Tracy for a moment. Too long a moment.

At least it was as far as Lulu was concerned. Unloved and unappreciated, she went skulking slowly off toward the pond, ears back, tail between her legs. Clearly, suicide was the only answer. She paused for a moment at the water's edge, considering the gravity of what she was about to do, then steeled herself and waded glumly in.

"Oh, God, there she goes again." Quickly, I unlaced my

ankle boots. She was already in over her ears, which doesn't take her very long.

"Don't worry, Mr. H!" Dwayne called out. "I'll save her!" He went running in after her, sending the ducks scattering. The pond's not deep, no more than three feet at its lowest spot, but by the time he'd waded over to her she'd already sunk to the bottom with a *glug-glug-glug*. He reached in and grabbed her by the scruff of the neck and yanked her back out, snarfling and barfling and yelping in protest. Then he carried her to shore, where she shook herself, shivering miserably. The water was damned cold now. She also didn't smell her best. She tends not to when she's wet.

Merilee ran in and got towels for both of them. I toweled Lulu dry and said a few stern, fatherly things to her I won't bother to repeat here. Dwayne refused his towel. Also our thanks. Just put his boots back on over his wet socks and went right back to work. He didn't even seem to notice that his jeans were soaked through.

"I'm taking Hoagy away from you this evening, Merilee," Thor announced with that familiar gleam of inspired lunacy in his eyes.

Merilee raised an eyebrow at this. "Oh?"

"We need to sit around a campfire," he explained. "Reestablish a feeling of common manhood."

"How cute," she said sweetly. "Will the two of you be pounding on little drums?"

"Thor's not into that," I answered her, also sweetly. "I suspect we'll mostly fart and spit and talk about girls."

"We girls will be having much more fun," Merilee assured us.

"We will?" Clethra said doubtfully. "What'll we be doing?"

"Putting up pickles and spiced pears," Merilee informed her brightly.

Clethra made a face. "No way. I don't *do* the kitchen thing."

"We'll be just like two pioneer women," Merilee plowed on gamely. "Come on, it's fun."

"It bites," Clethra snapped.

Merilee took a deep breath. "Okay, what would *you* like to do?"

"I wanna watch *The Brady Bunch*."

"Why would you want to do that?" I wondered.

"Do you have cable?" she asked Merilee, ignoring me.

"We have cable," Merilee said tightly.

"Cool. Then I'm good to go."

"You and I need to talk, Clethra," I said. "After your shower, I mean."

She curled her lip at me. "What about?"

"Your book. I'm going to help you with it." Either that or dunk her in the pond. Possibly both.

"Good man," exulted Thor, clapping me on the back. "I won't forget this, Hoagy."

"I don't believe I will either."

Clethra merely shrugged and mumbled, "Whatever." And went inside.

Merilee went in after her, pausing first to curl her lip at me. A flawless impersonation. I stayed outside with Tracy and Lulu, who was standing in between my legs, her front paws resting on my feet. She often gets a bit needy when she's been acting out.

Thor stripped to his waist and got to work chopping firewood. There was nothing lazy or casual about how he did it. This was work, hard work, and Thor Gibbs believed in hard work. He brought the ax down with thundering power, shaking the ground with his every swing, his huge muscles rippling. Sweat soon streamed down his barrel chest and flat, taut stomach. Me, I couldn't imagine being in such shape when I was seventy-one. Hell, I couldn't even imagine being alive. He was lucky to be alive himself. I couldn't help but notice the three-inch scar on his back, still fresh and pink, from when Ruth had tried to stab him to death.

"I can't believe it, man," Dwayne marveled, his voice hushed with reverence. "Thorvin fucking Gibbs. What a trip."

"That he is."

"And that Clethra . . ." Dwayne let out a low, admiring whistle. "Man, I sure would like to empty my scrotum in her monkey cave."

Lulu howled at the very thought of this.

"Thank you for sharing that with me, Dwayne. Thank you very much."

"Can't help how I feel, Mr. H."

"No, but you could shut up about it."

"Thing is, I meet a bazillion chicks over at Slim Jim's. And compared to her, they're pigs. I mean, she's different. She's *nice*."

I peered at him curiously. "She is?"

"Well, she's got a real nice smile, don't ya think?"

"Oh, so that's it."

Dwayne frowned at me. "That's what, Mr. H?"

"One of the three great misconceptions men have about women, Dwayne. Misconception number one is that if a woman has a nice smile she's nice. Number two is that if she laughs at your jokes she has a great sense of humor. Number three is that if she agrees with every intelligent thing you have to say she's smart."

Dwayne considered this a moment, scratching his greasy hair. "That's real interesting, Mr. H. Are there, like, any great misconceptions that they have about us?"

"Just one. That we actually *have* anything intelligent to say."

"I guess I'd just like to meet a girl where it's about something more than sex, y'know?"

"I do. The physical part is plenty at first, but after a while—"

"It'll blow over?"

"So to speak. In my experience the fever breaks in six or —how old are you again?"

"Nineteen."

"—eight weeks. After that, there has to be something more. Can I ask you a favor, Dwayne?"

"Sure, Mr. H."

"Could you keep it to yourself that the two of them are here? We don't want anyone else to know."

His face dropped. "You mean I can't tell anyone? Not even the guys?"

"One word gets out and the press will be all over this place. And then they'll have to leave."

He tugged at his scraggly goatee. "Well, if that's how it is then I'm cool with it."

"You're a good man, Dwayne."

His eyes were on Thor again. "Hope I get a chance to have some more talks with him. I mean, you're a bright guy and all, and I enjoy rapping with you about books and stuff, but Mr. Gibbs . . . he's like a true wise man."

I left that one alone.

Dwayne turned and looked at me. "Well, isn't he?"

"I suppose he is, Dwayne. I suppose he is."

I took Clethra to the mall for our little talk. The nearest was the Crystal Mall, which was about twenty miles away in New London, where the Coast Guard Academy and Naval Submarine Base were found. I hate the mall. Any mall. Something about all of those loud, tacky stores selling 163 different kinds of loud, tacky crap that people don't need and can't afford. Something about all of those fat, greedy housewives in polyester sweat suits elbowing and grabbing their way deeper and deeper into debt. Something about all of those brain-dead teenagers in reversed baseball caps milling aimlessly around, chewing on limp french fries, when they should have been in school learning how to spell. All it takes me is one trip to the mall and I want to flee this country for good. Sometimes, I want to do that anyway. But when I asked her where she wanted to go she said the mall. She needed clothes. So we went to the mall.

Lulu, of course, loves the place. They have a pet store there with tropical fish that's one of her absolute fave places to hang. Oh, well, at least she barked at the guy who was dressed up like Barney.

I sat on a bench drinking a tepid, oily brown coffee-like liquid while Clethra shopped. The Seventies, I noticed, were back again. Flared hiphuggers, body shirts, stacked platform heels . . . all back in fashion. Made me think I'd lost the last twenty years with the blink of an eye. I frequently feel that way—that I'm still twenty-one, still trying to figure the world out, positive that it will all make sense to me someday. I'm still waiting for it to make sense. Only now I know it never will. This, I am told, is maturity.

Clethra bought jeans at the Gap and flannel shirts at Eddie Bauer and some socks and tights and underwear at a place that sold socks and tights and underwear. She had to come looking for me when it came time to pay, what with Ruth having nuked her credit cards. I had to use mine. I started out in a hole with Clethra Feingold, to the tune of $317.64. And if you want to know the truth I never climbed out of it.

"This mall sucks." She flopped down on the bench next to me with her purchases. She had one of her new flannel shirts on over a gray gym shirt of Merilee's. "There's no Vicky's Secret, no Banana Republic . . ."

"Don't you have anything nice to say about anything?"

"Why should I?" she sniffed. "You don't."

"That's different. I've earned the right to be so utterly disillusioned."

"Hey, it's not easy bein' happy if you're a child livin' in this free world," she moaned. This was her being tragic and vulnerable, vintage Sylvia Plath by way of Kurt Cobain, with a generous side order of gag me with a spoon, Muffy. "Does Dwayne have a girlfriend?"

"He's never mentioned one."

"Like, don't you think he looks like T-Bone?"

"T-Bone?"

"Tommy Lee, the Crue drummer. One who's married to Pam Anderson from *Baywatch*. He used to be married to Heather Locklear. Is Heather really as big a bitch in real life as she is on *Melrose Place*?"

"You mean *Melrose Place* isn't real life?"

"Oh, go to hell."

"This is hell. Want to buy any more jeans?"

"Do you and Merilee fuck a lot?"

"Constantly. Like animals."

She sighed, the eternally suffering teen. "Geez, I'm like, why are you dogging me, homes? I'm totally fucking serious."

And she looked serious, too. Totally fucking serious. But this wasn't about serious. This was about her testing me, much the way a child tests a new baby-sitter. Nothing to do with her age. Every celebrity I've ever worked for has done it.

"That doesn't mean you're entitled to an answer."

"Oh, I get it." Now she copped a gangsta attitude, poking herself in the chest with her thumbs. "Like, I'm supposed to be straight up with you but you don't have to be straight with me? What bullshit."

"You're right, it is. But I'm not the one who's getting paid two million dollars."

"So why are you helping me?" she demanded.

"Because I enjoy getting crapped on. I'm a little kinky that way."

She let out a girlish shriek of a laugh, and immediately clapped her hand over her mouth, reddening. I had to keep reminding myself just how young she was. "I just wondered if the two of you got along together all the time, that's all."

"No one does."

"Thor and my mom sure didn't."

I glanced at her. She was twirling her hair around and around her finger. "They fought a lot?"

"Like, all the time. You two aren't married?"

"We were."

"But you're not anymore?"

"That's correct."

"So she's like your perma-date or something?"

"Or something."

"That's kicking," she said approvingly. "It's, like, you don't care what other people think of you."

"Now you're catching on."

She reached over and seized my hand. Hers was soft and rather hot. She turned mine over and squinted intently down at the lines in my palm, reading them with a look of spirited devilment on her face. This was her trying to be flirty and fascinating. I'm quite sure she thought she was, too. After all, she was eighteen—the zenith of female desirability if you go by all of the lingerie ads and rock videos. But that was image. Reality was quite different. Reality was that she hadn't done anything in life except go to school and buy and watch and listen to whatever we had told her to buy and watch and listen to. Reality was that she was nobody at all, just a pepper pot of attitudes still in desperate search of a person. Me, I was her tour guide.

"Whew," she gasped, dropping my hand. "You are *hostile.*"

Well, maybe she did know how to read palms.

I now became aware that three middle-aged chunkettes in stretch wear were standing there gaping at us.

"Omigod! It's *her!*"

"I don't *believe* it!"

"What is she *doing* here?!"

"Omigod!"

Others began swarming around us, wondering what the commotion was. And anxious to get in on it. Quickly, I hustled Clethra out of there, two dozen or more women in hot pursuit. We had to sprint the last hundred yards to the Jag. Lulu even had to show them her teeth, a sight known to throw terror into the hearts of fanzoids the world over. Then we hopped in and I floored it out of there.

"Jesus, why can't people just leave me the fuck alone?" Clethra cried, as we headed back toward Lyme. She seemed genuinely shaken by the frenzy she'd caused. She was used to Manhattan, where people go less ga-ga. In Manhattan, they've seen 'em all. "I mean, why do they even care?"

"Because your private life is public theater. They see you on TV, just like they see Heather Locklear on TV. It's all entertainment to them."

"Well, it's not fair."

"Life isn't, Clethra. Sorry to be the one to break it to you."

I got off the highway at Old Lyme and took the Shore Road down past the boatyards and salt marshes to Griswold Point, where the Sound and the mouth of the Connecticut River meet. The water was choppy that day, the beach deserted now that the summer folk were gone. I parked there and Lulu hopped out, the better to arf at shorebirds. We stayed in the Jag with the top down, facing the water.

"Do you love Thor?"

"Duh, yeah," she answered mockingly. "Like, what do you think?"

"I'm trying to figure out what to think."

She shook a Camel out of her jacket, stuck it between her teeth like a schoolyard tough and lit it, letting the smoke slowly out of her nostrils. "I've loved Thor for as long as I can remember," she said, her voice soft and dreamy. "Thor is a force within me, the great and eternal male, enveloping me, inside of me, part of me, *me.*"

From the rocks nearby, Lulu started coughing violently. Me, I was just staring.

"I love him with my body and my mind and my soul," she went on, and on. "Our love is timeless and life-af-firming. By loving Thor I am loving myself."

"I hadn't realized you were majoring in dramatic arts," I observed.

"I wasn't. History."

"My mistake. I take it you don't feel you've done anything wrong."

She shook her head. "I know I haven't."

"You don't think of Thor as your father?"

"He's *not* my father!" she insisted, flaring at me angrily. "God, why can't people get hip to that?"

"Because he raised you, that's why."

"Look," she said, with exaggerated patience, "if he was my father I wouldn't feel this way about him. I *have* a father. I mean, that's what people keep forgetting. *Barry* is my father. I see him all the time and I love him as my father and I would never, ever in a million years think about fucking him. Thor . . . He's just a man who used to be with my mom. And now's with me."

"About your mom . . . Is this you getting back at her?"

"Getting back at her how?"

"By taking her man away from her."

"She has shit to do with it. I love Thor. I *told* you."

"Do you love her, too?"

Clethra shrugged her shoulders inside the jacket. "I did, I guess. Back when I was little, I mean. But these last couple of years, man, she's just been all the time in my face, busting me, dissing me, telling me what to do."

"She's your mom. Moms do that."

"Not like her, homes," she argued. "Like, my mother happens to be the bitch of the century, okay? But I don't have to tell you that. You know her, right?"

I nodded. Because I did know her. And because I was well aware she could be damned hard on people. Ruth Feingold was a tough, demanding woman. Her outright belligerence had ultimately led to a big falling-out with Friedan and the others. And had dealt the women's movement a serious blow.

Clethra took a drag on her cigarette, staring out across the Sound. It was a clear day, clear enough to make out the north shore of Long Island on the other side. "I mean, nothing I ever do is good enough for her. Not my grades. Not how I look. Not who my friends are. I'm, like, she's always running me down. Thor's the one who kept me sane. If it weren't for him I'd have run away when I was fourteen. I'd be a hooker on the street somewhere. But I'm cool now. I'm free of her."

"Is it true that she has physically abused both you and your brother?"

"Half brother." She hesitated a moment before she nodded, swallowing. "All the time. With the back of her hand, with her fist. She's just so mad at the world. But, like, why does she have to take it out on us? Poor little Arvy, she'd smack him and scream at him until he'd just go running from the dinner table. And I'm, like, he shakes when she comes in the room. He's such a sweet, sensitive boy. I'm scared for him. What she'll *do* to him. Thor has to get him away from her. Has to." She tensed in her seat next to me. Savagely, she added, "I'd like to see her crash and burn. I'd like to see her dead."

"She will be soon enough."

Clethra frowned. "She will?"

"We all will."

She flicked her cigarette out onto the parking lot and stuck her chin out at me. "All the more reason to do what you want, right?"

"Is that your philosophy of life? Do what you want?"

She peered at me coldly. "Why are you dogging me again?"

"I'm not. I'm trying to help you formulate your voice for your book. Were you under seventeen when you and Thor started having sex?"

She shrank from me in horror. "Duh, what?!"

"I need to know this, Clethra. I have to know this. Because if you were, then we're talking about statutory rape."

"I was seventeen," she said earnestly. "And that's the truth. Not that I hadn't, y'know, been wanting him bad for a while."

"How long a while? When did you start to think of him that way?"

"I guess I was twelve or thirteen maybe. Like, I always had this crush on him, y'know? Sometimes when I was in bed I could hear the two of them playing Dick at Nite. Mom's this really intense moaner. Just like I am." She shot me a coy little glance. "And I'd think . . ."

"You'd think what?"

"That I could make him happier than she could. But I

didn't. We didn't. I mean, I didn't even know he felt that way about me, too. Not until that night she was, like, down in Virginia making one of her speeches. It was late and Arvy was in his room asleep. I was in my room studying . . ." Her eyes shined at me now. Her voice was nearly a whisper. "Thor came in and he just stood there staring at me for the longest time, not saying a word. Finally, I said, like, 'What is it?' And he said, like, 'I can't stand this anymore. My every fiber wants and needs you. I must have you this instant or I shall explode.' So . . . So we kissed. With, y'know, tongues." She ran hers over her plump lower lip. "And then he undressed me and I undressed him and we fucked our brains out all night long. It was *so* unbelievable. I mean, to know that I could give someone else pleasure—without inhibitions, without regrets, without *her* there telling me what a lazy cow I was. And to get pleasure back from him in return. I just felt sooo alive. And fulfilled, y'know? Maybe for the first time in my whole entire life."

"All seventeen years of it."

"It wasn't my first time, if that's what you're wondering."

"It's not."

"I mean, I'd done it all with Tyler, my ex-boyfriend. He was my first. But it all felt dirty somehow. Like he was, y'know, using me. Plus I never got off with him. With Thor . . ." She paused, searching for the words, a rosy, born-again glow on her face. "With Thor I felt *cleansed.*"

"Did the two of you ever get *cleansed* in front of Arvin?"

"That's tabloid bullshit!" she cried, outraged. "We'd never do that. That's, like, sick."

"Is it possible Arvin saw you two without you knowing about it?"

"I guess," she conceded. "But he never said anything to me about it."

"Would he?"

"Shit, yes. Arvy's my best friend. We're everything to each other. God, I miss him . . ." She eyed me suspiciously, her mouth tightening. "Thor wanted me and I wanted him. I make him feel good in bed. Raisin Tits can't. She's too old and dried up."

"She's fifty-six. That's not so old."

"Oh, yeah? Who would you rather fuck if you had a choice—her or me? That's cold, homes, I know. But who would you?"

I didn't touch that one. I didn't like what my answer would be. I especially didn't like that she *knew* what my answer would be.

She was eying me playfully now, the way she'd eyed Dwayne. "Y'know, you're kind of cute, in a dissipated, weary, older man kind of way."

Lulu immediately reappeared, a low, threatening growl coming from her throat. She's exceedingly territorial when it comes to other women. I let her back into the Jag so she could guard me as well as get as much wet sand as possible all over the floor.

"People will want the dirty details, Clethra," I warned her. "That's why the publisher is paying you this much money. Are you prepared to give them what they want?"

"Sure, I don't care," she said lightly. "I'm not, like, ashamed to talk about it. I just don't understand why people keep wanting to make it out to be something sleazy."

"We're a sleazy people. Something to do with our Puritan heritage, near as I can figure."

"But Thor and me aren't sleazy. Our love is timeless and life—"

"Life-affirming. I know, I know. Do you have anything

you want to tell the young women out there who'll be buying your book?"

She pondered this a long moment, frowning. "Like what?"

"Something you've learned from this experience, possibly."

"Okay, sure," she said eagerly. "Here it is: Just because your mama says it's so don't mean it is. Like, if you love somebody, you love him, okay? I mean, you have control over your own body and your own life. And so what if she says it's wrong? I mean, Romeo and Juliet's families thought what they were doing was totally wrong, didn't they? And it *wasn't*. It was totally excellent. Because they were in *love*. Girls just get so fucked up about what our moms or our friends think about the guy we're seeing. Y'know, like if he's too 'old' or too 'different' or—"

"Or your stepfather?"

"Well, yeah," she agreed readily.

I tugged at my ear. "So you see you and Thor as a Romeo and Juliet kind of thing?"

"Well, yeah. A little." She peered at me searchingly. "I mean, don't you?"

"And what about the women's movement?"

She made a face like I'd just asked her to eat raw liver. "Mom's thing? What about it?"

"Any thoughts?"

"Not really. Whatever you want to say is fine. Thor said you're real liberated and shit."

"Thor said that?"

"Uh-huh. Can we go now? He'll be wondering where I am."

"He misses you that much?"

"Well, sure. Plus he always likes to get him some in the afternoon." Her eyes flashed at me wickedly. "If you know what I mean."

"Yes, I'm afraid I do," I said, starting up the Jag.

Lulu, she just covered her head with her paws and moaned.

We left for Crescent Moon Pond before dusk, backpacking deep into the woods to get there. We came upon old stone walls erected before the Civil War by the hardscrabble Yankees who had tried to farm this stony soil before fleeing to the gentler pastures west of the Ohio. We climbed over huge trees downed by the great hurricane of '38 that still lay there, rotting on the forest floor, newer trees growing right up out of them. It was nearly dark when we finally arrived, and so quiet we could hear the fluttering of bat wings overhead. Lulu stayed very close to me.

Crescent Moon Pond wasn't much. Maybe a half mile across, with a severe crook in the middle and a few rickety shacks, deserted now that summer was gone. The place has powerful memories for me. One of those shacks belonged to Cam Noyes. I helped him write a book. Maybe you read it. Or about it.

I made a fire and got dinner started. We'd brought a quart of Merilee's chili and a loaf of sourdough. I started the chili heating and put water on for coffee. Thor, he was more interested in the pond.

"Just how cold is that water?" he wondered, rubbing his hands together with anticipation.

"Plenty cold. Forties, I imagine."

"Good!" he exclaimed.

"Good?"

He tore off his clothes and went running in, naked, roaring lustily. He dove for the bottom. And he didn't come back up. By that I mean, like, never. The man was down there so long I was getting ready to go in after him. Until suddenly he shot to the surface way out in the middle, sputtering and gasping. He treaded water there for a moment, catching his breath, and then he started back, his stroke strong and steady.

"I'm getting there!" he cried triumphantly when he'd reached shallow water.

"Getting where, Thor?"

He shook himself like a bear, toweling himself with his socks. "I'm in training, boy," he informed me, hanging them over the fire to dry. "Got to improve my stamina. I'm sailing solo around the world soon as spring hits. Journal should make for one helluva book."

I handed him the bottle of Laphroaig I'd brought along. It's a rather peaty single malt. Not to everyone's liking. "And what will Clethra do?"

He took a gulp, wiped his mouth with the back of his hand. "Whatever she wants. I don't own her. Although it's my hope she'll resume her education."

I watched him climb back into his clothes, thinking how so utterly typical this was of him. He was always stirring things up and then taking off, leaving nothing but roiling upheaval in his wake. Turmoil was the man's oxygen. Sure, this was vintage Thor Gibbs, all right. So I wasn't surprised. I just wondered if little Clethra knew the slightest damned thing about it.

He made himself comfortable next to the fire, grinning at me with boyish mischief. "Want to drop some acid?"

"Why, did you bring some?"

"Hell, no. Makes me too sane." He scratched his beard, studying me. "Just trying to figure out where your head's at."

"On top of my neck, last time I looked."

"See? That's your problem right there, boy. It should be bobbing along the surface of the River Ganges, or soaring high atop a Tibetan mountain with the holy men, or buried deep, deep inside the fertile, unknowable delta of some dark vixen who can tango until dawn with a knife between her teeth."

"Done it. Did that. Been there—except for the knife part." I crouched over the chili, stirring it. "Who says I've got a problem?"

"Let's talk man to man, Hoagy," Thor said gravely.

"Sounds good. Who's going to hold up my end?"

"You've gone soft, boy."

"No, I haven't. I was always soft."

"Like hell you were. You were one of the bravest wild men I've ever known."

"You must be thinking of someone else."

"I'm thinking of Stewart Stafford Hoag, who took the heroic journey. Stared your deepest fears in the face, even though it meant turning your whole being into one raw, gaping wound. That's where it all came from, boy. The good work. You bled for it, day in and day out. But now . . . now you've turned into the king of the mild frontier, all snug and contented. We got to get you out of here. We'll hit the road together, you and me. Revive the old Coast to Coast Bruise Band. Ride the rails, sleep out under the stars, hit every seedy barroom between here and Mendocino. What do you say?"

"I'll think about it."

He was silent a moment. I could feel his blue eyes boring through my head. "I'm disappointed in you."

"I said I'd think about it."

The chili was hot. I spooned it into tin bowls and gave him one with a hunk of bread. He took it, shaking his bald head at me. "And you wonder why your work has turned to shit."

"I don't wonder at all. I'm written out, that's all. Happens to everyone."

"Bullshit!" he thundered, startling Lulu, who'd been snoring before the fire. "They stop pushing themselves.

They stop asking why. Just go off in a corner somewhere and quietly form mold. I don't want that to happen to you. You're too damned talented."

"I was," I said, stroking Lulu. "I'm not anymore."

"Dangerous words, Hoagy," he warned, stabbing his spoon at me. "Damned dangerous. This is a horrifying age we live in, this post-modern age. We've become small and mean. We believe in nothing, quest for nothing, care for nothing. Our intellectuals are out of touch with reality. Our press revels in public executions. Yet we do nothing to stem the tide. Because that involves risk, and risk terrifies us. We've forgotten how to be brave. We've forgotten how to be *men*."

We ate, Thor wolfing his chili down hungrily and wiping his plate clean with his bread. He rinsed the dishes in the pond while I fed the fire and poured out our coffee. We sat drinking it and passing the bottle of Laphroaig back and forth, listening to the fire crackle and Lulu snore. Thor dug his ancient mouth harp out of his deerskin vest and played some old hobo blues for a while.

Then he sat back, hands laced across his belly. "You're just making the transition, Hoagy. Happens to all of us."

"Which transition is that?"

"From student to teacher. From asker of questions to provider of answers."

"I have no answers."

"And you're scared shitless about it. Because making a flesh and blood person and subjecting her to this world— that's a terrifying prospect. And not one goddamned bit like writing. Because when we write, we have control over things. They turn out how we want them to. Whole reason we do it."

"And here all along I thought it was to meet babes."

"Promise me something, boy."

"What's that, Thor?"

"Promise me you won't ever stop asking why. Don't give up the quest. Listen to your wild self." He got down on all fours and began pawing at the earth, rather like a madman. "Your wild self is your *wise* self, Hoagy. Pay heed to him." And with that he raised his head and let out a bloodcurdling howl, something of a cross between a coyote and Tarzan after a sex change operation.

Lulu opened one eye. She wanted to know whether I, too, was going to howl. Or at least get down on all fours and paw the earth. No way. No how.

"Pay heed to him, boy!" There was great urgency in Thor's voice now. *"Promise* me!"

"All right, Thor. I promise you."

"Good man." He dusted off his wild self and unhooked the hammered silver and torquoise bracelet that was on his wrist. "This was made by the Hopi from ancient cave drawings of bears and horses. It was passed to me by an elder. I've worn it for thirty years. Time to pass it on. Take it, boy."

"Why?"

"It's a symbol."

"Of what?"

"Just put it on, will you?"

I put it on. It felt heavy, like a shackle, and looked faintly silly on the end of my own arm. But I thanked him anyway.

"I'd like to father another child myself, when Clethra's ready," he informed me. "That's one of the reasons I had to leave Ruth."

"What's another?"

He stuck his lower lip out, thinking it over. "She was my equal, Ruth," he replied. "I used to relish the give-and-take, the disagreements, the battles. But I just got tired of her and her whole damned gender war. Tired of having to defend myself because I have a penis. Tired of listening to one feminista after another go on and on about the innate moral superiority of women. How men are greedy and selfish and immature, and women aren't. How men are afraid of intimacy, and women aren't. How women are caring, and men aren't. How men are obsessed with ego and power, and women aren't. What a load of shit. We're all people, some good, some not so good, all of us struggling to find our way. Men and women should rejoice in our differences, not get into this pointless blame game." He drank down his scotch and held out his cup for a refill. He'd probably downed the equivalent of four doubles and still wasn't showing the slightest effect. "Besides which, it's all their fault. Keep giving us too damned many conflicting signals. They want us gentle, they want us cruel. They want us strong, they want us weak. They want security, they want freedom. Christ, they don't know what they want."

"Yeah, not like us."

"We used to know."

"Did we? That must have been nice."

The air was much chillier now, fire or no fire. I unlaced my boots and climbed inside my sleeping bag for warmth; Lulu burrowed in gratefully after me.

Thor got up and watered a tree, then with a contented groan he climbed inside his own sack. "Man gets to be my age he wants rounded edges, not sharp corners. He wants peace."

"This is your idea of peace?"

"She fights with everyone now," he offered, as explanation. "She's grown sour and bitter. She's a frustrated woman, Ruth. The younger women in the movement, they don't even want to bother with her. Hard to blame them. Who wants to be screamed at day in and day out? So they've cast her aside. And she feels left out. Misses the limelight big-time."

"Well, she's back in it now, big-time."

"And loving every minute of it," he grumbled. "You ask me, that's what this whole mess is about—Ruth getting her name back in the news."

"You don't think she's fighting for her daughter?"

He let out a derisive snort. "Fighting for her? She can't stand her! Christ, she's an awful mother to those children. Never stops haranguing them, screaming at them—"

"Did she really hit them, Thor? Did she physically abuse them?"

Thor hesitated before he answered. "Not in my presence. Never."

"Did you ever see any evidence of physical abuse? Welts, bruises?"

"Clethra says she beat both of them," he answered carefully. "And I believe her. After all, the woman did try to kill me. Missed my left lung by a quarter inch with that knife. And that's no lie."

I sat up, peering at him across the fire. "Who's talking about lies?"

"Nobody," he said curtly.

He was silent after that, his chest rising and falling. Soon, he was snoring softly. I had to keep reminding myself he was seventy-one, and trying awfully hard not to be. I stretched out on my back and listened to the night. I gazed up at the stars, smelling the fresh air, feeling his bracelet on my wrist and Lulu on my hip. Feeling the pull of the open road, stronger than I'd felt it in years. I lay there, wondering what my old friend was getting me into. And how far I was going to let him take me. Eventually, I slept.

Three

HAPPILY, I was able to turn my head again after thirty minutes in a steaming hot tub and a torturous neck rub from Merilee. The shooting pains in my lower back were another matter. Those showed no interest whatsoever in leaving.

"Face it, mister," Merilee concluded. "You're getting too old to sleep on the ground."

"Am not," I grunted as I hobbled about the bathroom, stropping Grandfather's razor and using it. "There was a tree root under me half the night, that's all. And it was decidedly chilly out."

"I see." Her green eyes twinkled at me.

"In fact, I've been thinking I ought to do a lot more camping out—like in the old days."

"Which old days would those be, darling?"

"A long time ago. Before we met."

"Was that when you wanted to move to Oregon and raise peaches?"

"I was plenty happy then," I growled, somewhat defensively.

She glanced at me sharply. "Meaning what? You're not plenty happy now?"

I left that one alone. Limped into the bedroom to dress —the sixteen-ounce gray cheviot wool suit, a black cashmere turtleneck underneath it against the cold, drizzly morning. Tracy was gurgling happily in her bassinet. Lulu had staked out the bed, her kid sister be damned, and dozed there, grateful to be back in the world of flannel sheets and down pillows. Merilee had brought my coffee up on a tray, along with a sheaf of papers.

"You, sir," she reported, "have had three faxes already."

I hated that damned fax machine. It was always beeping and spinning, spinning and beeping. The paper was unpleasantly slick and smelly. To me it was the mimeograph machine revisited, except you couldn't get stoned from the fumes. "Who from?" I asked.

"Clethra's editor. She has questions. She has ideas. She has, apparently, nothing else to do."

"Which editor is it this time?"

"She's so excited about you being involved that she almost wet her pants."

"Oh, her." Actually, I could have done worse. This one was very tight-lipped about ghosts, preferring to hog all of the credit for herself. And she never, ever phoned. Had a pathological fear of human contact—and she didn't much care for dealing with writers either.

I sat down on the edge of the bed, groaning. "I don't get it. Thor's a lot older than I am, and he feels perfectly fine this morning. He even had a swim before we hiked home."

"Yes, he's probably out there right now picking up one

entire side of the barn all by himself," Merilee said drily. "With his jaws."

I took a sip of my coffee. "You don't like him, do you?"

"I don't dislike him." She sat next to me, suddenly uneasy. "I do think he drags you a bit close to the abyss sometimes."

"Maybe that's where I have to be—if I'm ever going to create anything decent again."

Merilee swallowed, her brow creasing fretfully. "Hoagy, has it ever occurred to you that whatever it is you're reaching for . . . that it's not there?"

"Only every day, Merilee. But it *is* there. It has to be there."

"What if it isn't?"

"I'll know."

"What then?"

"I don't know."

"Aren't you frightened?"

"Of course I am. The fear is what drives me."

"You frighten me sometimes, darling."

"Just sometimes?"

"You have this way of getting stuck inside of whatever you're searching for. You're like the mime in the glass box."

I stared at her. "Merilee Gilbert Nash, you've just compared me to a mime!"

She reddened. "I merely meant—"

"Why, that's positively the second worst thing you've ever said to me."

"What's the worst?"

"That night you said, 'Are you a devotee of the Brothers Gibb?' "

"Merciful heavens, Hoagy. I didn't *know* you. W-We'd only just met. I was trying to make conversation."

"You were trying to pick me up," I recalled, grinning at her.

"And I succeeded," she pointed out huffily.

"Only because I was easy." I slipped Grandfather's Rolex on my left wrist, and Thor's bracelet on my right, hefting it. It was a clunky damned thing. She noticed it, of course. "Thor gave it to me last night," I explained.

"You mean like some form of male bonding ritual? How cute. And *look*—it's got lions and tigers and bears, oh, my! Lions and tigers and—"

"I didn't expect you to understand," I grumbled. "It's a . . ."

"Yes, dear?"

"It's a guy thing."

"Yes, dear."

In the distance I heard the *thud-thud-thud* of death metal blasting from Dwayne's eight-inch woofers, followed by the crunch of his tires on the gravel drive. Through the casement windows I could see him hop out of the truck, clutching a Styrofoam cup of coffee from Bess Eaton donuts, his shoulders hunched against the cold. He began to unload his stuff.

The chapel door opened and Clethra came padding out in Thor's big fisherman's knit sweater and nothing else. She closed the door gently, sidled barefoot over to Dwayne and bummed a cigarette off him. She lingered there, smoking it, her head tilted up at him coyly. She was playing with him, much the way a kitten plays with a garter snake, Dwayne ducking his head bashfully. I couldn't hear what they were saying.

"Aren't they cute?" observed Merilee.

"Adorable."

"She's an extremely dull girl, actually. It's astonishing."

"What's astonishing? That she's so dull?"

"That Thor would give up everything for her."

"Strange things happen to us fellers when we get older, Merilee."

"Strange things happen to you when you're younger, too. Let's face it, mister, you're just strange."

"What did you two do last night?"

"Well, *I* pickled my cucumbers . . ."

"Careful, Merilee. You know what that kind of talk does to me."

"And then I made a nice roaring fire up here . . ."

"Whew, it sure is a good thing we have a fireplace up here."

"Stop it! And then I knitted. I'm still trying to finish that baby blanket for my cousin Abigail. That bovine girl, meanwhile, sat in the parlor staring at reruns—*The Brady Bunch, Gilligan's Island, The Partridge Family*—"

"My God, her brains must have oozed right out onto the sofa."

"All the while stuffing her face on potato chips and cheese puffs."

I frowned. "Where did she get those?"

"I let her take the Land Rover down to Reynolds', which I immediately regretted. She was gone so long I was afraid she'd driven it into a ditch." She shot me a worried look. "She's a flipper, you know."

"You mean she watches *Flipper,* too?"

Lulu stirred. Flipper happens to be her own personal favorite.

"I mean she throws up afterward."

"Well, who doesn't?"

"After she eats, you gherkin. She's a binger. Inhales a whole bag of chips and then tosses them. She refused any real food—wouldn't touch dinner. It's not a good thing, Hoagy. I know women who've ended up in the hospital from it."

"Did you two talk at all?"

"Well, she did ask me at one point if it was true that Flo Henderson and Barry Williams did the big naughty."

I shook my head disgustedly. "How can she waste her time on such crap?"

"It's from the past," Merilee replied mildly. "She's fascinated by our cultural heritage, much the same way we were fascinated by Bogart and Bette Davis."

"That's different. That stuff was *good.*"

"Darling, you're starting to sound like an aged foof."

"Only because I'm starting to feel like one."

In her bassinet, Tracy hiccoughed and started to let out distress signals. Merilee went over to her and gathered her up, cradling her in her arms. "Your mother called last night," she mentioned off-handedly.

"Why? What did she want?" I demanded.

She stiffened. "Don't bark at me, mister."

I sipped my coffee and tried it again. "What did she want?"

"She wondered if one of us could run over to the Department of Motor Vehicles for her. The registration is up on their Cadillac."

Always a Cadillac. New one every two years. Always bought, never leased. Leases were for salesmen and con artists. "What did you tell her?"

"That I'd be happy to take care of it."

"Great. And while you're waiting on line at the DMV you can fill out your application for sainthood."

Merilee's jaw tightened, red blotches forming on her cheeks. "Hoagy, I'm trying to be patient and understanding, because I understand just how painful this is for you. But you're not making it easy for me. In fact, you're not making it easy for anyone, including yourself." She waited for me to say something. When I didn't she took a deep breath and kept going. "She also wanted to know if we're coming by on Sunday. She said he really, really looks forward to it. Tracy makes him so—"

"I don't know," I broke in curtly. "I have to go to the city for a couple of days. To see Ruth."

"You're going to try and patch things up between them. Is that it?"

"I don't think anyone can do that."

"But you're going to try," she pressed.

"I'm going to see her. If she'll see me."

"And what of our guests?"

"They'll entertain themselves. Particularly in the afternoon."

"I didn't need to know that, darling. I really didn't." She poked at Tracy's tummy with a long, slender finger, eliciting giggles. "I do think it's rather odd, Hoagy," she said softly.

"What is, Merilee?"

"How you can care so much about the health and wellbeing of other people's families. And so little about your own."

"I don't think that's odd at all, Merilee. In fact, that's my idea of totally, perfectly normal."

The air got warmer as I got closer to town, the cool drizzle turning into a steamy tropical rain, with sudden gusts of wind and lightning crackling angrily across the sky. Most of it had blown over by the time I left the Jag in the garage around the corner from our seven rooms on Central Park West. Just the sticky heat was left. It felt like summer all over again.

It's always jarring to be back in the city after a while away. The people seem to move so furiously, with such grim intent and so little purpose. Briefly, I stand apart from them, wondering what invisible current propels them forward. But within moments the current lifts my own feet from the pavement and sweeps me along and I am one of them.

Pamela, our British housekeeper, was delighted to see me. Pamela's plump and silver-haired and possesses the most unflappable disposition I've ever come across. Lulu adores her. But then Lulu adores anyone who will make her kippers and eggs. I ditched the turtleneck for a lavender broadcloth shirt and cream-colored bow tie, and the cheviot wool for a lighter-weight silk and wool houndstooth. Then I sat down and picked up the phone and found out Clethra had just been Gilloolyed.

This was the day the home video broke, that infamous X-rated video of little Clethra performing her little striptease for Thor in some hotel room. One of the tabloid shows, *Hard Copy,* had gotten ahold of it and planned to show it in all its sleazy glory that evening. Already, there had been no small amount of horn-blowing on their part. Every television news outlet in the country had been rushed a tasty five-second snippet in time for the noon news. Plus, the tabloid's giddy producers had held a raucous morning press conference at the Grand Hyatt Hotel on Forty-second Street, where they flatly refused to say how they'd landed the tape—just that it came from a source close to the family. The tape went for between three and six hundred thousand dollars, depending on who you heard about it from. Me, I heard about it from Ruth, who claimed she'd known nothing about it until the producers called her that morning for her comment. She sounded worn down by this latest dirty installment. She told me I was welcome to come downtown for a talk, provided I was alone. She wasn't referring to Lulu.

Baby Ruth Feingold lived in the bottom two floors of a brownstone down on Greenwich Street, the same apartment she'd lived in back when she represented Greenwich Village in the U.S. Congress. Greenwich is all the way over

on the west side in the middle of the old meatpacking
district. There was still a meatpacking house right next
door to hers. Loud, burly men were busy loading and un-
loading sides of beef at the curb, a battalion of tabloid
cameramen and reporters competing with them for precious sidewalk space—and losing. You don't mess with
meatpackers. Not in New York. Not anywhere. These are
men who know what goes inside of hot dogs. And eat
them anyway.

A cop in uniform was watching it all with glum resignation. I elbowed my way through the crowd to him, my
Borsalino down low over my face, and told him I was
expected. The cop went into the vestibule and buzzed
Ruth. She let me in.

"It's been a long time, Ruth," I said, bending down to
kiss her cheek. The last time was when I had interviewed
her for *Esquire,* back in both of our heydays. "How are
you doing?"

"It stinks out loud is how I'm doing," Ruth fumed, her
voice a raspy, defiant snarl. "It's humiliating, it's painful
and it's *so* typical. He does whatever he goddamned wants
and I have to swallow it to the last drop and pretend I like
it, just like women have been pretending they like it for
centuries."

At our feet Lulu let out a moan. Any allusion to oral sex
has always horrified her.

"It's still a man's world, Hoagy," Ruth raged on.
"Nothing has changed. Not one thing. Did you know that
the average amount a divorced man pays in child support
has *fallen* by twenty-five percent in the past fifteen years?
That the number of women in domestic violence shelters
has *doubled?* That the largest percentage of working
women in this country are *still* entry-level clerks and typ-
ists?" Typical Ruth Feingold scream of consciousness, this.
Only occasionally did the woman come up for air. "Every-

one acts as if we won the war. Baloney. Working women all over this nation are still being shat upon."

"I've got some bad news for you, Ruth. We're all being shat upon."

She stood there in the doorway with her hands on her hips, scowling up at me. "Are you getting taller or am I getting shorter?" she demanded accusingly.

"Never fear, I'm getting taller. Deep down inside I'm still a growing boy."

She let out a snort and closed the door while Lulu and I tried to maneuver our way around her in the hallway. Not so easy. Ruth Feingold was very close to being a perfectly round human organism—no more than an inch or two over five feet and no less than two hundred pounds. You didn't know whether to go around her or over her. Not that you'd make it either way. There wasn't so much as a hint of give to Baby Ruth. She was pure attitude—blunt and passionate and tough. A New Yorker in the truest sense of the word. She was wearing a somewhat ratty cardigan over an EARTH DAY—DO MORE IN '74 tie-dyed T-shirt, slacks, and shearling slippers. Her shock of frizzy hair was silver now, and a pair of reading glasses was suspended from a chain atop her mountainous bosoms. But she'd lost none of her fierceness. The black eyes were still piercing. The fire still burned.

Her apartment smelled of chicken soup and mothballs. Lulu headed straight through the kitchen into the garden out back. She can't stand the smell of mothballs. Don't ask me why. Ruth and I went into the living room, which seemed a lot more Upper Montclair, New Jersey, than it did West Village. There were plastic slipcovers over the somewhat assertive chintz sofa and armchairs. There was thick gold shag carpeting on the floor. There were heavy burgundy velvet drapes over the front windows, blocking out any light from the street. Several lamps were on. There were more plastic slipcovers over the lampshades. One wall was nothing but framed photographs of Ruth with Bobby Kennedy and George McGovern and Eugene McCarthy, with Mailer and Breslin, with Gloria and Betty and Bella and the Shirleys, MacLaine and Chisholm. There were empty spaces on the other walls, outlines of where Thor's pictures used to hang. It was not a tidy room. Dirty dishes and newspapers were heaped on the coffee table, shoes and socks and jackets strewn about the floor.

"As you can see, there's a teenaged boy in the house." She sat, puffing out her cheeks. "Plus I'm still traveling two, three days a week on the lecture circuit. That's how I make my living now. And believe me, it hasn't been easy lately, being a public laughingstock. Women candidates all over the country used to beg me to come speak on their behalf. *Beg me.* Not anymore."

I sat, crossing my legs. "How's your law practice?"

"It sucks," she answered sharply. "Who the hell would hire me?"

"And Arvin?"

She hesitated, swatting at some crumbs on her sweater. "He's been better. We all have."

"I wonder if I could spend a little time with him this afternoon after school."

"Why would you want to do that?"

"To talk to him."

She bristled. "And maybe pass along a message from Thor?"

"Not at all. I have no message."

"Let's get one thing straight, Hoagy," she said, shaking her finger at me. "I regard you as in the enemy camp. I agreed to see you out of courtesy and because you're an old family friend and because I didn't have any other reason to get dressed today. But Arvin is off-limits, understood?"

"If you insist, Ruth."

"I do insist," she said, struggling to get comfortable on the sofa. It wasn't easy for her—her feet didn't touch the floor and she wasn't supple enough to fold her legs under her. She finally settled for a Humpty-Dumpty position, footsies swinging in midair. "I cannot believe that that man actually stooped so low as to peddle a film of Clethra taking her underwear off."

"You think he's the one who sold it?"

She stared at me. "Don't you?"

"I'm trying not to think."

She shook her head at me disgustedly. "Listen to yourself, Hoagy."

"I'm trying not to do that, either."

"There's nothing that man won't do to get what he wants."

"And he's got her," I pointed out.

"But he hasn't got Arvin," she fired back. "And I'll fight him all the way to the Supreme Court to make sure he doesn't get him. That'll cost him hundreds of thousands in legal fees. So wake up and smell the coffee, Hoagy. Ask yourself who else in this whole miserable affair has had their assets frozen. Ask yourself who else has—" She stopped short, her eyes bulging at me. "Isn't that his bracelet you're wearing?"

"It is." I twirled it around my wrist, examining it.

Ruth glared at me witheringly. "I can't believe you're helping him."

"Actually, I'm helping her."

Her face darkened. "What does the little tramp have to say for herself?"

"That she can't please you. That you're always in her face."

"Oh, *please*," she huffed, thrusting her chin at me. "I am what I am, Hoagy. My parents were German Jews who got off the boat in 1936 without three cents in their pockets or a word of English in their heads. My father, who pressed pants in Washington Heights until the day he died, taught me to aim high for myself. So I aimed high. I was valedictorian of my high school class, first in my class in Radcliffe, editor of the law review at Columbia. When I was twenty-five I defended a black woman in Little Rock who'd been accused of murdering a white man—a white man who happened to be raping her in the alley behind her beauty parlor at the time. When I was twenty-six I helped form the National Organization for Women in the ballroom of the Washington Hilton. We had a treasury of one hundred and thirty-five dollars. I've marched in every city in the world. I've been thrown in jail seven times. Elected to Congress four times. When I ran against Abe Beame for mayor of this city I lost by two percentage points. *Two.* Strictly because I wouldn't cozy up to the goddamned unions." She was waving her arms now, the words spilling out in a juicy torrent. "Am I in Clethra's face? You bet I am. She's a straight-A student with a first-class brain. I want her to use it, not sit around on her fat duff watching reruns on TV and spouting all of that Generation X crapola about how pointless and empty life is. I despise that whole goddamned mind-set. I despise laziness and self-indulgence. Do I expect a lot of her? Yes! I expect a lot of everyone." Bitterly, she added, "But this new generation doesn't want to listen to me. I don't tell them what they want to hear."

"Which is what?"

"That they aren't to blame for whatever happens to them in life. That it's somebody else's fault. That they're *victims.* Crapola! Crack babies are victims. Bright, healthy, middle-class women *aren't.* They're self-indulgent weaklings is what they are, weaklings who blame their mommy and their daddy and their nursery school teacher for every goddamned thing that goes wrong, instead of looking in the goddamned mirror. Let me tell you something, Hoagy. Before I came along, the women's movement was just a bunch of neurotic, overprivileged *kvetches* in search of the perfect orgasm. And that's precisely what it has gone back to. But don't listen to me. I'm old-fashioned. I believe if a woman wants equal rights then she has to take responsibility for herself and stop pointing fingers." She paused, a rare thing, and narrowed her eyes at me. "So you're helping Clethra with her book?"

"I am."

She sighed wistfully. "It was always my dream that she'd someday be an author."

I grinned at her. "Spoken like a true Jewish mother."

"Hey, I told you—I am what I am," she fired back indignantly. But with a hint of thaw, too.

I studied her face. "Did you ever physically abuse her, Ruth?"

Ruth studied mine, flaring her nostrils at me. "Never. That's something they cooked up so they can get Arvin away from me. Let 'em try."

"How about Arvin?"

"What about him?"

"Did you ever beat him?"

"I spanked him once when he was four," she answered, turning sardonic on me. "Does that count?"

"You said you expect a lot of people," I mentioned, shifting gears.

"So?"

"What did you expect of Thor?"

She puffed out her cheeks, considering this a moment. It was quiet in the room. I could hear the mantel clock ticking. I could hear the reporters outside joking and laughing. "I expected him to grow old with me," she replied. "I expected him to be by my side. To be true to *me*—instead of to that goddamned heroic quest of his. Which wears mighty thin as a daily diet, believe me. He's insane, you know. He's totally lost control."

"He claims he's in love."

"Oh, please! The man's phallus is in wonderland. He's found the proverbial honey pot. She's young. She's voluptuous. She's flattered by his attention. What college girl wouldn't be? He happens to possess one of the finest minds of the nineteenth century."

"Do you hate him?"

"Out loud," she affirmed. "He killed me, Hoagy. I'm dead inside. If he walked into this room right now I'd claw his goddamned eyes out."

"And Clethra?"

"She's just a child rebelling against her mother," Ruth said mildly, rocking back and forth on the sofa. "Nothing more, nothing less. How's Merilee?"

"Tired a lot of the time."

"Drag her away from that baby if you can," she advised. "Set aside one evening that's just for you two—flowers, wine, a romantic supper. It's vital for young couples."

"I wouldn't exactly call us a young couple."

"She was a wonderful campaigner," Ruth recalled fondly. "So passionate. When she believes in someone, she *believes.*"

"Yes, I suppose she does."

"Cherish her, Hoagy. What you two have together is priceless. You don't realize it until you've lost it like I have. Because you can never get it back. Never." She stuffed her hands in the pockets of her sweater, shuddering. "Know who's been like a rock through this whole thing? Barry. I guess because he knows from public humiliation. Went through so much himself when he came out after our divorce. Marco's been incredibly supportive, too. Gay men, they know what it means to be ostracized, to suffer. If it weren't for those two I'd never have made it through these past few weeks, believe me. Barry has a country place out near you, in Essex. He and Marco have invited Arvin and me out for the weekend."

"How do we fix this thing, Ruth?"

"Fix it?" She gaped at me, incredulous. I couldn't blame her. "We don't *fix* it, Hoagy. We go to court. When we do I'll win sole custody of Arvin. And I *will* win. And then, one of these mornings, Clethra's going to wake up and realize she has absolutely zero interest in sharing another day of her promising young life with an aging lunatic. And when that happens I'll take her in my arms and we'll cry and we'll laugh and then she and Arvin and I will get on with our lives. We'll survive. Hell, I don't blame Clethra. How can I? I just feel sorry for her, that's all."

"I feel sorry for Thor, too."

"You can afford to," Ruth Feingold pointed out. "He hasn't ruined your life. *Yet*."

Barry Feingold and Marco Paolo shared an airy twelfth-floor corner apartment in a pre-war building on Riverside and Seventy-ninth Street. Their view, which soared all the way up the river to the George Washington Bridge, was to die for. Their decor was not. You'd call it eclectic if you were being tactful. Kitschy if you were not. Not so much because of the marble cherubs and the gold-veined mirrors. Or the overstuffed, over-the-top Victorian rosewood chairs and the matched pair of fainting couches. No, it was their collection of antique dress mannequins from the 1930s—those two dozen life-sized plaster men and women, fully costumed, who were positioned about the living room as if in the midst of some scintillating smart set soiree. And who were exceedingly—well—unnerving. Unless, like Bill Clinton, you can get used to being watched over constantly by a Greek chorus of dummies. I know

Lulu found them totally unnerving. She never stopped growling at them the whole time we were there.

The sun was still rather high over the New Jersey Palisades but we decided on martinis anyway, heavy on the olives in my case. Marco went clomping off to the kitchen to make them while I sat across from Barry, who was draped languorously across one of the fainting couches with his ankles crossed. On the stereo Janet Jackson was going *ooh-baby-ooh* with what I suppose she thought was feeling. And, compared to Mariah Carey, I suppose it was.

"So how is old Thorvin these days?" Barry asked me politely.

"Not well, in my opinion."

"Perhaps," he suggested, "it was someone he ate."

Barry Feingold was in his early sixties, second-generation New York real estate money. His father, Herschel, built those awful brick apartment towers in Queens that are clustered practically on top of the Long Island Expressway, the ones you pass on your way to the airport and wonder how anyone could possibly live there. As far as I knew, Barry had never actually held a real job. During the Koch years, he had served as the Mayor's Commissioner of Cultural Affairs. Before that he'd been on some board or another at Lincoln Center. Lately, he'd been backing experimental theater, which is a graceful way of saying he was sleeping late most mornings. Not that Barry wasn't a self-made man. He most decidedly was. He'd made himself into what the British theater people call a laddy boy. Barry was trim and tanned, with a cultivated air of wry detachment and just a hint of the dissolute scamp. He had lovingly coiffed silver hair and a proud, aquiline nose and not a trace of sagging skin. Not under his eyes. Not under his chin. Not nowhere. We're talking multiple tucks. I think he was also wearing a girdle. Either that or he didn't exhale once while I was there. He had on a red velvet smoking jacket, white silk shirt, an ascot, gray flannels and black suede lounging pumps with little gold foxes braided on them. It was not an easy outfit to pull off, especially for someone who grew up in Douglaston, Queens. But Barry worked at it, and Barry Feingold was good at his work.

"That's a deliciously lugubrious little dog you have," he observed cheerily.

"Do you want her?"

Lulu jumped right up and let out a wounded yowl of protest.

Barry frowned—or tried to. Definitely multiple tucks. "Why, are you giving her up?"

"I may have to. We're having some sibling problems. She's not adjusting." This was me taking a stab at tough love. "I'm *hoping* she'll shape up, but if she doesn't . . ."

Lulu glowered at me, not buying one bit of it, then curled back up with a snide little grunt. This was her saying: *You couldn't make it without me if you tried, butthead.*

Marco came clomping in from the kitchen with our martinis. Marco Paolo, the former Mark Paul Humberstone of Grand Island, Nebraska, was a boy toy of the grade-A prime beef variety—six-feet-four and heavily muscled and still not yet thirty. Before Marco caused a stir in the fashion world with his Hasidic leisure ensembles he had been a bouncer at a downtown after-hours club, Mrs. Norman Maine, where he achieved modest renown for putting one of Madonna's entourage in the hospital with a ruptured spleen. It had taken all of Barry's considerable pull to smooth that one over. Marco had spiky hair, orange, and a two-day growth of beard, black. There was a diamond stud in his left earlobe. He wore a flowing black linen shirt, awning-stripe bombachas and no shoes or socks. He seemed edgy, as if he was about to either get violent or break into tears. He was also flushed and rather sweaty. When he handed me my glass his fingers were scalding to the touch.

"I was admiring your suit," he said to me, his voice unexpectedly hushed and demure. He reeked of that new vanilla scent everyone was wearing. Smelled very much like a bakery.

I thanked him and he sat and the three of us drank and talked about my suit, which I'd had made for me in London at Strickland's. And then my brogans, which were also made for me in London, by Maxwell's.

"I've just ordered my first pair of customized orthopedics from T. O. Dey on East Thirty-eighth Street," Marco informed me, mopping at his brow with a red bandanna. "They're costing me six hundred and fifty dollars, but I can't believe I ever lived without them. They're dope. So well made, and just for me. Everyone's getting their shoes made there now—Sly, Cher, Liza . . ."

"That's everyone, all right," I agreed pleasantly.

Yes, it was all very pleasant. Me, I can drink martinis and talk about clothes, especially my own clothes, for hours.

But Barry's glass was empty. "Make us another round, would you, dear?" he said, holding it out to Marco.

Marco got to his feet and started back to the kitchen, moving rather unsteadily. The big guy crashed right into a pair of those non-mobile plaster partygoers, knocking them flat and sending himself sprawling. "I'm okay, I'm okay," he said quickly, scrabbling back to his feet. "Don't fuss."

"Poor bastard's running a fever," Barry clucked as we watched him stagger from the room. "I just know it."

"Is it something serious?"

There was a narrow wooden box of small cigars on the table next to him. Barry removed one and lit it. "Do you mean, is it AIDS?" he asked, arching his brow at me. Or trying to. "He won't go to the doctor to find out. Too afraid. He's HIV positive, you see." He puffed on the cigar, watching the smoke rise toward the chandelier. "We both are."

"I'm sorry to hear that, Barry."

"Ruth doesn't know, by the way," he said airily. "In fact, no one in the family knows."

"Why tell me?"

"Just felt like it, I guess. Maybe I've had too much to drink. We started with wine at lunch and haven't stopped since. Have you noticed how no one drinks in the afternoon anymore? I do believe there's a clear connection between the decline of Western civilization and the death of the two-martini lunch. What do you think?"

"I think no one has any fun anymore. Which, I suppose, is another way of saying you may be on to something."

"It's not as bad as I thought it would be," said Barry, drawing on his cigar. "A certain peace of mind comes with knowing it can all end just like that. I spend a lot of my time thinking about what I haven't done. Do you know I've never been to Niagara Falls or the Grand Canyon?" He paused, in case I wanted to toss anything in. I didn't. "What I've come to realize is that there's no sense getting upset about anything. Just enjoy what and who you have."

"You don't have Clethra," I pointed out.

"I never did," he countered. "Thor's her dad."

"She says *you* are."

"Of course she does. It suits her to say that. Otherwise, she'd be doing something terribly dirty, wouldn't she?"

"I rather thought that was the whole idea."

"I *am* her biological father," Barry conceded. "But he's the one who's been there for her through the years—bandaged her scraped knees, wiped away the tears." He let out a mirthless chuckle. "Awfully strange, the two of them ending up playing hasta la grab ass together."

"Does it upset you?"

"I don't condemn them for it, if that's what you mean. I don't feel I have a right to. I don't feel anyone does."

"That sounds suspiciously like the voice of experience."

"Oh, it is, Hoagy. It most assuredly is."

"Ruth told me you've been a big help through all of this."

"I've tried. Ruthie and I were good together, early on. I just wasn't being me, that's all. It wasn't easy for her, when I came out. People made fun of her, laughed at her. But she was nothing but supportive. She understood. So now it's my turn. Whatever she needs. Hell, it's the least I can do."

There was a crash in the kitchen—glass shattering.

"I'm okay, damn it!" Marco cried out angrily. "I'm *okay!*"

Barry's face fell. Or tried to. "His apparel line is in the toilet, too. Loans up to his ears. The Hasidic look came and went. As a fashion statement, I mean. And I know exactly what you're going to say next . . ."

"How can you when I don't?"

"If he's flat broke what's he doing spending six hundred-some bucks on a stupid pair of shoes, right?"

"Not at all. In the world we live in, appearances are everything."

Barry eyed me approvingly. "You're very perceptive."

"I'm a thin entering wedge, all right. Getting back to Marco . . ."

"I'd much rather talk about your thin entering wedge," he joked.

"Down, boy."

"I may have to sell my country house to bail him out," he confessed wistfully. "I'll miss it terribly. It's so quiet out there you can hear a cliché drop. And we tool around the back roads in this dear little old bug-eyed Sprite. I suppose that'll have to go, too."

"What year is it?" I asked, tugging at my ear.

"A '59. Are you interested?"

"Does it have any rust?"

"Don't we all?"

That one I let him have.

"My money is in a trust, you see," Barry continued. "Can't be touched without being okayed by a committee of bean counters. Bailing out Marco's line would not be their idea of sound investment strategy. And even if it were, I'm quite certain they'd demand a blood test of him. Anyone who's backing fashion these days does. And that would be the end of that."

"I'm sorry to hear you say all of this, Barry. It gives you a motive."

He stared at me. "A motive for what?"

"Peddling this tape of Clethra. Lots of money involved."

"But I didn't," he insisted, reddening. "I couldn't. I wouldn't. The girl's my own flesh and blood. I'd never do something like that to her."

"You wouldn't be doing it to her. You'd be doing it to him."

"Thor?"

I nodded. "This is bound to throw even more public sympathy toward Ruth. Hard for people to root for a man who makes videos of his teenaged lover taking her clothes off. It's unseemly."

"Maybe so," he admitted. "But how would I even get hold of that tape?"

"You tell me."

He turned chilly on me. "I don't think I like what you're insinuating, Hoagy."

"Okay, if you didn't do it, then how about Marco?"

Barry shook his head. "All butt, no brain. Dumb as a

salt cod, that one. Actually, I was thinking it was Thor who did it."

Marco returned with our martinis. "Thor who did what?" he demanded.

"Nothing, dear," Barry said hurriedly, reaching for his glass.

"Goddamned caveman is what he is," Marco spat angrily. "He saw a piece of meat and he took it!"

"Marco, sit down and drink your—"

"Like one of those animals who rub up against school-girls on the subway and come in their trousers!" Marco thundered, clenching and unclenching his big fists. He was shaking with rage. "Someone ought to cut the old bastard's schlong off for what he did to Clethra. And to poor Barry, too. Hurting him this way. Barry doesn't deserve this, especially . . ." Marco trailed off; his features darkened.

"Especially now?" I put in.

He shot a look at Barry. "You *told* him?"

Barry gave him a mild shrug in reply.

Marco breathed in and out several times rapidly, his eyes wild. Man looked like he was about to explode. Then he let out a wounded sob and went running off to the bedroom, knocking over several more partygoers en route. He slammed the door behind him. The whole apartment shook.

Barry sipped his martini, totally unfazed.

I got to my feet. So did Lulu. "Thank you for your time, Barry," I said.

Barry frowned, or tried to. "But you've not touched your drink, Hoagy."

"You drink it. For some strange reason, I'm not thirsty anymore."

. . . .

I walked up Riverside to my old apartment, the drafty fifth-floor walk-up on West Ninety-third Street I'd had since before I met Merilee. And still kept as an office. It had little or nothing in the way of heat, and hadn't been painted since the seventies. Or cleaned, for that matter. Something of a dump, if you want to know the truth. But the apartment on Central Park West was *ours*. The farm was *hers*. This place was *mine*. What can I tell you—it's a guy thing.

Lulu made right for the fridge. There wasn't much in there besides her jar of anchovies and a half loaf of pumpernickel with a bull's-eye of blue mold growing on it. I threw her an anchovy. Then I called home.

"How's my little girl?" I asked when she picked up.

"Fine, darling," she answered wearily. In the background I could hear small splashing noises.

"And how's the midget?"

"A holy terror. We're having a bath. And when I say we, I mean *we* . . . No, sweetness, please don't kick! Mercy, I've gotten soap in my eyes six times already. I should start wearing goggles."

From the floor next to me Lulu started whimpering. She always knows when it's her mommy on the phone. Don't ask me how.

"I've been thinking, Merilee. We haven't had an evening out alone in quite some time."

"We've never had an evening out alone. That was all a dream."

"We'll dress to kill. Something black and low-cut and slinky."

"Sounds perfect for you, darling. But what shall I wear?"

"We'll eat caviar, we'll drink champagne, we'll paint the town until we drop. Tracy can stay with Pam for the night. What do you think?"

"I think you've just saved my life. But what of Thor and the bovine girl?"

"Oh, him. I would have words with him, if he's available."

"They're out in the chapel, darling." She lowered her voice. "It's the afternoon, you know."

"It's important, I'm sorry to say."

"I'll have Dwayne fetch them out a cordless phone. Hang on . . . Oh, darling?

"Yes, Merilee?"

"You're not too terrible."

"You're not too terrible yourself."

Thor got on in a few moments. "How's the big city, boy?" he boomed, all hale and hearty.

"I take it you haven't heard the latest news."

"Which news is that?"

I told him. And he hadn't known about it. Or at least he gave a very good imitation of not having known about it.

"I would never do such a thing, Hoagy," he protested, his voice turning thin and strangely high-pitched. "Clethra's body is a sacred temple. I would never, ever defile it in such a way."

"You didn't sell the tape?"

"I don't even own a video camera," he insisted. "You must believe me, boy. You *must*." He sounded genuinely shaken. And old. He sounded old.

"Thor, would you mind putting Clethra on?"

I heard heated words between the two of them. Couldn't make out what they were. Then she got on.

"I don't know anything," she whined right off, like a kid who'd just been caught with a couple of joints in her sock drawer.

"Clethra, you know who filmed you taking your clothes off, don't you?"

"Duh . . . yeah."

"Well, then we have to have a talk about it."

"But—"

"When I get back."

"But—"

"Just you and me."

"Oh, okay," she said glumly. "But I don't know much."

"That much I already figured out."

I hung up and went digging in the bedroom closet. The old metal strongbox was up on the top shelf, back behind the shoeboxes full of tax returns and canceled checks, the files full of old contracts, the bound galleys and manuscripts and other paper entrails of my so-called adult life. I got the strongbox down and set it on my desk, staring at it a moment. Then I opened it.

It was all in there. The journals, the notebooks, the photographs. All just as I'd left them. Hadn't looked at them in, what was it, ten years? Longer? But leafing through them took me right back. Back to Amsterdam and Istanbul and Lisbon and Barcelona. Back to Cadaques, where I tended bar for my keep and fell in love eight times every night. Back to Port Vendres, where I went out with the fleet before dawn. Back to London: *This is a city of smells —diesel fuel, stale ale, cigar smoke and the rancid odor of forgotten ambitions and failed dreams."* Whoa, heavy, man . . . To the Isle of Skye: *"The light is different here. Perhaps it is the clouds. Or perhaps it is history itself. The world is so much older here."* Step aside, Bill Faulkner . . . I glanced through the snapshots—a Portuguese girl whose name I didn't remember but whose breasts I did. A gang of six kids I stayed with in Truro, helping them fix up a thatched cottage that had no heat or running water . . . I flipped through my sketchbooks—not that I was ever going to be an artist. This was an exercise Thor had taught us. First you looked at something, then you tried to draw it with your eyes closed. It was a way of strengthening your powers of observation. Opening up your mind, or expanding it, or . . . it was supposed to do something to your mind.

It was Thor who'd urged me to take the year off before I started my career. The world, he assured me, would still be there when I got back. Father had a much different plan for me. He expected me to come take my place at the old brass factory on the banks of the Housatonic River, the one that had been in the family since 1823. But I wanted to see the world first. And I did. And Thor was right. It was the greatest year of my life. And Thor was wrong. My world wasn't there when I got back. The factory failed. Not that I could have saved it. No one could have. But you couldn't tell Father that. He'd never forgiven me for deserting him. And I'd never forgiven him for not understanding me. Nothing had changed between us to this day. I still thought he was a rigid, close-minded, sanctimonious prig. He still thought I was a juvenile, irresponsible hedonist. He had never even read my two novels.

And now it was too late. Now he never would.

I sat there, sifting through my artifacts of the road and feeling the old wanderlust. Maybe Yucatán this time. Sleeping on the beach. Living on grilled fish and iced *cerveza*. New sights. New sounds. New voices, other than the ones already up inside my head. Maybe Thor was right once again. Maybe it was what the novel needed.

Maybe it was what *I* needed.

One glance at Grandfather's Rolex brought me back— from the old and the restless to the young and the sleazy. Time to watch Clethra on *Hard Copy*. I flicked it on just in time to catch her. She was standing there in a T-shirt and tight jeans, giggling at the camera. She was in what appeared to be a hotel room. There was a mirrored dresser and a bedspread made of something shiny. Her hair was frizzier than she wore it now, and she seemed a bit chubbier. She also seemed to be drunk or stoned or both—her eyes were half shut and she was staggering. A muffled male voice from behind the camera was egging her on. I couldn't tell if the voice was Thor's or not. I kept watching for a glimpse of him in the mirror over the dresser, but there wasn't one. There was only Clethra. Slowly and self-consciously, she started shaking it. And since there was no music, she started singing it, too. That old Aerosmith chestnut, *Walk This Way.* Soon she was strutting and grinding and doing her best Steven Tyler, which is not much worse than Steven Tyler's best Steven Tyler. The T-shirt came off first. She had a bra under it, and no belly button ring. The bra came off next. The producers of *Hard Copy,* being such upholders of moral decency, blurred out her nipples. She unbuttoned her jeans next, but when she tried to wiggle out of them she lost her balance and fell over with a thud, clapping her hands together and screeching with laughter. And then it ended, all thirty seconds of it. It wasn't much. It certainly wasn't sexy. Mostly, it was embarrassing and pathetic and sad. And now everyone in the United States had seen it. The show's anchorperson capped it all off with some slavering speculation about just how long ago this little striptease show was filmed and whether it might prove that Thor and Clethra's illicit love had been consummated when she was still underage.

My phone rang two seconds after I turned off the TV.

"Oh, good. I found you." It was Ruth. She didn't sound pleased.

"You saw it?"

"I saw it. And I hope he's awful goddamned proud of himself."

"He swears he didn't film it, Ruth. And, to be fair, there's no proof it's him."

"It's him," she declared with utter certainty.

"How do you know?"

"I know him."

"Did you recognize the room?"

"Nah. Some hotel room. I'm going to hire a private detective to track down which hotel and when they stayed there. The date's crucial. If we can prove that sick old bastard laid so much as a finger on her when she was under seventeen then he's going to jail for statutory rape. Hoagy, I've changed my mind."

"About what, Ruth?"

"You and Arvin. He . . . got into a fight with one of the boys at school today. And he won't talk to me about it. Not a word. Maybe you he'll open up to. He could sure as hell use a mature male in his life right now."

"Wait, I thought you wanted him to talk to *me.*"

"Do you want to or don't you?" she barked impatiently.

"I'll be right over."

"What are you, some kind of therapist?"

"I'm a writer. Still trying to figure out which kind. Would you like another hot dog?"

"What are you, kidding?"

"Yeah, I'm a human whoopee cushion. Feel free to sit on me. Everyone else does."

Not that I could argue with his taste. The hot dogs were limp and flavorless, the buns stale. My beer was flat and he still hadn't touched his Coke. Great seats though, right behind third base. Of course, great seats weren't hard to come by at Shea in October. Not with the Mets falling out of play-off contention by Mother's Day. They were just playing out the string on another long, losing season now. I doubt there were more than two thousand people in the whole stadium, counting the players, coaches and vendors, all of whom seemed really bored. Some non-touted prospect was laboring out there on the mound in the hazy, heavy air, falling behind to every Marlin he faced. He gave up three runs before he got his first out, the flop sweat streaming from him. Dallas left him out there anyway. For seasoning.

I couldn't blame Arvin Gibbs for being hostile, either. Which he was. He had plenty to be hostile about. Thor's son was also confused and tightly wound, a pent-up basket case with an oversized Adam's apple that jumped up and caught every third or fourth word he tried to get out. He spoke in quick gulps, almost like he had the hiccoughs, and he had very little control over which octave he was in. He was a gangly kid, nearly six feet tall, with thick wire-rimmed glasses, a pubic mound of curly black hair on his head, mournful eyes and ears he hadn't grown into yet. He had pimples scattered across his face in a connect-the-dots fashion and braces on his top and bottom teeth. He looked much more like a nerd than he did a brawler. But his battle trophies—the fat, tender lip, the welt under his left eye— said otherwise. He wore a Barnard sweatshirt, jeans and scuffed Air Jordans, and had not objected to eating out with me, even though I was a complete stranger. He seemed to have accepted that he had no control over his life, which is a sad thing to already know and accept when you're only fourteen years old.

He was not a big baseball fan. Didn't know who was on first and didn't give a shit, which is true of a surprising number of kids his age. Mostly, he just stared out at the field in sullen silence. Lulu, on the other hand, was clam happy. She has a major thing for Ryan Thompson, the Mets' outfielder. Or, more precisely, his tush. Plus the housewife next to us had left a half-eaten tuna sub under her seat when she and her husband bailed in the fourth inning.

"I'm also a family friend, Arvin. Clethra and your dad are staying with me in the country."

His eyes stayed on the field. "You must be writing her book for her."

"I'm helping her."

"Nah, you're writing it. She's a total doof when it comes to books. Doesn't read a bit."

"Do you?"

"A ton. Sci-fi, mostly." He pulled a tattered paperback out of his back pocket. The cover featured a large, distasteful insect lost in cyberspace. "I could care less about the hardware. I'm just really into fantasy."

"It sure beats the hell out of reality."

He shot me an appraising glance, but said nothing more about it. Or anything else.

I ordered a bag of peanuts from one of the vendors and another beer. Out on the field, Dallas was finally pulling his pitcher, who was trailing 5–2 in the fifth. The kid got a polite hand from the tiny crowd when he left the mound, except for the six beery pinheads behind the dugout who started screaming obscenities at him. Six more rushed to the kid's defense. Soon the whole bunch was throwing beer and wild punches at each other. They all got taken away in handcuffs by security. No one seemed particularly alarmed. Just another night at the ballpark, '90s style.

"Looks like you got in a fight today," I said, munching on the peanuts, which were stale. "Somebody give you a hard time about Clethra?"

Arvin shrugged. He colored slightly. "This dick Stan Passey, he heard about . . . he wanted to know if my dad let me watch while he filmed her dropping her clothes."

"Did he?"

"No!" Arvin cried indignantly. "I wasn't even there."

"But you were there when it all started between the two of them."

"Says who?"

"Clethra. She told me you were home the evening she and Thor made love together for the first time."

Arvin gulped some air, his plaintive eyes on the field. "If I was, I didn't see anything or hear anything," he muttered.

"How about the other times?"

He didn't answer me.

"Did you ever see the two of them kiss?"

"You mean like father and daughter or the other kind?"

"The other kind."

"No. Not ever. I just wish . . ." He halted, his voice a strangled quaver.

"You just wish what, Arvin?"

"People would leave us alone!" he blurted out, loud enough to turn the heads of all the fans sitting near us. All three of them.

I drank some of my beer. "Arvin, your dad was real nice to me once, back when I was younger and kind of confused. I think he's kind of confused now. So I'm trying to help him. Friends do that for each other."

"So what's that got to do with me?"

"He told me how much he misses you. Is there anything you'd like to say to him?"

"Sure." He craned his neck uneasily, fingering his tender lip. "That I hate his fucking guts for what he did to Clethra."

"What did he do to her?"

"He took her away from me. I miss her. She's my best friend."

She'd said the same thing about him. "You're not friends with the guys at school?"

"I'm not friends with anyone." He said it glumly.

"So you think all of this was your dad's doing?"

"Don't you?" he shot back.

"Clethra seems to feel she had as much say about it as he did."

"I miss her," he repeated earnestly.

"And that's why you hate your dad?"

His Adam's apple bobbed. He didn't reply.

"How about your mom?"

"What about her?"

"Do you love her?"

"I guess. She's gone a lot of the time, making speeches and stuff. Clethra always used to be around. Now there's nobody. Just some dorky woman I don't even know who stays with me. She's Mom's publicist's secretary. It's really lame. It's not like I need a baby-sitter anymore. Mom . . . she can be hard to take a lot of the time. But she's okay."

"Are you afraid of her?"

He frowned at me quizzically. "Isn't everyone?"

He had a point. "Has she ever smacked you around? Beaten you, punched you?"

"She spanked me once when I was little," he replied, gulping. "I called her a bad word is why. I called her a cunt. That's a bad word, right?"

"Yes, that's a very bad word."

"How come?"

"Something to do with the way it sounds coming out." I examined his bruised and battered face. "Arvin, did your mom give you that fat lip?"

"I got it in a fight at school. I told you."

"That's right, you did."

"Mr. Hoag?"

"Make it Hoagy."

"Is it wrong what Clethra and my dad are doing?" he wondered. "Is it a bad thing?"

"The world certainly sees it that way."

"How do *you* see it?"

I tugged at my ear. "People aren't always going to do

what's right, Arvin. Or smart or responsible or any of those sane, worthwhile things. A lot of the time they just fuck up. They don't mean to, but they can't help themselves. I know you're pissed off right now. That's part of the deal when you care about somebody. Not much of a deal sometimes, but in the long run it beats being all alone."

He sorted through this, nodding miserably to himself.

"Which of your parents would you rather live with?" I asked him. "In a perfect world, I mean."

"Neither of them," he answered. "I'd like to live on a deserted island somewhere, just me and Clethra. We don't need anybody else."

"That's your idea of happy?"

"That's my idea of awesome."

"I understand you're heading out to Barry's this weekend."

"Yeah . . . ?"

"Care to see her?"

"*Could* I?"

"Sure, why not?"

"Mom won't like it," he pointed out.

"I can handle her," I assured him.

He looked me up and down. "You?"

"Don't kid yourself. I'm a lot tougher than I look."

Lulu promptly started coughing at my feet.

"Why's she doing that?" he asked, frowning at her.

"Peanut shell. Would you like to see your dad, too?"

"Never," Arvin snapped. "Not as long as I live. I can never, ever forget what he did. Not *ever.*"

"It's true, Arvin. You won't forget. But you will forgive."

"No, Hoagy, I won't."

Arvin Gibbs said this with total conviction. In fact, I'd never heard anyone sound more certain of anything in my entire life.

Four

S HE WAS SITTING out there waiting for me with the porch lights on
when I pulled up outside the carriage barn. She'd heard
the Jag coming. There wasn't much other noise out
there at 2 A.M., not unless you count the raccoon fights.
She was planted rather ripely on the hood of the Land
Rover in her black leather jacket and nothing else, strik-
ing a pose straight out of a Snap-On tool calendar.

"Don't you ever wear any clothes?" I asked her. From
closer up her hair was uncombed and she gave off a
pungent smell of sweat.

"Why?" she wondered, puffing on a cigarette, one
bare foot swinging up and down, up and down. "Don't
you like looking at me?"

Right away Lulu let out a low, menacing growl.

Clethra let out a laugh. "She hates me, am I right?"

"She tends to be wary around animals she considers
predatory."

"Is that what you think I am?" she asked, running her index finger slooowly along the Rover's hood.

"Let's just say I'm trying to keep an open mind."

"That's real decent of you, homes."

"Not really. Thor asked me to. Is he asleep?"

"Sort of." She glanced unhappily at the chapel. "Like, he drank up a whole bottle of your scotch after dinner and did the George Bush thing."

"The George Bush thing?"

"Passed out in his own vomit."

"Better his own than someone else's." I leaned against the Rover with my arms crossed. "So much for his training regimen, huh?"

She flicked her cigarette butt off into the darkness with a cascade of orange sparks. It glowed there a moment, then went black. "Like, which training regimen?"

"He's sailing solo around the world next spring."

She stared at me. "He's *what?!?*"

"He didn't tell you, did he?" Somehow, I wasn't surprised.

"No, he *didn't* tell me," she whined fretfully. "What am *I* supposed to do?"

"He's hoping you'll go back to school."

"But I don't wanna go back to school!" she cried, her voice turning high and shrill. "I wanna be with him! I can't *believe* him! Gawd, I hate guys sometimes. I mean, they just go off and they do whatever they wanna do and then you have to find out about it from their friends. And if you have a problem with it, then, like, it's *your* problem."

"Why did Thor get so drunk tonight, Clethra?"

She looked away, her face tightening. "He was real upset about that video."

"I can well imagine. You weren't?"

She shrugged her shoulders inside her jacket. "Not really. I don't get upset anymore."

More of that blasé Generation X nihilism. Briefly, I wanted to throw her over my knee and spank it out of her. But that prospect made my face tingle and my palms sweat.

A romantic night. We definitely needed a romantic night.

"Let's go inside and talk."

She shook a cigarette out of her pack. "Can I smoke in there?"

"Let's stay out here and talk."

"Okay," she agreed, lighting it. "Only, I didn't have shit to do with it."

"Who did?"

"We were goofing is all. I mean, God, it wasn't like it was ever for somebody else to look at." She squirmed unhappily there on the hood, much the way Lulu does when she has a personal itch. "But I guess now that I'm some bizarre public figure the temptation is too big for some people."

"Which people, Clethra?"

She hesitated, her eyes glistening at me in the porchlight. "Like Tyler."

"Your boyfriend?"

"Ex-boyfriend."

"Want to tell me about it?"

I heard a skittering noise in the carriage barn. Lulu stayed put, not so much as a woof out of her—Sadie was stalking a mouse. Or, even worse, a bat.

"Well, it wasn't filmed in some hotel, okay?" Clethra said. "We made it in his parents' bedroom on East Seventy-second Street—one night when they were out of town. Their place just looks like a hotel is all. We were smoking a joint and drinking some peppermint schnapps and Tyler, like, found this video camera of theirs and so we decided to do it. Y'know, for fun?" She pulled on her cigarette. "I didn't even know he still had it. I mean, I figured he'd thrown it out or something."

"Well, he didn't. Is Tyler at Columbia?"

"Uh-huh. He lives in Furnald Hall. His last name's Kampmann."

"Are you still seeing him?"

"No way!" she answered hotly. "He kept dicking other girls behind my back. He's just a total snake. But I guess that's pretty obvious, am I right? His father used to have big bucks. Lost it all in the stock market crash, not that I'm trying to make excuses. Tyler's really into the ambition thing. Has all these big plans for law school and shit. So I guess now he'll be able to pay for it. I still think the only real reason he went out with me was so he could meet my mom. He was just, like, totally impressed by her."

"I saw her today."

"Oh, yeah?" she said, feigning a lack of interest.

"Arvin as well."

"You saw *Arvy?*" she cried, her brow creasing with tender concern. It was the first genuine, human reaction I'd gotten out of her. "Oh, man, how's my sweet baboo?"

"Confused and upset. He misses you."

"God. Like, me, too."

"Would you like to see him this weekend? I might be able to arrange it."

"I'd kill to."

"That may not be necessary. Of course, I'll expect something in return."

She peered at me, instantly suspicious. "Like what?" she demanded, giving her jacket a huffy little tug.

"I don't like surprises, Clethra. In this business, they can be just about the worst thing there is. So I want you to tell me what you haven't told me."

She considered this a moment, plump lower lip fastened between her teeth. "I don't know what you mean."

"Don't you?"

"No, I don't," she insisted heatedly. "I really, really don't."

"There's nothing you want to tell me? Not one thing?"

She ducked her head. "Well . . . I guess there's something I wouldn't mind *asking* you, if you wouldn't mind. I thought about asking Merilee but she already thinks I'm some kind of bimbonic whore slutsky . . ." She glanced nervously over at the chapel. "Do you think it would be bad for me to see other guys? Like, since I'm with Thor and everything. I mean, if you were him, would you mind if I went out with somebody else?"

I stood there studying her face. She seemed incredibly sincere. Also incredibly young. She was still only eighteen years old, no matter how fast she was growing up. I had to keep reminding myself of that. "Yes, I would mind," I said slowly. "As a general rule, it's not a good idea to sleep with more than one man at a time."

"Y'see, that's just it," she said, nodding. "We're not."

"You're not what?"

"Sleeping together. I mean, we are but we aren't—if you can dig where I'm coming from."

I tugged at my ear. "I'm afraid you'll have to help me."

"Look—how well do you know Thor? I mean, you're his friend, right? So when do you think we'll . . . y'know, get busy?"

"You mean you're not?"

"Like, I don't think so."

"Like, you're not sure?"

"No, I'm plenty sure, homes. We're not. We *sleep* together. We hold, we hug, we kiss. But no sex. Not yet, anyway. He won't. He just plain won't." She pulled on her cigarette, squinting at me through the smoke. "You're surprised."

"Every once in a while. In fact, this one may make my

highlight reel." Not that I should have been surprised. One of the chief characteristics of the work I do is that just when I think I understand what's going on I realize it doesn't make the least bit of sense at all. In that regard it's a lot like the films of David Lynch. "So let's get this straight, Clethra. Everything you told me before was bullshit? That whole seduction scene? How it was *different* than it was with Tyler? How Thor made you feel *cleansed?* How you two like to get *cleansed* every afternoon? Lies? All lies?"

"I guess it maybe comes off that way," she replied uncomfortably. "But it's, like, if you keep on telling yourself enough times that it's happening you start to believe it is, even if it isn't."

I nodded. She wasn't wrong there. This was the entire basis of Reaganomics.

"It's like we *should* be," she went on. "I *want* us to be. I guess I'm hoping that by saying it *is* I can somehow make it real. Only, why won't he do me, Hoagy? Is it because he's so old?" She lowered her eyes. "I mean, I heard a lot of men his age can't get a chubby."

"And what about your mom?"

"Huh?"

"Has she actually abused you and Arvin? Or is that just more of your Disneyfied reality?"

"She terrorizes us," Clethra replied harshly.

"That's not an answer," I said.

"That's the *truth,*" she insisted, her voice trembling.

"I see." Was it? Who the hell could tell? Not me. This teenager was the consummate liar—she believed in her make-believe as much as she did in the truth. If not more. "Have you spoken to Thor about this?"

"Like, yeah. Constantly."

"And what's his response?"

"He says we'll do it when I'm ready. That's what he

keeps saying—*when I'm ready*. Shit, I'm so ready I could die. I mean, sometimes after he's fallen asleep next to me I have to—"

"I don't need to know this part."

"Will you talk to him for me?" she pleaded. "Will you ask him when we get to fuck?"

"Clethra, may I ask you a stupid question?"

"Duh, yeah."

"Why did you run off with Thor?"

"I thought it would be excellent," she replied simply.

"You thought it would be excellent to destroy your entire family?"

"I guess I just thought, like, people would be more cool about it. That they wouldn't freak out so much. And I thought that when we did split that we *would*. Get it on, I mean. Like, that the only reason we hadn't was because we were still living at home."

"Do you love Thor?"

"Uh-huh."

"No second thoughts?"

"Uh-uh."

"Then why do you want to see other guys?"

"I don't," she insisted. "I just . . . I'm frustrated, that's all."

"Clethra, why did you really run away with him? Was it to get back at your mom? To hurt her? Is that what this is all about?"

She rolled her eyes, greatly annoyed. "No!"

"Then why?"

"You really, really don't get it?"

"I really, really don't get it."

She stared at me like she thought I was a major doof. And replied, "He asked me to."

. . . .

There were two faxes from Clethra's editor waiting for me on the kitchen table. One said: *"What do you think about Clethra topless on the cover?"* The other said: *"Disregard previous fax."* Me, I value my independence. I disregarded them both.

I tiptoed up the stairs with Lulu in my arms so as not to wake Tracy. Stripped off my clothes and climbed into bed next to Merilee, who was all long and warm and cozy. She stirred, snuggling against me.

I lay on my back with my arm around her. I could feel her breath on my neck. "Merilee?"

"Yes, darling?" she murmured heavily.

"I just reached a somewhat startling conclusion about us."

"Wait, don't tell me . . ." She yawned. "You think I'm the cutest human life-form on the face of the planet and you can't live without me."

"No, I've always known that."

"Why, darling, that's absolutely the second nicest thing you've ever said to me."

"What's the nicest?"

"That time you told me I could count Velveeta as a vegetable." She reached for her water glass and drank some, the nursery monitor on her nightstand mercifully silent. "So what is it?"

"We lead an extremely sane life."

"Well, that was rather the whole idea, wasn't it, darling?"

"Yes, I suppose it was," I said quietly. Too quietly. I could feel her eyes searching for mine in the darkness. "I brought you a pile of stuff from the city. Scripts they want you to read."

"Ptooey. Not interested. I've got better things to do than get disemboweled by those lousy sons of sea cooks." She plumped her pillow. She had herself another drink of water. She lasted a full seven seconds before she said, "Anything good?"

"The new Spielberg."

"I said anything *good.*"

"The Shuberts are bringing *The Miracle Worker* back to Broadway."

"For Mac Culkin," she sniffed. "They're still looking for their Annie Sullivan."

I frowned. "Who's Mac Culkin playing?"

"The child, naturally."

"Isn't he a little old?"

"He plays young."

"But it's a girl child."

"Not anymore it's not."

"But it's *Helen Keller.*"

"Correction, darling, it's *Broadway,* and Mac is a tourist attraction, which is all they care about anymore." She sighed regretfully. "They're destroying the theater in this country. Turning it into a satellite of Las Vegas—garish and mindless and not half as entertaining as *Hard Copy.*"

I glanced at her. "You saw it?"

"The three of us watched it together. She was enthralled, he was ill. All I kept thinking was that there's no point in being a performer anymore. You're better off if you commit some crime."

"She didn't," I reminded her.

"People don't want to see *Hamlet.* They want to see Joey Buttafuoco."

"Me, I want to see Joey Buttafuoco in *Hamlet.*"

"This is serious, darling," she said gravely. "I'm obsolete."

"Talent and beauty never go out of style, Merilee."

"Craftsmanship does," she countered. "If everyone is a performer, then no one is." She paused. "Does it bother you much?"

"You being obsolete?"

"Us leading this so-called sane life."

"Come here, I want to show you something."

I took her in my arms and kissed her. She kissed me back and then the furnace kicked over and, slowly, the heat started to come on all over the place. We slid deeper down into the bed, and each other, her breathing becoming deeper and steadier, my own more rapid and fervid. I heard her groan softly under me. And then I heard something else.

From the baby monitor.

I heard the Monster Gulp.

We called it that because it sounded exactly like the startled gulp Frankenstein's monster made the first time he caught a gander at himself in the mirror. This was Tracy's way of letting us know she'd been activated and was now lying there in her crib pondering what she could do for amusement. Chances were now nine out of ten she would choose: Cry. There wasn't much else on her personal menu.

We both froze, hoping she'd fall back to sleep this once. Just this once. Hoping, hoping . . .

She didn't.

"Let's ignore her," I suggested over the din. "Let her cry herself out."

"Are you saying this because you consider it an important aspect of child rearing?" Merilee wondered, her eyes gleaming at me. "Or because you're desperate to slip me your frightful hog?"

"I adore your quaint little expressions."

"Is that all you adore?"

"Come here, I want to show you something else."

"I'll tell you what, darling," she offered, struggling to climb out from under me. I wasn't exactly helping. "Keep my side warm and I'll be back before you know it."

She was right, too. Kind of. I didn't know it when she got back. I'd been fast asleep for an hour.

"Why did you run off with Clethra, Thor?"

Thor downed his shot of Wild Turkey and washed it down with a gulp of Rolling Rock. "I told you, boy. I love her." He wiped his mouth with the back of his hand, grinning at me contentedly. "I feel reborn. Possessing that fine, firm young flesh of hers. Feeling her heat around me, squeezing me, pulsing around me like a—"

"Shut up, Thor."

He peered at me, taken aback. "Shut up?"

"You haven't laid a hand on her and we both know it. So why don't you drop-kick the reconstituted Henry Miller and tell me what the hell's going on?"

Thor hesitated, scratching at his beard. Then he gave me a brief nod and signaled the proprietor, Slim Jim, for another shot. They called him Slim Jim because he was circus fat, 350 pounds easy. His place, which was up past Rogers Lake on the old Boston Post Road, was our nearest watering hole. A rustic log cabin with a potbellied stove that served shots and beer and corn nuts. Sort of a biker bar, only without the glamour. The slack-jawed boys all hung there, grungy and unshaven; the air was thick with their cigarette smoke. There was a pool table and a jukebox and a TV. It being a Saturday afternoon, Notre Dame was busy running up the score on some patsy. The dozen or so regulars were hunched over their beers watching them in bored, dumb silence, all of them young and big-boned and sullen. More of Thor's Lost Boys. I recognized them. They were the ones who mowed the lawns and pumped the gas and rounded out the paving and roofing crews during the paving and roofing season. Most of them still lived with their folks, although if you wanted to contact them the best way was to dial 1-800-HUH?. This was where they hid out. Us they ignored, just as they ignored the pair of low-rent bar floozies who were shooting pool, both of them short and fat and forty, with raccoon eye makeup and bleached-out, sticky-looking hair.

"I can do this cool trick," one floozie announced hoarsely to no one in particular. "All I need is two balls and a straight stick."

None of the gang reacted, no doubt because they'd all heard it before eight or nine hundred times. Lulu, who was curled up at my feet, ignored her completely.

Even when she sidled over to me and said, "Hey, mister, can I borrow your balls?"

"Sorry, they're in use."

She let out a wicked laugh, which I suppose she thought was sexy, and which quickly turned into a hacking cough, which decidedly was not. And then Slim Jim waddled back with Thor's whiskey and chased her off.

Thor stared moodily down into his glass, cupping it in his big scarred mitts. "I love her, boy. That's all there is to it."

"Then why won't you have sex with her?"

"That," he replied, "is none of your business."

"Wrong, Thor. You made it my business when you showed up out here, begging me to help you. Besides which, she asked me to ask you. So I'm asking you."

He tugged at his lower lip, his big chest rising and falling. His eyes were on the TV over the bar. "I'm over seventy years old. You're barely forty. You can't possibly understand it, boy. Maybe when you get to be my age you will. But not now."

"Not good enough, Thor. Let's try it one more time: Why did you run off with Clethra?"

"Just shut up about Clethra."

"I'm sorry, Thor. I can't do that."

He tossed back his whiskey and smacked the shot glass

down hard on the bar. "Bartender!" he roared, waving his big arms in the air. "A round for the house! Drinks for all my friends!"

This seemed to make everyone in the place happy. Everyone except me. It was my money. Slim Jim passed out the beers and the guys raised their bottles to Thor and he raised his to them. "To all of you lost little boys," he toasted, launching into one of his lusty orations. "With your pickup trucks and your jet skis and your flaccid little dickies in your hands. You confused, misbegotten little jack-off artists, out of touch with your wild selves, afraid of women, afraid of your own manhood—"

"Ooh, this dude's twisted!" cried one of the floozies.

"Far fucking out!" cried the other.

"I think he just called me a faggot," one guy grunted, with acute Beavian logic.

"I think he did, too," his friend muttered.

All of them were growing hard-eyed now. They knew when they were being dissed, free beer or not.

"Thor," I cautioned. "Now wouldn't be a good time to do this."

"Nonsense," he huffed. "We have nothing to fear from these little lonnie limp dicks."

"Watch your mouth, pops," snarled a hulking kid in a flannel shirt and jeans.

"Or what, you little twit?" Thor snarled back. "You'll punch me? Go right ahead. This I'd pay cash money to see!" Not that he had any cash money. He swaggered down the bar toward the kid, his hands loose at his sides. A man on a quest, all right. He was trying to prove to himself he was still rough and tough. He was also, I was well aware, trying to duck my questions. "Or *what*, pussy boy?" he jeered, shoving the kid in the chest.

"Keep your hands to yourself," the kid warned. His face reddened.

"Or *what?*" Thor shoved him again. "Tell me what you'll do. Go on, tell me."

"This guy's mouth needs shutting," the boy threatened, clenching his fists angrily.

"Think you're the man for the job, do ya?!" screamed Thor, going face to face with him. His eyes blazed. Sweat glistened on his bald dome. "C'mon, pussy, show me what you've got."

"All right, cool it!" ordered Slim Jim, coming out from behind the bar with a baseball bat. "Leave the man alone, Kirk."

"He's the one's hassling me!" Kirk protested.

Thor shoved him again, backing him up against the jukebox.

"I don't want to fight you, old man," Kirk warned between gritted teeth.

"I may be old," bellowed Thor, "but I'm still *twice* the man you'll ever be. Christ, boy, don't you have any capacity for human outrage? Don't you know you have the right to remain violent? Don't you even know when someone's calling you a worthless piece of dogshit to your face?!"

Three of Kirk's husky friends were edging toward Thor now, jaws and fists clenched. If Kirk didn't want a piece of him, they did.

Slim Jim turned to me. "Mister, get him out of here right now or I'm calling the trooper."

"C'mon, Thor. You're already violating your parole by being in here. You don't want to get in a fight or they'll send you back."

Kirk's eyes widened. "You been doing time?"

Thor let out a laugh. "No, he's just playing mind games with you."

"He's right, I am," I admitted. "Unfortunately, it takes two to play." I tossed some money on the bar. "Let's go,

Thor. These guys are twenty years younger than I am. They'll kill us both."

Lulu certainly knew this. She was already halfway out the door.

But Thor wouldn't budge. "Not until this here boy gets up on his hind legs and howls."

"Call me crazy but I don't think he's going to." Indeed, I think at that point we had a better chance of getting ol' Kirk to dress up in a red velvet dress with white stockings, a garter belt and matching pumps. "So let's go."

But by now a half dozen of them were circling us.

By now I realized we weren't going anywhere.

Kirk moved first, charging Thor and ramming him into the bar, fists digging into his ribs. Someone grabbed my arms from behind me. Someone else punched me in the nose, which immediately went numb. And then in the stomach, which didn't. I struggled free and did a little damage. I know I hit someone square in the mouth. And I know Lulu, the noted barroom brawler, had her jaws clamped around one kid's ankle, snarling like a stuffed animal possessed. But I'd have to say the three of us were, well, getting killed. Until, that is, one kid jumped in on our side.

Dwayne Gobble was a fearless scrapper. He punched, he kicked, he hurled guys bodily over the pool table. "C'mon, Mr. Gibbs," he gasped, pulling Thor from the fray. "Man of your stature shouldn't be mixed up in this shit."

"Wait, what about a man of *my* stature?" I wanted to know.

I can't tell you if Dwayne answered me or not, because that was when Slim Jim knocked my head clean over the left-field fence with his Louisville Slugger and the crowd cheered and they turned off all the lights in the stadium.

· · · ·

When I came to I was lying out in the gravel parking lot with blood on my shirt and Cole Slawski standing over me looking most imposing and certainly no more than twelve feet tall.

Actually, Lyme's resident state trooper was a chiseled six-feet-six, not counting his broad-brimmed, rather silly hat. And he was a celebrity anywhere he went in the state of Connecticut. He'd been a swingman on UConn's 1990 dream team, the one that would have made it to the Final Four if Duke's Christian Laettner hadn't drained that buzzer beater and broken the entire state's heart. Tate George and Scottie Burrell were the stars of that team, Slawski a scrapper with no outside shot who played tough defense and hustled after every rebound and loose ball. Not a lot of natural talent but a world of desire and blah, blah, blah—all the usual coach-speak you hear when they're trying to say something nice about the white kid who comes in off the bench. Except Cole wasn't white. He was black. And his name wasn't Cole. It was Tyrone. Until, that is, ESPN's resident genius, Chris Berman, dubbed him Tyrone "Cole" Slawski one night on *SportsCenter* and it stuck. Not that Slawski was what you'd call much of a kidder. He looked like he'd tried to smile exactly once in his entire life, when he was perhaps three, and didn't like it and vowed never, ever to do it again. The man had a pair of hot coals for eyes and shoulders out to here and a nineteen-inch waist. His uniform, of two contrasting shades of muck, looked like it been painted on. It was somewhat unusual to have a black resident trooper in such a rural part of the state, but Slawski was a big hit. Not just because he was a former basketball star but because he was bright, efficient, courteous and fair. Everything you'd want in a resident trooper or scoutmaster. He had everyone's respect. He also had a master's in criminology and ambitions to move up. As was standard throughout the state, the community provided one half of his salary and a house. Slawski's was a snug, two-hundred-year-old cottage across the road from Lyme Town Hall, where he lived alone.

Unless you counted his K-9 Corps partner, a 135-pound German shepherd who was even more no-nonsense than he was. Lulu, the little flirt, was yapping at the four-legged officer girlishly. He just stood there at Slawski's heel, ignoring her big-time. Probably preferred tawny, long-legged show bitches. Or maybe he just didn't go for girls who got in bar fights in the middle of the day.

"Will you be requiring the services of an ambulance?" he barked at me. Slawski, not his partner.

I shook my head, which was a big mistake. Something rattled around in there, like it does inside an aerosol paint can.

Thor and Dwayne were over leaning against Slawski's kidney-colored Ford Crown Victoria cruiser. Dwayne's shirt was torn to shreds and Thor had lost himself another tooth. But both of them seemed to be in better shape than I was. In fact, Thor seemed positively juiced, laughing and crowing like a boy.

The Lost Boys were crowded into Slim Jim's doorway, watching us. Especially watching Slawski, who got down on one knee so as to look me over. My head wasn't bleeding. My nose was.

Lulu was still trying to turn his partner's head. She was over on her back now, dabbing at the air with her paws. It was a shameless display, really. I know I was embarrassed for her.

"What's his name?" I asked Slawski hoarsely.

"Whose?" he asked, frowning at me.

"Your partner."

"Klaus."

"Klaus?"

"You got some particular degree of difficulty with that?" he demanded, his voice booming and most authoritative.

"Not at all. Klaus is a nice name. Aryan."

"It's a dumb name. Fool trainer give it to him." He glanced down at Lulu irritably. "She may as well knock that off. He's a trained police officer. Won't pay her no mind while he's on duty."

"What about when he's off duty?"

Slawski climbed back up to his full height and took off his hat and examined the brim. He wore his hair in a hightop fade that looked like it had been shaped with a T square. "Why, you looking to mate her?"

Lulu gulped and let out a whimper. She'd witnessed firsthand what Merilee went through—and that was to produce a litter of merely one.

"I just thought maybe they could get together sometime. She's going through a rather rough transition, and she doesn't know many dogs out here who she can relate to."

"Uh-huh." Slawski gave me a knowing nod. "Okay, I done *heard* about you." Ah, yes. One of the non-joys of small town life. Everyone knows you—or thinks they do. "You're that writer dude's married to Miss Nash. Got you a farmlike configuration up off Joshua Town, all the time goofing on people and talking piffle."

"Piffle? I didn't know anyone still used that word."

"Yeah, well, there's a lot you don't know. Like how to behave yourself in public. That goes for you, too, Mr. Gibbs," he added, raising his voice for Thor's benefit. "Don't know how you figure into this but—"

"He started it," I said.

"Now don't you be passing the blame off on some old man," the trooper fumed.

"No, no, he's absolutely correct, officer," Thor said. "It's all my fault—if you wish to call it that."

"What you call it?" demanded Slawski, peering at him.

"An awakening," Thor answered, beaming.

Slawski turned back to me, perplexed.

"And you thought I was the weird one," I said.

"They're fast asleep," Thor explained, gesturing to them. They were still crowded there in the doorway, yucking it up. Although when Cole looked their way they grew silent. "I was trying to wake them up."

"You was chumping them down's what you was doing," Slawski said with frosty disapproval. "Except you picked the wrong bunch. Half of them just got laid off over at Electric Boat and they're itching to get in a knuck game with someone. I'm in a serious avoidance mode regarding this particular situation, Mr. Gibbs." The man was positively fluent in cop-speak. Most impressive. "Folks in town don't want to see them awake. And I don't want to see you in here again, either of you. I hear you are, I'll throw your sagging gray butts in jail. Understood?"

"My sagging butt happens to be pink," I pointed out defensively.

"Understood?" he repeated, louder.

I said I understood. "Any chance you could keep Thor's name out of your report, Trooper? He's trying to keep a low profile."

"He's got a funny way of showing it," Slawski snarled. "You got somebody can drive you home?"

"I can drive," I assured him. "I only had one beer."

"And one conk on the head," Slawski reminded me. "No way."

"I'll run 'em home," Dwayne offered, hitching up his sagging jeans. "I didn't have nothing to drink."

The trooper eyed Dwayne's stitched-up face and torn shirt dubiously, Dwayne growing more and more resentful the longer the lawman scrutinized him. Slawski went over to him and sniffed his breath. Grudgingly, he said okay.

Then he put his hat back on, straightened his shoulders and started toward the gang in the doorway. They backed inside, cowed.

We piled into Dwayne's pickup, brimming with testosterone, and took off around Rogers Lake for home. The truck rode very high and bouncy. The interior was strewn with beer cans, junk food wrappers and dirty laundry. It was as if the kid lived, ate and slept in the damned thing. Thor rode in the middle, clutching his broken tooth in his big hand. Lulu got to ride in back with the scrap lumber and tools just like a real country dog, one of those big retrievers named Travis or Justin that chase Frisbees and have no allergies. It was a real thrill for her, almost enough to make up for Klaus blowing her off. But not quite. Trust me, a father knows these things.

"Good thing you stepped in when you did, Dwayne," Thor declared. "No telling when I might have hurt someone."

Dwayne's eyes flickered across him at me, then back out at the road. "I got no use for them dumb shits."

"Still, it wasn't your fight," I put in.

"Anytime Kirk and them are involved it's my fight," Dwayne said, his jaw muscles hardening. "Been mixing it up with them guys since I'm ten years old. They're ignorant and close-minded and mean. Gave me hell over my mom. If I was you I'd watch out for 'em. They hold a grudge. And they smoke that shit, that illy."

"Illy?" Thor asked.

"It's new," I answered. "Marijuana soaked in embalming fluid."

"Good Lord," gasped Thor. "That sounds . . . *great.*"

"It's not," warned Dwayne. "It's bad, dangerous shit. Makes you crazy—violent crazy. Like getting dusted, only worse."

"You've tried it?" I asked him.

He glanced at me uneasily. I was, after all, his employer. "Maybe once or twice."

"Good man," Thor said approvingly. "You should try everything in this world once or twice."

"Do they buy it around here?" I wondered.

"No way, Mr. H," Dwayne replied. "Not as long as Slawski's around. He can spot a dealer a mile away. Have to go to New Haven you want illy." He punched his cigarette lighter, fished a bent Camel out of his shirt pocket and lit it. "Wasting your breath on them boys, Mr. Gibbs, you want my opinion. All they care about's their next paycheck. Give 'em six cold ones and some wet pussy on Saturday night and they're happy."

"No, they're not, boy," Thor countered. "They think they are, but they're not."

Dwayne furrowed his brow thoughtfully. "I guess maybe they don't realize they have the power to reach for more, like you say."

"And so," Thor added somberly, "they gulp their beers in sullen silence and they drug themselves and every once in a while they erupt in spasms of frustrated violence. Because they are men, and deep down in their wild selves, they cannot accept limits. Cannot accept unhappiness. Men must act, Dwayne. It is in our nature to act."

"To act," Dwayne recited, as if he were trying to memorize it. "To act."

Merilee was working in the garden when we pulled up, Tracy next to her in her buggy. Clethra was sprawled in an Adirondack chair looking supremely bored. Merilee gave me her fiercest stare when she saw my bloody nose. It was practically enough to turn me into a pillar of salt.

Clethra, however, lit up. "I'm, like, what'd you guys *do?*" she squealed, jumping excitedly to her feet.

"Kicked some butt, girl," Thor boasted, offering her his tooth like it was a trophy cup.

She took it, thrilled. He went inside to wash up.

I asked her if she'd mind driving back to Slim Jim's with Dwayne to fetch the Land Rover. No problem. She hopped in and I tossed her the keys and off the two of them went down the driveway, music thumping from his stereo. Dwayne had not, I realized, played it when we were with him. This made me feel even creakier than I already did.

I went upstairs and climbed into a hot tub, which I seemed to be doing a lot of on this particular non-assignment. Merilee came up a few minutes later with an ice pack for my nose and a brandy and soda for the rest of me.

Plus a few choice words: "Look at you."

"I'd really rather not," I said.

"You know what you look like?"

"I'd really rather not."

"An aging patrician club fighter who's taken one punch too many."

"Looks are not deceiving."

"What is this, some kind of *guy* thing?"

"Some kind."

"Are you happy now?"

"I'm not unhappy."

"And why is Lulu acting so weird?"

"Weird how?"

"She just growled at me from under the bed."

"Oh. She may have met someone, that's all."

"Do you suppose it's for real this time?"

"I doubt it. He's a cop."

"Oh, dear."

I shifted my ice pack and had a sip of the brandy. "I thought we'd go to Essex tomorrow."

Merilee froze, startled. "Essex?"

"We may have to make one or two stops along the way, if you don't mind."

"I don't mind," she said carefully.

We were silent a moment. She was gazing at me, her green eyes brimming with tears.

"What is it, Merilee?"

"Nothing, darling," she sniffled, swiping at them.

"Tomorrow *is* Sunday, isn't it?"

"Yes, darling," she said gently, squeezing my hand with hers. "Tomorrow is Sunday."

Five

WE CROSSED the Connecticut River at Hadlyme on the little car ferry that steamed back and forth there in the shadow of Gillette's Castle, that immense, storybook rock pile built by William Gillette, the actor who popularized Sherlock Holmes on the Broadway stage at the turn of the century. From there it was a short jog down to Essex, which was the prettiest village in the area, and my least favorite. Too quaint, too precious, too much.

Clethra rode next to me in the front seat of the Woody with her sunglasses on, even though the morning was gray and drizzly. She was tapping her foot, wringing her hands, dying for a cigarette. But this was a no-smoking car—Tracy was riding directly behind her in her baby seat, Merilee next to her. Lulu was behind them in back, grumbling sourly. She hates the whole suburban dog thing. Hates it.

We drove in tense silence. This was Sunday, a day for

deception, for intrigue, for treachery. A day for family, in other words. First, I'd had to arrange the clandestine meeting between Clethra and Arvin. This had meant taking Barry into my confidence and keeping Ruth completely in the dark—Clethra did not, repeat not, wish to see Ruth. Barry's assignment was to take Arvin out with him to buy the Sunday papers. On their way back, they would decide to stop for breakfast at Debbie's Diner, which would explain why they were gone for an hour or more. We would drop Clethra there on our way to my own personal hell. She and Arvin would have breakfast together. Barry would get lost. And Marco, who was in on the plot, would feed and entertain Ruth back at Barry's house. Barry would then pick up Arvin and take him back home, and we would do the same with Clethra on our own way back home.

It was airtight, provided no one at Debbie's recognized Clethra and notified the media. But I was willing to take that chance—Sunday mornings in Essex nearly everyone was in church or hung over or both.

The deception didn't end there, though. Because there was Thor to consider. And Arvin did not, repeat not, want to see Thor. So we'd needed a credible reason for taking Clethra with us and leaving Thor behind. Merilee came up with it: Clethra had volunteered to look after the baby for us. Feeb city, but Thor bought it. Mostly because he was up for some solitude. Said he wanted to go for a swim in Crescent Moon Pond and do some meditating and communing with his wild self.

Me, I envied him.

Debbie's Diner was attached to a drugstore directly across the road from E. E. Dickinson, where they've been making witch hazel since 1866. Barry's canary-yellow bug-eyed Sprite was parked out front with its top down and no one in it. Clethra took a deep breath, hopped out and started inside. Through the plate glass window I could see Arvin jump up from a table and run toward her. They hugged tightly next to the muffin case. She gave Barry a hug, too, and then she and Arvin sat together and Barry came sauntering out, looking a bit frail and worn. He had on a baggy navy blue turtleneck, stained white duck trousers and tattered deck shoes. He paused at the Sprite to recover a beer mug that was half full of what looked to be a Bloody Mary. He came over to us, swigging from it.

"I'm soo glad we decided to do this thing, Hoagy," he purred, after he'd said hullo-hullo-hullo to Merilee and given me a dead fish handshake, along with a whiff of his morning breath. A Bloody, all right. "I'm driving over to the Black Seal now to chat up a fellow who's interested in the Sprite." He arched an eyebrow at me, or tried to. "Shall we synchronize our watches?"

"Let's not," I replied. "And say we did."

We drove on, the Woody heavy and smooth, Lulu grunting at me from the back. She wanted to ride shotgun now that Clethra had split. But we weren't going far.

They were living that season in a two-bedroom condo in Essex Meadows, an ultra-posh Q-Tip colony tucked discreetly into several hundred acres of woods off Bokum Road. You could mistake Essex Meadows for a country club if you didn't know better. There was a nine-hole golf course. There were tennis courts, indoor and outdoor pools, a health spa, an elegant dining room, library, billiard room. There were 189 luxury apartment units with gourmet kitchens and air-conditioning, a full-time staff of gardeners, plumbers and electricians all of whom were polite and efficient and spoke English. It cost several hundred thousand to get in. And there was a hell of a waiting list, too. You could mistake it for a country club, like I said. Except for this one dirty little secret—no one got out of Essex Meadows alive. They'd all been tried, convicted and sentenced, with no hope of a reprieve. This was death row with white shag carpeting, complete with twenty-four-hour nursing care. Exit Meadows, I called it. And, personally, I'd rather get run over by a bus tomorrow than end up there thirty years from now.

Mother was gamely digging away in the narrow flower bed that edged their patio, a brave smile set firmly on her face despite all the pain and the fear. Or maybe because of it. This was her role, after all—to be cheerful and supportive and to let no one know what she was really feeling. They had taught it to her at Miss Porter's School, just as they had taught it to Merilee a generation later. Although Merilee, I'm happy to say, had rebelled in her own quiet, tasteful way. Mother was seventy now, still straight and trim and vigorous. Swam for an hour every day. She'd broken down only once so far—in front of Merilee, not me. Never in front of me.

He sat under the overhang in his wheelchair with his nurse next to him and a blanket over him, his long, narrow face as familiar as my own. In fact, it was my own. Except the nose seemed longer and bonier now. The teeth stuck out more, his dry, chalky lips pulling back from them in a grimace. And his expression was different, too. It was as if the muscles had been pulled and stretched like soft, wet clay.

Plus somebody had turned out the light in his eyes.

He sat there staring straight ahead like he had ever since it happened—the stroke, that is. A right hemiplegia, they called it. His right arm and leg were paralyzed, his memory was like Swiss cheese. He could see some, though he had double vision, and he could speak, only it was slow and halting, as if he were trying to communicate in some new, unfamiliar language. Sometimes he was with you. Sometimes he was unreachable. Sometimes he'd start sobbing weakly and for no apparent reason, aside from the most obvious one.

This was not my father. My father had been icy and rigid and dictatorial. My father had been decisive and strong. He had inspired terror in me and he had inspired hate. This man I didn't know. This man was a stranger.

Mother made a big fuss over Tracy and hugged Merilee and oohed and aahed over the black hollyhock she'd brought her from her garden. She paid zero attention to Lulu, which peeved Lulu to no end.

Actually, I thought she'd forgotten about me, too, until she finally came into my arms and kissed me. "Thank you so much for coming, Stewart," Mother murmured softly in my ear, the way she used to when I'd come running to her after some bully had knocked me off my bicycle. "Seeing you, even for a little while, makes his day so special."

"Now there's a depressing thought."

"Don't you be churlish," she commanded sternly. "You're his only child, Stewart. He has no one else he cares about. And very little to look forward to."

Just his own exit, which might come tomorrow or in a few months or even a few years. No one knew. In the meantime he was on blood thinners and physical therapy. In the meantime he was a turnip in a wheelchair. He wasn't even aware that we were there.

Mother tilted her head at me. "What happened to your nose?"

"Merilee hit me. She's a big meanie."

"I know why you haven't been coming, Stewart."

"Do you?"

"It pains him greatly."

I said nothing.

"Are you ready to say hello?"

"Yes, Mother. I'm ready to say hello."

She took my arm, and steered me over to him. His nurse smiled up at us. He continued to stare straight ahead.

Mother mustered a smile. "Look who's here, Monty," she said, raising her voice. "It's Stewart. And Merilee. And your granddaughter, Tracy." And Lulu, who was sitting out in the grass all by herself getting really pissed.

"Hello, Father," I said, hearing the strain in my voice—and hating it. "How are you doing today?"

He moistened his lips with his tongue but didn't respond. Or blink.

"We're doing fine," his nurse assured me. She was plump and hearty and really upbeat. I hated her. "We ate all of our oatmeal today. We watched some television. We—"

"Who's this *we* you keep talking about?" I snapped at her.

She recoiled as if I'd slapped her, then got up and marched inside. Merilee shot me her warning look. I breathed in and out slowly. I sat down next to him. I patted his bony knee. He gave off a sickly sweet aroma, like rotting flesh. I smiled at him.

Abruptly, he turned and nodded hello to me as if I'd just been away a few minutes, not many, many weeks. "Why d-don't you . . . you bring Stink around anymore?" he said. His voice was different, hollow and trembly.

Stink had been my best friend in elementary school until he and his family moved away. That was in 1961. I hadn't seen or heard from him since.

I glanced up at Mother. She smiled at me encouragingly. She wanted me to humor him, to say something, anything. This part I found difficult. This part I found excruciating.

"Always l-liked . . . Stink," Father went on, grinning crookedly. "Good little p-pal for you, Bucky."

That was my childhood nickname, Bucky. He'd taken to calling me by it again. I'd taken to letting him.

The invasion was under way now—the widows from the neighboring apartments inching toward Merilee, fluttering excitedly. The widows loved to get their picture taken with her, to coo over the baby. Merilee was gracious about it. She's always gracious with her fans. Within moments they surrounded the patio, a dithering cloud of blue hair and fruity perfume. Mother suggested I take Father for a walk.

I did, wheeling him slowly along the cart path to the golf course, Lulu trailing us forlornly. I wheeled him like he'd once wheeled me back when I was vulnerable and afraid and needed him. Now he needed me. All part of the big cycle, I suppose. Only nobody warns you about it and they sure as hell don't give you lessons. They ought to give proper lessons, goddamnit.

There was a faint drizzle in the air. I pulled up by a bench next to the putting green, tucked his blanket around him against the damp and sat there with him, thinking what a shame it was we'd never had the chance to be adults at the same time. We'd never been men together. Men who listened to each other, learned from each other. Men who didn't hate each other. And we never would be. That was never going to happen. Not now. Not ever. And I knew, way down deep inside, that this would be one of the biggest regrets in my life until the day I died.

"Bucky?"

"Yes, Father?"

"When are you going to g-get . . . ?" He trailed off, trying to remember the word. "Get . . . married?"

"Married?"

"You and M-Merilee. You have the baby now. Should b-be married."

Well, well. Here was clarity, briefly.

"We were married once before, Father, and it didn't work out. We like it better this way."

"Should be a . . . big wedding," he said stubbornly. "In a-a church."

"We'd rather keep it a small, quiet affair."

"You're g-getting married at the house?"

"No, we're having a small, quiet affair."

"But you have T-Tracy n-n-now," he sputtered, frustrated by his impaired speech. And possibly by his impaired son. "What happens when she . . . g-gets older?"

"We'll have to buy her bigger clothes."

"I m-mean, what'll she tell her . . . friends?"

"That she has really weird parents. But I'm fairly certain they will have already figured that out for themselves."

"You never could make a c-c-commitment." His voice was heavy with reproach. "That's always b-been your . . . problem. Always."

"So that's it," I said sharply. "I always wondered."

We sat there in brittle silence for a moment. Something we were both used to.

"G-Got some numbers in the mail from Gene," he mentioned offhandedly, meaning his accountant. "One of my CDs . . . it's a-about to roll over. He's got . . . other options. Can't m-make head nor tail of them. Mother . . . n-never could."

"Only because you never let her learn how."

"Gibberish. All of it's g-gibberish."

I said nothing more. I knew what he wanted. He wanted me to take a look at it for him, tell him what to do. But I wasn't going to. Not until he said the words. He didn't have to beg me. All he had to say was: "What should I do?" A small thing, I suppose. But it meant a lot to me. And until he said it, until he admitted out loud to me that he valued my opinion, I would be goddamned if I was going to help him. I was not proud of this. It gave me no satisfaction or pleasure. But I couldn't help how I felt.

We sat there in silence some more, until I realized he was sobbing.

I knelt before him, dabbing at his eyes with my white linen handkerchief. "What is it, Father?"

"I don't w-want to go!" he wailed, clutching at my arm with his good hand. "Don't let them t-take me away, Bucky! P-Promise me . . . you won't! I don't w-want to die!"

"I know you don't," I said, between gritted teeth. "I know."

He calmed down after a moment. Stared out at the golf course—at least that's where his eyes were. I had no idea where his head was. Not until he said, "I-I always liked Stink. B-Bring him around again. We'll . . . play some . . . touch out in the yard, okay? W-Will you do that, Bucky? Will you b-bring Stink around?"

"Of course, Father," I replied, my voice husky. "I'll bring Stink around."

Clethra was sitting there smoking a cigarette on the bench out in front of Debbie's Diner, ultra-impatient.

"Like, I've been waiting forever," she informed us with supreme annoyance.

"Like, we got here as fast as we could," I informed her back. "Barry picked up Arvin?"

"Half a fucking hour ago." She climbed into the front seat next to me.

"And how did it go between you two?" I steered us back toward the farm.

She shrugged her shoulders, looking out her window. "He's *so* mixed up. Like, he's convinced it's somehow all his fault. Y'know, like somehow he drove Thor and Mom apart."

"That kind of reaction is typical when parents split up," Merilee put in from the backseat.

"God, I'd give anything to get him away from her," Clethra said angrily. "The three of us belong together—Thor, me and Arvy. We could really have something together, y'know? If we could only get that bitch out of our lives."

"She's your mother, Clethra," I reminded her.

"She's a bitch."

"Did you have any breakfast?"

"Breakfast?" She frowned at me, perplexed. "Like, no. Why?"

"It's not good, the way you eat."

"It's bad for you," Merilee chimed in.

Clethra heaved her chest. "Who are you guys, the food police?"

"It's bad for you," Merilee repeated. "Your system can't tolerate it."

"So what, y'know? So fucking what?"

"Fine, whatever," I snapped. I'd had more than enough of her. She was hard and she was unyielding. A chip off the old block. Whether she knew it or not.

"Arvy said you were real nice to him," she said, her eyes back out on the road.

"I'm nice to everyone—just as long as they aren't related to me." I glanced at Merilee in the rearview mirror. She was sticking her tongue out at me.

"Well, thanks," Clethra said grudgingly. "I mean it."

"Careful, I may faint and drive us right off the road."

"Why are you being such a shit today?" she demanded.

"I always let my guard down on Sundays. Say hello to the real me."

A light, steady rain was falling by the time we got back. The gravel drive up to the house was shiny and wet. I parked the Woody next to Thor's motorcycle and let Lulu out the back. Merilee went into the house with Tracy. Clethra went into the chapel to see if Thor had returned from getting in touch with his wild self. As for poor un-loved Lulu, she decided to set off on another of her death marches. I called to her but there was no stopping her. She was on her way out to the middle of the pond again, so as to end it all. Cursing, I tore off my shoes and socks, rolled up my trousers and went wading in after her, sending the ducks scurrying for cover in the marsh, quacking at me furiously. Just as I reached her I tripped over something solid there on the bottom. Solid and large. I reached down and tugged at it.

And raised up an arm. It was Thor's arm.

He was down there getting in touch with his dead self.

Six

UH-HUH. *You* again. Somehow, I ain't surprised."

"Real nice to see you again, too, Trooper."

I was still trying to pull Thor out of the pond. I couldn't lift him out—he'd been weighted down with something—so I had the Rover backed up to the edge of the water with a heavy chain hooked to its bumper. I was just about to tow him out when Resident Trooper Slawski came driving up in his Crown Victoria and jumped out and told me to cool it.

"Don't you be messing with this here scene," he ordered me sternly. "Not until we're able to ascertain if this was an accidental drowning or perhaps—"

"It was murder, Trooper. And there's no perhaps about it."

He stood there in the rain with his arms crossed, scowling at me. He had a slicker on over his uniform, and wore a clear plastic thing that looked like a shower cap over his broad-brimmed trooper hat. Klaus was watching us from the backseat of the cruiser, dry and cozy. Merilee and Clethra were watching us from the kitchen porch. Grief etched Clethra's soft young face. "Why you so sure?" Slawski demanded.

"A man like Thor Gibbs doesn't drown in three feet of water."

"Man maybe had a heart attack," Slawski stated. "Or got drunk and passed out. I seen it happen, I'm saying it."

"A man doesn't die elsewhere and then dump his own body in the pond, Trooper." I showed him the cart tracks that cut deep into the soft, wet earth between the gravel drive and the edge of the pond. Then I showed him the second, shallower set. Both belonged to our garden cart. "Someone killed him elsewhere and wheeled him down to the pond. Those would be your deep tracks. The shallow ones are from when they wheeled the cart back, empty. It's standing up over against the carriage barn, where it usually is. There are shoe prints, too."

Lots of shoe prints, none very distinct. There were too damned many of them one on top of the other in the squishy mud.

He looked down at them, then up at me. "Who you be —Mr. Bob Shapiro?"

"You'll want to check the cart's handles for prints, of course. Lulu's searching for the murder site as we speak. I'm quite certain she'll—"

"She better not be tampering with no physical evidence."

"If you'll toss me that chain we can get the body out," I said, wading back in.

"Don't you be telling me my business!" Slawski snarled. "This is my 'hood!"

"And this is my property, my pond and my friend," I

snarled back at him. "So either give me a hand, Trooper, or call someone who will."

He didn't budge, flaring his nostrils at me. Then he said, "I'll get the fire department. One of 'em's got a truck got a big winch on it."

Lyme's fire department was an all-volunteer one. Slawski raised somebody over the radio in his cruiser. Then he reported in to the Westbrook Barracks of the Connecticut State Police. Two members of the fire department showed up in less than five minutes, one of them behind the wheel of the mondo tow truck from Doug's Texaco. Dwayne Gobble came zipping up the drive in his own truck a few seconds after them, greatly agitated.

"Billy here's my neighbor," he explained to me in a frantic, high-pitched voice. "I-I was helping him with some yard work when he got the call. I-I can't believe it's him. I mean, it *can't* be Mr. Gibbs."

"It's him all right, Dwayne. I'm sorry."

I moved the Rover out of the way and Billy backed up the tow truck. Dwayne waded in and felt around in the water until he found something to hook the winch chain onto. Then he gave Billy the signal and they pulled Thor Gibbs out. He didn't come out easily. He'd been chained by the waist to one of the old iron wagon wheels that had been part of the carriage barn's vintage contents. He was facedown; the back of his bald head was bashed in. His jeans were down around his ankles. Slawski motioned for Dwayne to turn him over. That's when we made the unpleasant discovery that Thor Gibbs had been Bobbitted—his penis had been cut clean off.

"Damn!" Dwayne gasped.

The rest of us just stared.

Clethra started screaming. Merilee immediately took her inside.

"Damn!" Dwayne gasped again, louder this time.

Slawski shook his head. "Why would somebody want to do that?"

"You don't really need an answer to that, do you?" I said.

He shot me a look. "Lousy hiding place for a body, water being so shallow. Bound to happen on him eventually."

"There are several possible explanations for that," I suggested.

"Such as?"

"Whoever did it was in a real hurry. Or they panicked. Or they wanted us to find him." I tugged at my ear. "Or maybe they were just really stupid—you have to consider all of the possibilities."

Another uniformed trooper pulled up the drive in his cruiser, followed by an EMS van. They got out, radios squawking.

"Gibbs was here all alone?" Slawski asked me.

"From ten until noon." I frowned. "The driveway was all wet when we got home."

"It be raining," he pointed out, his eyes on the heavens.

"I know that, Trooper. But it hadn't been raining for very long when we pulled in. If someone had come here and gone you'd think there would have been a dry patch where their car had been parked. But the driveway was completely wet."

"Meaning what, exactly?" he asked me, with mounting impatience.

"I'm not sure, exactly."

Lulu started barking like crazy from the direction of the woodshed. I made right for her, Slawski trailing me. She was standing in the open doorway yapping at the six-pound sledgehammer that hung on the wall next to the ax, caked with dirt and blood and hair. Blood was splattered all over the shed's dirt floor. A path had been smoothed out from something heavy, like a body, being dragged across it.

"Whoever did it used that sledge, Trooper," I said. "Then wrestled him into the cart and wheeled him down to the pond."

Lulu snarfled at me from my feet. She wanted some stroking. I patted her and told her she was a good girl, my eyes scanning the shed. There was no sign of the weapon that had been used to Bobbitt him. No sign of his severed penis either. But there was an empty holster hanging inside the doorway. The Felco spring-action pruners that belonged in it were missing.

"When you drag the pond for his penis you may find a pair of Felcos," I informed Slawski.

He took off his hat and examined the brim. He looked much closer to twenty than thirty with it off. "Wonder why he'd hide them but leave the sledge here?"

"You're thinking it's a he?"

He stuck out his lower lip, considering it. "Victim was a big man. Take a big person to move him."

"Or more than one person," I countered. "After all, more than one person wanted Thor dead." Like Baby Ruth, who'd already tried to kill him once. Like Marco, who'd specifically told me he thought someone should rid Thor of his troublesome schlong. Like Barry, whose daughter the old lion had defiled—or so everyone had been led to believe. All three happened to be out for the weekend. No way this was a coincidence. No way.

"Like who?" he wondered.

Lulu moseyed shyly over to Slawski's cruiser, anxious for some approval from Klaus. He was, after all, a pro. But he ignored her completely, the bum.

"Like who?" Slawski repeated, louder.

"Like lots of people, Trooper," I answered. "Don't you read the newspaper?"

"Why, don't you think I can?" he demanded icily.

"That's not what I meant and you know it."

"I know shit."

A whole convoy came tearing up the drive now—a cruiser, an unmarked cruiser, a medical examiner's van and two big blue-and-white Major Crime Squad cube vans. Four burly investigators wearing Connecticut State Police windbreakers and baby blue latex gloves jumped out of those and went to work sealing off the area. They worked soundlessly and efficiently, wasting no time. They had done this sort of thing together before. A distraught Dwayne lingered there on the periphery in his wet clothes, watching them, wanting to do or say something. But there was nothing to do or say, so he got in his truck and drove off.

A plainclothesman climbed out of the unmarked cruiser, hitched up his trousers and looked around at the place as if it were not quite up to his standards.

Slawski stiffened noticeably at the sight of him. "Damn, this be about bad shit now." He glanced at me uncertainly, as if he wanted to confide in me but had no reason to believe he could. "Watch my back, will ya?"

"Your back, Trooper?"

The plainclothesman spotted Slawski. He started across the yard toward us, not moving particularly fast.

"Don't be dealing your piffle on me now, man," pleaded Slawski, his voice rising with urgency. "We be about team now. About sticking together. Just do this for me, okay? I'll school ya after the man's gone."

The man was in his mid-forties and none too happy about it, or about something. His whole face was a gray mask of dread and anxiety. He had a wet, puckered scar of a mouth that turned down at the corners, worry lines like crinkles in old newsprint, eyes that were bleary and pouchy. And the left one had a tremor in it. He had thinning hair of no particular color and a body of no particular shape, unless lumpish counts as a shape. He had on a three-piece suit made out of something cheap and shiny and a raincoat made out of something cheap and dull. "Well, well, if it isn't my homeboy, Tyrone," he jeered in that flat, nasal working-class New England accent that belongs to New Britain, Connecticut, and nowhere else. Nowhere else wants it. "How they hangin', superstar?"

"Lieutenant Munger," Slawski grunted. Nothing more.

"What you got for me?" Munger growled at him irritably. "What's so hot, vis-à-vis I gotta get outta my nice warm fucking bed on a fuckin' Sunday?"

"What you've got, Lieutenant, is a murder," I said.

He eyed me with cold contempt. "The fuck are you?"

"Stewart Hoag," Slawski said. "He the one found the body."

"Stewart Hoag, the writer?" He looked me and my wet clothes over, unimpressed. "Geez, you're not what I expected."

"That's funny, Lieutenant. You're exactly what I expected."

"What, you live here?"

"What, I live here."

"You fucking kill him?"

"He was my friend," I replied, hefting the clunky bracelet on my wrist.

"That's not what I asked you. I asked you if you fucking killed him."

"May I have your full name and badge number, please?"

"What for?"

"I want to report you to your superiors for being rude and abusive and for using foul language at the scene of a crime when one of the victim's relatives is well within earshot. I don't know where you usually are when you behave in this manner, Lieutenant, but you aren't going to behave this way here."

Slawski drew his breath in and stared straight ahead, stone-faced.

Munger held his hands up in a gesture of surrender. "Hey, hey, no need to get your bowels in an uproar."

"My bowels are perfectly fine. I'd like your name and badge number, please."

"Chick Munger," he said between his teeth, which were yellow. "Central District Major Crime Squad, out of Meriden." He took his badge out and held it so I could see the number. "You got any complaints, you go ahead and you call 'em. But I just pulled the week from hell, okay? Didn't get to bed until five in the morning. Sorry if I came off insensitive."

"You didn't come off insensitive, Lieutenant. You *were* insensitive."

He grimaced wearily. "I apologize, okay? We cool now? You got it all out of your system?"

"Drained and flushed," I said curtly.

"Beautiful." He turned his red-rimmed eyes back to Slawski. "Talk to me."

Slawski talked to him, Munger making notes on a small pad as the resident trooper hit the high points. When he got to the part about the woodshed Munger went and had a look for himself. "Victim in any fights lately?" he wanted to know.

Slawski cleared his throat. "Well, yes."

"Where and when?"

"In my professional opinion," Slawski replied, "I would regard that particular altercation as inconsequential."

Or was it? Kirk and the others were plenty mean, according to Dwayne. Especially if they smoked illy. I wondered if Slawski knew they did. I wondered if they'd de-

cided to finish what Thor had started yesterday. I
wondered.

"I don't recall asking you for your professional opinion,
Tyrone," Munger informed him brusquely. "Where and
when?"

Slawski swallowed, his jaw muscles hardening. "He got
in a big fistfight yesterday with a bunch at Slim Jim's, on
the Old Post Road."

"You file a report on it?"

"I did."

Munger peered at my swollen nose, his left eye tremor-
ing as if someone had poked at it with a sharp stick. "You
were in it?"

"I was."

"Talk to me."

"He tried to get them to reach out and touch their wild
selves."

"Their what?"

"He was taunting them," I explained.

Munger considered this, brightening. "Well, maybe he
struck a nerve."

"He often did."

"Okay, good," concluded the lieutenant, pocketing his
notepad. "We move fast we can button this up by nightfall." He seemed eager to prove Slawski wrong. Most eager.

"I should like to remain an active participant in this
investigation, Lieutenant," Slawski spoke up. "I believe I
can be of some particular assistance."

"Appreciate the offer, Tyrone," Munger said pleasantly.
"Only, resident troopers give way to Major Crime vis-à-
vis all homicides, unless otherwise requested. And I'm not
otherwise requesting, okay? So stay out of my way,
okay?" he added, not so pleasantly. "Next of kin been
notified?"

"They're in Essex," I said. "I can tell them."

"*We* can tell them," Slawski corrected me.

"Beautiful." Munger started back toward the pond, then stopped, scratching his head. "Guy was a celebrity, right? One who slipped it to . . . who ran off with his own daughter?"

"Stepdaughter," I said.

"That explains it, then." Munger pointed down to the road, where a dozen news vans were already crowded into the ditch. "TV stations in Hartford and New Haven listen in on our calls. Tabloid shows'll be here soon. Place is gonna be a zoo." The prospect of so much media attention seemed to tickle him. I did not, I decided, have much use for this man. "We can keep a trooper at the drive if you like," he offered.

"I'd like."

He grimaced. He did that a lot. "Consider it done."

Slawski watched him go back to his car, glowering at him. "That dumb ass Slim Jim's lead oughta keep him out of my hair for a while anyway. Gimme a chance to find out what really went down. C'mon, we'll take my ride." He started toward his car, moving briskly.

"So what exactly are you, Trooper, some kind of hot dog?"

Lulu let out a low growl. She hates that expression.

"Man got hisself done in my 'hood on my watch," Slawski replied. "That makes it my responsibility. I take my responsibility very serious—and what Munger or anyone else says about it don't mean shit to me." He shot me a look. "Why, you got some particular difficulty with that?"

"Not at all. In fact, we may even be birds of a feather."

He let out a snort. "I be disbelieving that."

I ducked into the house before we left. Merilee and Clethra were drinking coffee at the kitchen table, Merilee holding Clethra's hand and talking to her in a low voice.

They both looked up when I came in—Clethra hopefully, as if maybe I was about to tell her it was all some kind of terrible mistake, that Thor wasn't dead, that he was still out there roaring like a lion somewhere. But then her eyes clouded back over and she ducked her head, sniffling.

"I'm going to Barry's house with the trooper to tell everyone what happened," I informed her. "Would you like to come?"

"I want to stay here with Thor," she moaned.

"He's not here anymore, honey," Merilee told her gently. "His body is, but *he's* gone."

"I wanna stay!"

"That's perfectly okay," I assured her. "But your mom has to be told, and it would mean a lot to her if you—"

"What do you mean, *told?!*" Clethra cried scornfully. "She's the one who *did* it!"

"You don't know that," I said.

"Oh, yes I do," she said with cold certainty. "She couldn't stand it, okay? She couldn't stand that he wanted me more than he wanted her, okay? So she *took* him from me, okay?" Tears were streaming down her face, which had become red and blotchy. "The bitch. The horrible, dried-up bitch. I hope they *fry* her!"

Merilee and I exchanged a look.

"I have some bad news for you," I said to her. "The press has descended on us. They're stationing a trooper at the foot of the drive, but . . ."

She let out a huge, unhappy sigh. "Very well, darling. We'll stay in the house." She wanted to say more. I knew that. She wanted to blame me for bringing all of this into our lives. She wanted to blow. But it is at moments like these that you measure a person's worth, and Merilee Nash was twenty-four-karat gold.

I changed into dry clothes. When I came back outside

Slawski was sitting behind the wheel of his cruiser, watching the Major Crime people photograph the body.

"Will Klaus mind if I bring my partner along?" I asked him through the open window.

Slawski looked around, puzzled. "Partner? What you talkin' about, partner?" Then he froze, a pained expression crossing his face. "Uh-huh. You be talking about yo dog, don't ya?"

Lulu showed him her teeth.

"What's her problem now?" he wanted to know.

"She prefers not to be called a dog."

"Well, I don't care what she prefers. She ain't coming."

"We're a team. We always work together."

"Maybe so, but she ain't coming," he said stubbornly.

"She found the murder weapon, didn't she?" Which was a helluva lot more than Klaus had done so far.

"Look, it's against regulations for me to transport another canine when Officer Klaus is in the vehicle."

"Like it's against regulations for you to pursue a case on your own when you've been told not to?"

"Get in," he muttered, exasperated.

"If you'd rather I can take my own car and—"

"Get in!"

We got in. He rammed it into gear and took off down the drive, barreling right through the gaggle of pushy reporters and cameramen clustered down there at the edge of the road. *The Enquirer* and *The Star* were there now. *Hard Copy* and *A Current Affair* and *Inside Edition* were there, too. They'd traveled fast. Birds of prey tend to.

Lulu rode in between us, sniffing gleefully at Slawski's radio and shotgun. She loves riding in cop cars. Klaus remained in back, ignoring her. He was on duty and—let's get it out in the open—Mr. Warmth he wasn't. We're talking somewhat less personality than a horse and somewhat more than broccoli rabe. I hoped she didn't get impatient with him and blow it. I hoped he didn't mind them short and neurotic.

"Tell her not to be messing with my stuff," Slawski said irritably. "Don't see Klaus sticking his nose where it ain't wanted. He's a trained police officer. And, damn, what's that smell?"

"She has rather unusual eating habits."

"What's she eat, pond scum?"

"Why, you got a problem with that?"

"Won't catch Klaus eating nothing but red meat."

"Raw or cooked?"

"Cooked good and proper."

"Do you ever pet him or make kissy-face noises at him? In an appropriately manful manner, I mean."

Slawski hit the brakes, bringing the cruiser to a screeching halt right there in the middle of Joshua Town Road. "Look, man, I ain't in the mood for none of your piffle," he said with quiet menace. "So just stop flapping them gums and you and me'll get along fine."

"You mean there are people who actually get along with you?"

"Eventually. Unless they be disrespecting me."

"You mean like Munger?"

At the mention of the lieutenant's name, he tensed up. "If this was my investigation," he said between his teeth, "we'd be taking soil samples from these folks' shoes right now."

"You consider them suspects?"

"Oh, yeah," he affirmed. "I consider them suspects."

"So why don't you take them?"

"You heard the deal."

"I heard it."

He resumed driving, gripping the wheel tightly in his huge hands. He sat ramrod straight, his bare head grazing the top of the car. The rain had weakened to a drizzle. "How about you?"

"What about me?"

"Anyone get along with you?"

"From time to time. The problem is they usually end up dead." I smiled at him faintly. "Sorry to be the one to break it to you, Trooper."

Barry Feingold's place was hidden away at the end of a long, narrow dirt road that snaked back through several hundred acres of Nature Conservancy forest before it dead-ended at the bank of the Connecticut River. The house backed right up on the water. It was an exceptionally private house. It was not a particularly nice or interesting one—just a faded gray two-story cape from the early Sixties set behind a ledge of granite. His bug-eyed Sprite sat in the garage, a Ford Tempo rental car parked next to it.

Lulu immediately sniffed at the tires of both cars, in search of familiar scents. Or maybe she was just showing off for Klaus. She found zip. Klaus stayed in the cruiser. I was really starting to wonder what he did.

The back of the house was mostly glass, and there was a pool that had a lot of dead maple leaves in it. A jungle of wild berry bushes, forsythia and lilac tumbled down to the edge of the river, where there was a private dock but no boat.

We found them back there on the terrace seated around a table under an awning, eating salad and talking. They stopped doing both of those things as soon as they saw us. And how we looked.

Ruth dropped her fork. "What is it? What did he do to her?"

Slawski took off his hat and examined the brim, his jaw muscles tightening.

"The bastard!" Marco jumped to his feet, kicking his chair over violently. He was still exceptionally hulking and exceptionally flushed. He wore a beret over his orange hair. "I'll tear his head off! I'll kill the—!"

"I'm afraid someone's beaten you to the punch, Marco," I said quietly. "Thor was murdered this morning."

Arvin let out a strangled yelp.

"Christ, I didn't mean it!!" Marco cried, panicking. "It was just something to say. I didn't mean it!"

"Shut up, dear," Barry said to him, not unkindly. "Sit down and shut up."

Arvin ran to his mother and fell to his knees at her feet, his face scrunching and puckering like the skin on a baked apple.

Ruth clasped him tightly. "How, Hoagy?"

"Someone smashed in his head with a six-pound sledge-hammer and dumped him in our pond."

"Is Clethra okay?" she asked.

"She's upset, of course. But she's fine. Merilee's with her."

"Can I call her, Mom?" Arvin pleaded, his voice rising. "I have to call her. She *needs* me."

"Of course you can, Arvy," she said tenderly. I saw nothing but kindness from her toward him, by the way.

I gave him the number and he ran into the house. Then I introduced Slawski around.

The resident trooper squared his shoulders and cleared his throat. He seemed extremely ill at ease. "Naturally, we will require your cooperation so as to enable us to ascertain where each of you were at the time of Mr. Gibbs' death," he said, most carefully.

"Any particular reason, Trooper?" Barry demanded, climbing up on his high, rich horse.

"There's every reason to believe that the crime was car-

ried out by a perpetrator of the victim's personal acquaintance," Slawski responded, retreating all the way into the
stilted, multisyllabic comfort of cop-speak.

"What reason?" Ruth demanded, scowling up, up, up at
him.

"His person," Slawski replied, glancing down, down,
down at her, "was mutilated in an extremely graphic and
sexual manner."

Barry and Ruth both frowned at me.

"They cut his penis off," I translated.

Marco clapped his hand over his mouth, staggered. Or
gave a damned good imitation of it.

Through the French doors I could see Arvin on the
phone in the kitchen with Clethra, pacing back and forth,
gesturing wildly.

"Such mutilation is not, as a rule, considered consistent
with a break-in or other random act of violence," Slawski
went on. "Thus suggesting he was murdered by someone
of his acquaintance."

"You mean me?" Ruth huffed.

"I mean someone of his acquaintance," Slawski answered stiffly. "Consequently, this necessitates we ascertain the whereabouts of those particular individuals
who—"

"Since when do resident troopers handle murder investi-
gations in this state?" Ruth wanted to know. No one had
ever accused her of being slow on the uptake.

"The Major Crime Squad has asked myself to assist,"
Slawski maintained, avoiding eye contact with me. "Given
the complexity of the investigation."

"Unless now isn't a good time," I put in tactfully. "We
could come back later, after you've had a chance to—"

"Nah, nah." Ruth waved me off. "Let's get it over with.
None of us have anything to hide."

We sat. Lulu got busy working her way around the table

sniffing delicately at everyone's shoes. Ruth didn't seem to mind it. Barry didn't seem to mind it either. But Marco minded it plenty. Kept fussing with the cuffs of his khakis and shifting his feet—he even bonked her on her large, black schnoggin with his sneaker, hoping she'd go away and leave him alone. She wouldn't. A kick in the nose brings out her stubborn streak, and it's some stubborn streak, if you know anything about bassets. Finally, he jumped to his feet, sweating freely, and fled inside, mumbling something about iced tea.

He came back a moment later carrying a tray with a pitcher and glasses on it. He was wearing a pair of sandals now. Lulu peered at them and at him while he poured, his eyes guiltily avoiding hers. Then she curled up under me with a triumphant grunt, a.k.a. her pickled herring grunt. I patted her gently. That would have to do for now.

"Now, what time was he killed?" asked Ruth, immediately seizing control.

Slawski replied, "The victim was alone between the hours of 10 A.M. and noon. We can't be any more specific until we receive our preliminary findings from the medical examiner."

"I was right here that whole time," Ruth declared, stabbing the table with a fat index finger.

Slawski focused his hot coal eyes on her. "Can anyone vouch for you?"

"Marco can," she snapped. "We were having coffee together."

Slawski took out a pad and made a note of it. "Anyone else see you?"

"Look around you, fella," said Marco, his gaze taking in the forest that all but engulfed the property on three sides. "There's no one else around."

Slawski turned to Barry. "Where were you, sir?"

"Barry and Arvy went out for breakfast together," Ruth answered.

I looked at Barry. Barry looked at me.

"That's not exactly true, Ruthie," he said slowly.

She gave her ex-husband a withering glare. "What do you mean?"

"I mean . . . I left him at Debbie's Diner for an hour," he said gingerly. "With Clethra."

"What the hell was he . . . ?" She whirled and glowered at me. "This was all your doing, wasn't it?" she snarled.

"Arvin did tell me he wanted to see her," I acknowledged. "It was mutual. I didn't see any harm in it."

"And you were where while they met?" Slawski pressed Barry.

"Having a Bloody at the Black Seal." Barry left it at that. He didn't say he was seeing a man there about his Sprite. Possibly, he didn't want Ruth to know he had money troubles. Or, possibly, he hadn't been there at all. Possibly he'd sped over to the farm and bashed in Thor Gibbs' skull. True, the ferry boat captain would remember him if he'd taken the car ferry. But he could have taken the bridge at East Haddam instead, which also had the advantage of being faster. Only, Lulu hadn't turned up anything on his tires. How to explain that?

"I see you have your own dock," I observed, glancing down at the vacant slip. "Your boat's already out of the water for the winter?"

"Sold it this spring," Barry replied offhandedly. "Wasn't getting much use out of the damned thing so I gave it up." He reached for his iced tea, eying me over the rim of his glass. "Why do you ask?"

"Just curious."

Slawski was eying me, too. Most disapprovingly. He

wanted me to let him handle things. I gestured for him to go ahead.

He went ahead. "Mrs. Feingold, it has been well documented that you tried to take the life of the victim once before in New York City. Seeing as how your individual presence here in this community coincides with his demise . . ."

"What kind of idiotic bim do you think I am?" Ruth blustered at him angrily. "You think I'd be stupid enough to schlepp all the way out here and kill him!? Huh?"

"I w-wouldn't know, ma'am," Slawski mumbled, clearly flustered. "I merely . . . is there anything you'd like to tell me? Anything that you feel might shed some light on this particular situation?"

"No, there isn't." She paused, softening. "Except . . ."

"Yes, ma'am?" Slawski leaned forward anxiously.

"Except that I'm sorry he's gone. I loved the man once."

Slawski nodded grimly. "This topless videotape that appeared on television . . ."

"I knew nothing about that," she claimed.

"And neither did Thor," I spoke up, in his defense. Someone had to.

"I see." Slawski thumbed through his notes in thoughtful silence. He was either groping for an angle or stalling. I couldn't tell which.

Arvin came back now and folded his gangly self in his chair, gazing at the river out beyond the berry bushes, lost in his thoughts and his grief.

"If there's nothing else, Trooper, we'd like to drive back to the city this afternoon," Ruth said anxiously. There was an edge of desperation to her voice. It was as if she needed to get away from this place as fast as possible, to get back home, to get where she could close the door on everything and everybody.

"Unless, of course," Barry added graciously, "you'd rather we stick around."

Slawski considered this carefully. "No, that shouldn't be entirely necessary. Long as we know how we can contact you. We will be requiring formal statements. We may also wish to pursue other, more specific lines of inquiry once we have completed our examination of the physical evidence." He passed his notepad around so that they could write down their addresses and phone numbers. Then he gave each of them one of his cards. "There's also the disposition of the deceased to be facilitated. I assume you'll be wanting to transport your husband's body back to New York for burial."

"He wasn't my husband anymore," Ruth pointed out.

"Perhaps not, ma'am," Slawski conceded. "But legally speaking, he was still—"

"Don't tell me about the law, Trooper!" she raged. "I'm a goddamned lawyer, okay?"

"Yes, ma'am," he mumbled, chastened.

We sat there in silence a moment.

"Hell, I'll bury him," I offered. "If no one else will, I mean."

"He wanted to be cremated," Ruth said hoarsely, her eyes filling with tears. "He always said so. He didn't believe in crowding the earth with wooden boxes filled with bones and old clothing and . . ." Her voice caught. "Will that be a problem?"

"Shouldn't be," Slawski replied crisply. "Provided there's nothing inconclusive in the medical examiner's findings that would require further laboratory analysis of the body. The body's evidence, y'understand."

"I really wish you would stop calling him 'the body,' " she fumed. "That's a cold, dehumanizing way to talk about someone."

"I'm sorry, ma'am. Didn't mean to disrespect nobody."

"Of course not," Barry said with a smile, to let him off the hook.

Marco just sat there mopping at his brow and sneaking looks down at Lulu. Arvin was still watching the river, not really with us.

Slawski got up out of his chair, towering over everyone. He started to say something else but decided to leave it be. He tipped his hat. Then he headed back to his cruiser. Lulu and I followed him.

"One of these days, Trooper," I said, "I'm going to have to talk to you about your bedside manner."

"What about it?"

"You haven't got one."

"I'm working on it."

"It doesn't show."

We got in the car with Lulu in between us. Klaus was fast asleep in back, which wasn't much of a change from when Klaus was wide-awake in back.

Slawski started up the engine, shooting an uneasy glance at me. "Can you keep a secret?"

"That's one of the things I'm best at."

"Rich white people like them scare the shit out of myself."

"I'll let you in on a little secret, Trooper. You have more money in the bank than all of those rich white people put together."

He raised his eyebrows at me, surprised. "How you know?"

"I know."

"What, you make it your business to know?"

"If it has anything to do with my business."

"And what is your business?"

"That's my business." I looked at him curiously. "Tell me something, why is it that Munger doesn't want you anywhere near this case?"

"Because it's prime time, that's why. Put your whole career on the fast track—provided you can make the play, if you know what I'm saying."

"Is that why you want in?"

"I want in because it went down in my 'hood," he replied gruffly. "Like I done told ya."

"And because he dissed you."

"I'm used to that," he said mildly. "Comes with the pigment." He sat there with his hands on the wheel, the engine idling. We still hadn't moved. "What about you?"

"What about me?"

"What's your interest here?"

"Thor was my friend, like I told you."

"Uh-huh. What else?"

"I'm helping Clethra write her book."

"That's all?"

"That's all."

"Then why do I keep getting the feeling you be looking to create your own shot for yourself?"

"You must be scared a lot of the time, Trooper," I suggested, sidestepping him. "Working around this part of the state, I mean."

He sat there in uncomfortable silence a moment, not touching it. I think he was sorry he'd shown himself to me. I wasn't exactly sure why he had. "Not a whole lot to go on here, huh?" he ventured, nodding at the house.

"I wouldn't say that, Trooper. I wouldn't say that at all."

"What, you got some ideas?"

"I have too many ideas. That's one of my biggest problems."

He heaved a sigh. "Man, I can't tell when you're goofin' on me and when you ain't."

"You have my sympathy."

"Miss Nash . . ."

"What about her?"

"She elevates any production with which she's associated."

"That she does." I glanced at him. "So how come *I* don't?"

"Don't what?"

"Scare the shit out of you."

"First time I laid eyes on you," he reminded me, "you was facedown on the floor of Slim Jim's."

"Go ahead," I sniffed, fingering my tender nose. "Rub it in."

"I may do that. I just may indeed." He rammed the cruiser into gear and hit the gas. "A man's got to find his pleasure somehow."

It took us twenty minutes to get back to the farm by way of the bridge at East Haddam. I timed it. There were even more press vans crowded along Joshua Town Road than before. The three networks, determined not to be outhustled on a story of such pure schlock value, were now camped out there shoulder to shoulder with the tabloiders, groveling for the same greasy crumbs. This was something new. When I first got started in my second career, the networks steered clear of sensation. Not anymore. They couldn't afford to.

Shoreline Sanitation was almost done sucking the water from out of the pond into a tanker trunk. Two of the Major Crime Squad investigators were sifting through the bottom muck with their trousers rolled up, looking very much like they were panning for gold. Two more were taking careful stock of the cart trails and squishy footprints between the pond and the driveway.

One of the goldminers let out a triumphant whoop as we pulled up. He'd recovered the Felco pruners.

"Where will I find you?" Slawski asked me from behind the wheel.

"I don't know. Why?"

"I may wish to talk to you," he said, turning authority on me.

I tugged at my ear. "You don't think *I* killed Thor, do you?"

"I don't know what to think," he said grimly. "Nothing's making too much sense to me right about now."

"You'll get used to that," I advised him. "In fact, pretty soon you won't even remember what it was like when you thought life made sense."

"Do me a favor, will ya?"

"Of course, Trooper."

"Get the hell out of my car!"

I did, wasting no time. Him, he wasted no time getting out of there.

Clethra was in the front parlor watching *I Dream of Jeannie* and eating a bag of Doritos. She grunted hello at me. She did not ask me how it went with Ruth.

Upstairs, Tracy was in her nursery, crying irritably, and Merilee was in our room, packing up for the city. No small operation this. Traveling with Tracy meant taking along extra diapers, something to put her wet diapers in, something to wipe her clean and dry with, something to wipe yourself clean and dry with after you'd wiped her clean and dry, her blanket, her change of clothes, her various and sundry recreational devices . . . It was a lot like traveling with Elizabeth Taylor, except Liz is less self-centered.

"I'm sorry, darling, I just can't handle all of these people being here," Merilee announced, her voice stretched tight, as she swiftly crammed things into her oversized Il Bisonte gym bag, her movements precise and practiced. She was replaying her getaway scene from the Alec Baldwin thriller —all that was missing was the loaded Glock and the briefcase full of cash. She always fell back into some role or another when she got rattled. Take it from me: Don't ever get mixed up with an actress. Or if you do, make sure she chooses her parts awful damned carefully. "They've got Tracy riled. They've got me riled. The phone's been ringing non-stop . . . I'm filling up the Woody and I'm fleeing back to the city." She zipped the bag shut and hoisted it over her shoulder. She had changed into a cashmere turtleneck and flannel slacks. "You don't blame me, do you?"

Outside the window I could hear the cops and technicians hooting instructions at each other, hear the steady throb of the press corps down at the foot of the drive. It was like living under a state of siege.

"No, I don't, Merilee. Do you blame me?"

"For what, darling?"

"Bringing all of this down on you." I wrestled the bag from her and took her in my arms. "After all, this was our refuge from the world. Our safe haven."

"No, it wasn't, darling," she said softly. "That was all just an illusion. A sweet, sweet illusion."

"I didn't realize I still had any of those left."

"A few," she observed. "We started out with so many, after all."

"Tracy's not going to be like us, is she?"

"I don't see how she can be. It's a completely different world than the one we grew up in."

"Bother you much?"

"Only enough to make me cry if I think about it." She kissed me tenderly, gazing at me with her brow creased. "Will you be okay without me tonight? I know Thor was someone you cared about. I'll stay if you need me."

"I'll be fine. No big deal."

"Gosh, you're tough."

"Yeah, I'm a hard guy of the old school, all right," I

said, wondering when we'd have our romantic evening
together. *If* we'd have our romantic evening together.

"How's Baby Ruth?"

"Angry."

"Did she kill him?"

"I don't know, Merilee." One fine strand of her long
golden hair had worked loose from her ponytail and tumbled across her forehead. I smoothed it back over her ear.
"Clethra's going with you?"

Merilee shook her head. "She wants to stay here."

"She belongs with Ruth and Arvin."

"You know that and I know that, darling," Merilee
agreed. "But Clethra has to reach that conclusion for herself, and . . ."

"And?"

"We have to let her."

"Why, Merilee Gilbert Nash," I exclaimed. "You're going to make somebody a good little mother someday."

She sighed. "So I keep telling myself."

She and Tracy took off for the city at dusk. I figured the
investigators would clear out about then themselves for
the night. I figured wrong. They merely brought in floodlights so they could keep right on working. The press vans
stuck around, too. As long as there was some activity, any
kind of activity, they were going nowhere. The phone kept
ringing—reporters trying to wheedle an exclusive out of
me, tabloid television producers trying to buy one. I took it
off the hook and left it that way. There was no one I
wanted to talk to.

The cops found the severed penis of Thor Gibbs a little
before 7 P.M. I'm sure it was a great source of triumph for
them. I'm sure it was also a great source of sick jokes, but
they didn't share those with me—partly out of respect for
my feelings and partly because Munger and Slawski were

both on hand, growling at each other. I sat at the kitchen table glumly drinking a Samuel Adams Cream Stout and watching them through the window. I didn't go out there to talk to them. They didn't come inside to talk to me. Munger was the one who went down to the foot of the drive to speak to the press under more bright lights. Their ranks did thin somewhat after that. And then the Major Crime Squad investigators and their vans cleared out, too, leaving the crime scene cordoned off and us in semi-peace.

By then Clethra had moved on to *Green Acres* and Orcos. She still wasn't saying much. She tossed her cookies and her Doritos at eight, then curled back up on the sofa and stared at *The Partridge Family*. When I mentioned dinner she just curled her lip at me.

Lulu, on the other hand, was a woman of appetite. She inhaled the pickled herring treat I'd promised her, as well as a full ration of her 9-Lives canned mackerel for cats and very strange dogs. The thrill of the chase always enlivens her. So does being away from Tracy. She was so juiced she didn't even mind contributing a half dozen of her precious anchovies to my own supper—provided I made a little extra for her, of course. I drank another Cream Stout while I put on water for linguine and chopped up enough garlic to ward off every evil spirit in southern New England. I sautéed it in extra-virgin olive oil, threw in some hot pepper flakes, Merilee's Italian parsley and Lulu's anchovies. When it was just about done I added a half cup of homemade fish broth to the skillet and let it simmer awhile—a trick I learned from my landlady in Montalcino a while back. Then I dumped the cooked pasta in the pan and tossed it and topped it with fresh grated pecorino romano. I made enough for all three of us but Clethra still wasn't interested so Lulu and I ate the whole batch ourselves. I washed mine down with most of an ice-cold bottle of Sancerre. For dessert I had one of our ripe pears smeared with soft goat cheese. I ate at the kitchen table, feeling spent and empty and lousy.

Afterward, I took a walk, Lulu ambling along next to me. The clouds were gone and there was a full moon out and stars and all of that. The air was bracingly cold and smelled of fallen, rotting apples. I walked down the driveway, thinking about how this place would never be the same. A place never is after there's been a murder. I walked, thinking about Thor. Trying to remember what he looked like before I'd found him face down in the ooze with his head caved in and his dick snipped off. I walked, trying to forget.

There were still a dozen or so vans parked down at the road. Local crews from the New York and Connecticut stations mostly, hanging around until they could do their live, latest, up-to-the-minute *bupkes* for the eleven o'clock news. Our sentry, a thick-necked young bull of a trooper, was stationed in his cruiser reading what appeared to be a comic book.

The phone was ringing when I got back up to the house. Clethra had put it back on the hook while I was outside. She must have used it. But she wasn't answering it. Just staring at the TV in the parlor. I took it in the kitchen, hoping it would be Merilee checking in from the city.

It wasn't. It was Barry Feingold. "How's that dear, sweet daughter of mine?" he inquired thickly. Man was somewhat in his cups.

"She's resting uncomfortably. And you folks?"

"We're just getting ready to leave for the city." He lowered his voice. "I felt I should speak to you about a certain personal matter, Hoagy. By that I mean . . . I felt you were someone I *could* speak to."

"Yes, of course."

"The unwashed truth, you see, is that I simply can't account for my whereabouts when old Thor was murdered. By that I mean . . . I can but I can't." I heard muffled voices at his end. "Coming!" he called out. Into the phone he said, "Are you following me?"

"Not even a little."

He let out an exasperated sigh. "What I'm trying to say, dear boy, is that I was *not* at the Black Seal seeing a man about my car. It so happens the bartender there knows me quite well and if the police go there and question him he'll *tell* them I wasn't there. And so they'll have no choice but to think I lied to them."

"You did lie to them, Barry."

"I had to," he insisted. "At least in front of Marco I did. You see, I had a personal appointment this morning. One that I didn't wish for him to know about. One that I *don't* wish for him to know about. He just gets *so* jealous he'd . . . Believe me, Marco can get very rough when he's angry. He mustn't know. He can't know."

"Barry, are you seeing someone else?"

"God, no! Not anymore, at least." He hesitated. "There *was* someone who I was close to, briefly, a few years ago. He's been working abroad for a while, for a German bank. Just got back. And he didn't know about . . . that I've come down with the virus, you see. I had to tell him, didn't I? I owed it to him. So I met him this morning outside the Black Seal and we went for a drive together. That's where I was."

"I don't see any problem here, Barry. If the police talk to him I'm sure he'll back you up."

"But I don't *want* the police to talk to him! He's married. Always has been. And his wife, she doesn't know anything about us. When he and I were together, they were having their problems. But now they've worked them out, and they've got a good thing together. This would destroy it. Her finding out about us from some cop, I mean. She should hear about it from *him*. And he *will* tell her. He has to tell her. Only . . . Oh, God, what messy, messy lives we lead."

"The only tidy people are dead people."

"Do you understand now why I had to lie?"

"Yes, I suppose I do."

"Can you protect him, Hoagy?" Barry pleaded. "Can you shield him from Slawski and the others?"

"I can try. But I have to know who he is."

Barry drew his breath in. "Must you?"

"I'm afraid so."

"Can I trust you to—?"

"You can trust me to do what I can. That's all I can promise."

Reluctantly, Barry Feingold gave me his ex-lover's name. Also how the man could be reached in New York and in Essex. Again, he begged me not to tell Marco.

I promised him I wouldn't. "Provided you do me a favor in return."

"Favor?" Barry was instantly on alert. "What favor?"

"Marco was afraid to let Lulu sniff his shoes this afternoon. He even went inside and changed them. Why is that? Was he afraid she'd recognize the mud on them?"

Barry laughed, relieved. "Good heavens, no. Nothing so sinister as that. You want me to tell you why?"

"I'd rather hear it from him."

"Marco!" he called out. "It's Hoagy! He wants to know why you changed your shoes at the table."

I heard Marco groan and say, "Why is that any of his fucking business?"

And Barry say, "Just tell him."

And Marco say, "Why the fuck should I?"

And Barry say, "For me, okay? Will you do it for me?"

And Marco growl, "Christ, okay." Before he got on the phone and said, "That was just me being paranoid, Hoagy."

"Paranoid how, Marco?"

"We grow some marijuana down by the river, okay?" he answered testily. "Down behind the blackberry bushes, in a sunny spot where no one can see them. Nothing major. Eight or ten plants, tops. I was down there just before lunch harvesting some leaves to take back with us to the city. When your dog started getting all interested in my shoes I started wondering if maybe she was trained to sniff dope . . ."

"She's not."

"And then I looked up and saw Trooper Slawski sitting there and I freaked. He can be a genuine hard-ass—especially if he thinks you're selling the shit."

"Are you?"

"No! But we grow enough that, technically, they could say we do. And, Christ, they can take your *house* away for that. Anyway, I freaked. I guess it didn't help that I was stoned off my nut at the time."

"When did you smoke it?"

"After breakfast."

"You and Ruth?"

"God, no!" He lowered his voice to a whisper. "I can't stand being alone with her when Barry's not around. She's never liked me and I've never liked her." He sniffled, resuming his normal voice. "I smoked it by myself in my room. Just stretched out and listened to some music until Barry and Arvy got back."

"How long were you in there?"

"Maybe an hour."

"What was Ruth doing?"

"Fuck if I know."

"Was she in the house?"

"She may have been. She may have been out back. I don't know."

"Could she have left?"

"Left?"

"Taken the rental car and gone."

"You mean gone and bashed his head in?"

"Could she?"

I heard muffled voices. He was conferring with Barry. "I guess she could have," he allowed after a moment. "I do crank up the stereo pretty loud."

"Who were you listening to?"

"Miss Diana Ross, who Barry hates. I don't know why. She's such a survivor."

I felt thirsty all of a sudden. Lulu's anchovies. I filled a glass with cold well water from the tap and drank some. "How are you feeling these days, Marco?"

"Feeling?" An edge crept into his voice. "Why?"

"No reason. Barry told me you've been—"

"Fuck what Barry told you," he snarled. "I'm fine, okay? There's nothing wrong with me. I'm *fine*."

"Do you smoke a lot of dope?"

"Why not?" he replied defensively. "It helps keep me even."

"Does Barry smoke, too?"

"He likes his drinks more. What the hell does this have to do with—?"

"Ever smoke any of that illy?"

"Not a chance. I'm trying to stay pure and clean. That's why I grow my own. Illy's got poison in it. Besides which, it makes you mean. And that's not where I want to be anymore. That's the last place in the world I want to be." He was getting impatient. "Anything else?"

"Not a thing, Marco. Could you please put Barry back on?" When he did I said, "How's Arvin doing?"

"He seems terribly lost," Barry replied heavily. "Not that he's cried. He hasn't shed one tear. Just sits there on the sofa like a resolute little soldier. I wish I could say something to him, but what on earth is there to say?"

Not a thing, except our goodbyes.

Once again, I left the phone off the hook.

Clethra was still staring at the TV when I went up to bed. She'd moved on to *F Troop*. Everyone grieves in their own way. Hers was to watch Larry Storch. As good a way as any, I suppose.

"You might be more comfortable in the guest room tonight," I offered. "You're welcome to move inside."

"I'll stay out in our room" was all she said, her voice wooden and far away. Her eyes never left the screen.

"Suit yourself. Goodnight."

I built a fire in the bedroom fireplace. Got into the soft white cotton broadcloth nightshirt from Turnbull and Asser. Climbed into bed with Lulu and Ring Lardner, who is someone I re-read every couple of years just to remind myself what good writing is. But I didn't read and I sure as hell didn't sleep. I had too much on my mind. Like who had killed Thor. Munger was going with the gang from Slim Jim's. Me, I agreed with Slawski—I doubted Kirk and those other chowderheads were involved. Unless, that is, they'd gotten high on illy and decided to get even. It certainly wouldn't have been hard to find out where I lived. Anyone in town could tell them. Only, it still didn't play. Say they had done it—why Bobbitt Thor? Why leave him —and it—there in the duck pond? Why not bury him— and it—way off in the woods somewhere, never to be found? I wondered. There was so much to wonder about.

Thor's murder had been a violent one. It would take someone strong to smash in his head. A good-sized woman could swing that six-pound sledge. Merilee could, for instance. But to load him into the garden cart, chain him to that wagon wheel, shove him into the water . . . no one small could have done that. Ruth couldn't have done it. At least, not alone she couldn't. But what if she had help? What if Marco helped her? What if the two of them killed

Thor together while Barry and Arvin were gone? Marco was certainly strong enough and volatile enough. Then again, maybe it was Barry who'd helped her. Maybe that whole story about meeting his ex-lover in Essex was baloney. Maybe he and Ruth had banded together to save their young, helpless daughter from Thor's evil clutches. Or maybe Barry had acted alone. Or maybe Marco had. Or maybe Barry and Marco had acted together. Neither of them had much to lose, to be blunt about it . . . *"Don't let them take me away, Bucky!"* . . . Or maybe the two of them *and* Ruth had been in on it together. So many possibilities. And so little I knew for certain.

Except that whoever had murdered Thor Gibbs had hated him something fierce.

I lay there gazing at the fire and thinking about him. He'd never answered me. Never told me why he'd run off with his own stepdaughter. What had he been trying to do —hang on to his youth? Piss off the world? Cause a stir? Or was he genuinely in love with the girl? If so, why hadn't he touched her? How could he be so cruel to Ruth and to Arvin? He hadn't explained. Wouldn't explain. All he'd said was that I wouldn't understand—not for another thirty years. But I could think about it. Hell, yes, I could think about it.

I lay there thinking long past midnight, the fire crackling, Lulu snoring contentedly on my head. Until finally I slept.

It was past two when Lulu woke me, growling softly. Something had awakened her. Something she didn't like. The glowing embers and the moon outside the windows threw an eerie half-light over the room. But I saw nothing. And I heard nothing. I shushed her and listened harder. And then I heard it—a creak on the stairs. Footsteps. Someone coming up. Someone inching down the hall toward us . . . Nearer . . . Pausing outside the bedroom door . . . Slooowly, it opened. A figure started across the room toward the bed. A figure clutching something shiny and sinister in one hand, gripping it overhead like a weapon . . .

I flicked on the light.

It was Clethra. And the weapon was a claw hammer. Only the light startled her so much she dropped it. "Oh, shit!" she cried, as it crashed to the floor. "Did I wake you? I'm so fucking sorry." She stood there, wide-eyed and shivering. She had on a T-shirt and nothing else.

Lulu bared her teeth, snarling. I told her to behave herself.

"What's with the hammer, Clethra? Planning to install some drywall?"

"I-I was just so scared." She was breathless, her teeth chattering. "I had this nightmare—that the killer was right outside the chapel. That he came back for *me*. And I was just . . . I felt so alone. I-I'm sorry I woke you. I just got so *scared*." She sounded like a frightened little girl. She *was* a frightened little girl.

"There's no need to be. A trooper's at the foot of the drive."

"I know that. I do. I'm sorry. I'm really, really sorry." She stayed there at the foot of the bed, trembling.

There was an extra blanket over my feet. "Here, put this around you."

"Could I get in there with you, Hoagy?" she blurted out. "For a little while? Please? I just need to . . ." She let out a jagged sob. "I j-just need to *be* with somebody."

It was pretty much Lulu's call. She considered it a moment, weighing if this chilled, semi-naked semi-celebrity was any threat to her unhappy home. She stirred and had herself a leisurely stretch. Then she moved over to the rocker by the fireplace and curled up in it with a grunt.

When push comes to shove she has a pretty good heart. Just don't ever tell her I said that.

Clethra dove in gratefully. "Oooh, it's so nice and warm in here," she gasped, burrowing in. Her feet were two blocks of frozen hamburger.

I reached over and turned off the light. She turned on her side, facing me. I could see tears on her cheeks in the moonlight. And I could smell her. She smelled of the Crabtree and Evelyn avocado oil bath gel Merilee kept in the guest bath. She inched closer to me, hesitant but insistent. I sighed inwardly and raised my arm. She immediately snuggled under it with her head on my chest. Then she broke down. I held her while she cried, stroking her hair, feeling the scented warmth of her there. I held her until she grew still and silent, our chaperone watching us carefully from the chair.

"Hoagy?" she whispered, after a long while.

"Yes?" I whispered back. I don't know why. We were alone in the house. At least I sincerely hoped we were.

"I miss him."

"I do, too."

"There's nobody in the whole wide world I can trust now. Not one person."

"There's Arvin."

"I meant a grown-up." She raised her head, her eyes searching my face. "There's *you*."

"I thought you said a grown-up."

Her breath caught. She needed the words.

"There's me," I assured her. "And there's Merilee."

"I like her."

"So do I."

"You guys really have it all together, y'know?"

"You must be thinking of another couple." I knuckled my eyes, yawning. "There's Ruth," I suggested.

"No way." She shook her head vehemently. "I can't ever trust her. Not after this."

"You really think she had something to do with his death?"

"She *caused* it, Hoagy. By hating him so much. By hating *us* so much."

"What about Barry?"

"What about him? Like, he's never been for me. Not ever."

"Has Marco?"

She reacted with surprise. "Marco?"

"Are you and he at all close?"

"Like, why would we be?"

"No reason. I just wondered."

"Hoagy, is it okay if I stay out here for a while? I don't want to go back to her."

"Stay here as long as you like."

"Even though I'm, like, an annoying little brat?"

"Even though you're, like, an annoying little brat."

She let out a giggle. "You weren't supposed to agree with me."

"My mistake. Sorry."

"Will you still help me with my book?"

"If you want me to."

"I want you to."

Slowly, I became aware that she wasn't lying completely still anymore. She was a living, breathing girl, her body warm and pliant against mine, stretching, arching . . . Her hand was on my stomach. My hand was on her round, firm hip. And she had nothing on under that shirt. And all I had to do was pull her over on top of me and . . .

"What are you doing, Clethra?"

"Nothing," she insisted.

"Well, stop doing nothing."

She lay still. From the chair I could hear Lulu snoring softly. Some goddamned chaperone.

"Did you and Arvin stay at Debbie's Diner that whole time?"

"Well, yeah. Barry only left us there for maybe an hour."

An hour. Was that enough time for Barry to get to the farm and do Thor and get back? Was an hour enough time to kill? "You didn't go anywhere else?"

"Like, how could we? We didn't have a car."

"That's right, you didn't. And how long did you have to wait for us by yourself after Barry came back for him?"

"Maybe half an hour."

"What did you do?"

"Um, I went to the ladies' room, did some magazine grazing at the drugstore . . . Shit, I don't remember. Why?"

"Just curious," I said, thinking she sounded vague and evasive. Or was that just my imagination?

"Geez, you don't think *I* killed Thor, do you?"

"I don't know what to think, Clethra."

We were silent then, her chest rising and falling more evenly as she started to drop off. But as soon as she did she let out a startled yelp and was awake again, remembering it all. "Hoagy, if I tell you something will you promise not to hate me?"

"I promise."

She sniffled. "Mom never beat me and Arvy. Not really. I-I just said that to piss her off. Kind of a shitty thing to do, I guess."

"Kind of."

"I'm sorry, Hoagy."

"I'm not the one you should be apologizing to."

"I know. But I'm still sorry." Her eyes were searching my face again. "It hurts, Hoagy. It really, really hurts."

"I know it does, Clethra. And it's going to keep hurting for a long, long time. But eventually you won't feel it anymore. In fact, you won't feel anything at all."

"What do they call that?"

"Being middle-aged."

"Sounds a lot like being dead."

"It's very similar, except it doesn't last as long."

"Hoagy?" she said drowsily.

"Yes, Clethra?"

"You take some getting used to."

"So do you."

She held her face up to mine. "G'night, homes."

I kissed her on the forehead. "Goodnight, sweetheart."

She lowered her head to my chest and slept. We both slept.

Seven

I T WAS THE SOUND of dishware breaking downstairs that woke me. The morning sun was streaming in the windows, and I was alone in the bed. Not so much as a trace of Lulu. A moment later I heard footsteps coming up the stairs, and then the door swung open and Clethra Feingold burst in carrying a breakfast tray, Lulu scrabbling along behind her, tail wagging happily. Dogs, it has been my experience, always wake up in a good mood.

"Well, well, what's the occasion?" I said, sitting up.

"I thought it was time for me to start earning my keep," Clethra replied brightly, up as a pup herself. Her hair was brushed, her cheeks flushed. She had on a flannel shirt and jeans. The top button of the jeans was unbuttoned, as were the bottom buttons of her shirt— the better to show off her belly button ring. "Um, there was this little white milk pitcher? With, like, these daisies on it? I hope it wasn't too valuable . . ."

"What, that old thing?" That old thing had originally belonged to Merilee's great-grandmother and had been handed down from daughter to daughter ever since. Merilee would weep. "Not to worry."

Clethra set the tray down on the bed next to me. There was orange juice. There was coffee. "I didn't know how you took yours," she said, meaning the coffee.

"Black is fine." I took it from her and sipped it.

"How is it?"

I really did try to answer her, but no way. Not without airmailing it all over Aunt Patience's quilt, which would have meant the ruination of Merilee's second heirloom of the morning. I'd never tasted coffee quite like it before. But I certainly knew what to call it—Mocha Drāno.

"It sucks, doesn't it?" she agreed sheepishly. "I wasn't sure how your coffeemaker worked, and I don't usually make—"

"It's fine," I croaked. "Really."

She sat on the edge of the bed, wringing her hands, suddenly very unsure of herself. "I-I put some food out for the cat. Lulu seemed hungry, too, only all I could find was the cat's food. Where do you keep Lulu's?"

"I'll take care of her. You're in much too fragile a state to know the truth."

"Actually, I'm fine," she insisted. "Last night was a big, big help. You're a sugar, even though you try to pretend you're not."

"Actually, I'm flavored with NutraSweet."

"Anyway, thanks. I mean it."

"No problem. That's what collaborators are for."

She swallowed nervously, poking at the quilt next to my leg with her finger. "That's what we are, huh?"

"That's what we are," I affirmed, wondering just exactly what was going on. Was this her trolling for a new daddy? She did have me here all to herself. And she had

already worked her way into my bed. What next? Bust up
a second family? First the mentor, now the pupil? Or was
this all my sick imagination? After all, she was eighteen
and alone and the roof had just caved in on her. I took her
soft little hand and squeezed it. "And we're friends as well.
Thor was my friend, and you're my friend. Okay?"

She nodded, blushing, and lingered there clutching my
hand. "I guess you'll be wanting to get dressed and stuff."

"And stuff."

"Cool." She released my hand and got to her feet. "I'll
start your breakfast."

"What am I having?" I asked warily.

"Irish oatmeal. I found it in the pantry. That okay?"

"Only if you're going to join me."

"I don't *do* the breakfast thing."

"Then forget it. No way."

"But—"

"That's my deal. Take it or leave it."

She rolled her eyes—the all-suffering teenager bit. "Well
. . . okay," she said with great reluctance, as if this were
some totally major sacrifice. Then she smiled at me quickly
and went back downstairs.

I showered and shaved and doused myself in Floris. I
dressed in the suit of dark brown wide-wale corduroy I'd
had made for me in Milan. I wore an aged blue denim shirt
and Fair Isle cashmere knit tie with it, the suede balmorals
from Maxwell's, Thor's bracelet. By the time I made it
downstairs a pair of Major Crime Squad investigators had
shown up to paw around in the bottom of the pond some
more. And the Irish oatmeal, which was on high heat, had
boiled over and was streaming across the floor like high-
fiber molten lava. Clethra was busy in the parlor watching
That Girl with Marlo Thomas and Ted Bessell. I turned
the stove down and mopped up the spilled oatmeal and
dumped Clethra's pot of coffee down the kitchen sink,

which had been draining rather sluggishly of late anyway. Then I made some genuine coffee and leafed through the stack of faxes her editor had sent. That morning's coverage of the murder in the New York newspapers: SNIPPED AND DIPPED screamed the *Post*. THE FINAL BLOW cried the *Daily News*. LEGENDARY AMERICAN AUTHOR DIES IN RURAL CONNECTICUT POND yawned the *Times*. Also three faxes of her own devising: *"Are we still on?"* asked the first one. *"How soon can you deliver?"* asked the second one. The third one declared: *"We'll stand by her* no matter what, *if you know what I mean."* Oh, I knew what she meant, all right. Even if we're sitting on the killer's very own confession was what she meant. And no doubt hoped. Which explained why the woman liked sending faxes so much. The whirring noise helped drown out that nagging sound of Maxwell Perkins spinning in his grave. I tore the faxes up into tiny pieces and threw them out and put the phone back on the hook. Would have been unprofessional not to.

It started ringing right away—crazed, feverish producers for *Hard Copy, A Current Affair* and *Inside Edition* offering me up to $750,000 for the exclusive story of Thor's last days. When I said no they immediately asked to speak to Clethra. When I hung up on them the crazed, feverish producers for Paula and Diane and Katie called offering me a sober, responsible network face time with Paula and Diane and Katie, like this somehow beat out three quarters of a mil and the chance to appear on the same show as Bob Barker's sex slave. When I hung up on them a crazed, feverish editor of *The New York Times Book Review* called asking me if I'd contribute a twenty-five-word remembrance of Thor Gibbs for a special tribute they were putting together. So far they'd lined up Erica Jong, Bret Easton Ellis, Jerry Seinfeld, Simpsons' creator Matt Groening and supermodel Naomi Campbell. I said no to this, too. I said no to everybody. If the grand-high-exalted Tina Brown herself had called and asked me out to lunch I would have said no.

Then Dwayne Gobble checked in. "Just wondered if you'll be wanting me this morning, Mr. H," he said, his voice over the phone somber and respectful. "I mean, I figured maybe you folks would be wanting to be alone today . . ."

"Let's make it tomorrow, Dwayne. The police are still poking around. Oh, and Dwayne?"

"Yessir?"

"The tabloid TV shows may start phoning you."

"No shit, man. They, like, already have, but I . . . Wait, can you hang on a sec?" I heard a muffled exchange before Dwayne said, "In a *minute,* Mom, okay?" Sounding weary and annoyed. "Sorry about that, Mr. H. Where was I?"

"The tabloid TV shows."

"Oh, right. Told 'em all to get fucked. Mr. Gibbs was a great man. Man like that, you're supposed to treat his death with reverence, not try to cash in on it."

"You're a good man, Dwayne."

"Be seeing you tomorrow, Mr. H. And please give my best to Clethra."

I left the phone off the hook after that. Served up the porridge, put out the maple syrup and honey. She came when I called her and flopped down at the kitchen table, twirling her hair distractedly around her index finger.

"Dwayne sends his best."

She played with her food, her plump lower lip stuck out. "He's a lot smarter than I expected. Reads a lot of serious books. He even reads *you.*"

"I make for a nice break from the serious stuff."

"He said I should try reading you. Should I?"

"Not if you intend to become a healthy, productive

member of society." I tried her oatmeal. Not too terrible, actually. Would be perfect in between those troublesome loose bricks in the chimney. "He thought we'd want to be alone today."

Her eyes sparkled at me with flirty mischief. "Do we?"

"That's entirely up to you. We could start working together."

She set her spoon down, her breakfast untouched. "Like how?"

"Like I could ask you questions and you could answer them."

"That doesn't sound so bad," she allowed. "Only, I wanna talk about you first."

The old role reversal bit. I've gotten it from every single celebrity I've ever worked for. They need to know they can poke and prod at me the same way I'm poking and prodding at them. It makes them feel less vulnerable. "If you'd like," I agreed.

"Okay, how long have you and Merilee been together?"

"Twelve years, off and on."

"Like, how come?"

"How come the off or how come the on?"

"The off, for starters," she said.

"Sometimes we can't stand to be together."

"Okay, how about the on?"

"Sometimes we can't stand to be apart. Eat your oatmeal."

"It's boring." She curled her lip at it.

"Do you want me to make you something else?"

"How come you two won't get married again?"

"Why, have you been talking to my father?"

She let out a giggle. "Do you get it on with other girls?"

I finished my oatmeal, somehow, and put the bowl down for Lulu to lick. She doesn't care for oatmeal, but she likes to reserve the right to change her mind at any time. In this sense she is very much like a cat or the head of a film studio. "Other girls?"

"Like when you and her aren't getting along, I mean. Do you?"

"Not lately, no."

"Does Merilee?"

"Get it on with other girls?"

"You know what I mean."

"I wouldn't know. We respect each other's privacy." I poured myself more coffee and sat back down with it. "Why, did Tyler go out on you?"

"*All* the time!" she flared, her little fists clenching. "He'd, I'm like, bail on me because he had this big paper due, okay? So I'd show up at some party somewhere, okay? And there he'd be with some bitch—like his tongue down her throat and everything, okay? One time it was one of my best friends even. I mean, that's just so shitty."

"What if you wanted to see another guy?"

"I'd be straight up about it."

"What if he minded?"

"Then I'd tell him, like, Tyler, you're being a dick, okay? I'm my own person, okay?"

"Did you tell him you were seeing Thor?"

"No way!" she replied sharply. "I mean, me and Tyler were history by then."

"He didn't know about you and Thor?" I persisted. "Before it all blew up in the press, I mean."

"That's right," she said, her eyes avoiding mine across the table.

She wasn't telling me the truth. This much was obvious. Meaning what? That she'd continued seeing Tyler even after she and Thor had become a famous couple? Or that Tyler knew her relationship with Thor had begun *earlier* than she and Thor had admitted—like when she was still sixteen? Not that this mattered, of course. She and Thor had never actually had sex.

Or *had* they . . . ?

"Are you and Tyler still friends?"

"No, he's not like that."

"Not like what?"

"There's guys who you like as friends but don't wanna fuck and then there's guys like Tyler who you do wanna fuck but you don't like. I mean, you just *want* them, y'know?" She sighed mournfully. "It's just so hard to find guys who are good-looking and not schmucks. I sure haven't."

I tugged at my ear. "Except for Thor, you mean."

"Right. Except for Thor." She was starting to squirm in her chair. My questions were making her edgy.

I got up and poured myself some more coffee, watching her. "Are you still holding to the story that you and he never had sex?"

"It's not a story," she insisted. "We hugged and kissed, that's all."

"Nothing happened between you two when you were still underage?"

"Nothing happened *period.*"

"He never touched you where you shouldn't have?"

"No!"

"And you never touched him where you shouldn't have?"

"No! I *told* you the truth. Geez, why won't you fucking *believe* me?"

"Because that's my job, Clethra."

She puffed out her cheeks impatiently. "This, like, sucks. I'm not having fun."

"They aren't paying you two million dollars to have fun. This is work, not the MTV Spring Break."

"How much longer do we have to keep doing it?" she demanded.

"We can stop anytime."

"Cool." And with that she got up and flounced back into the parlor to the TV.

"Not to worry," I called after her. "I can take care of the dishes."

Which I did. Afterward, I went upstairs and packed my briefcase and came back down to the parlor with it. She'd moved onward and downward to *The Beverly Hillbillies.* "I'm going to New York," I informed her.

Her eyes stayed on the TV. "What, right now?"

"What, right now."

"How come?"

"Things I have to do."

"How long will you be gone?"

"A day or two. Care to come?"

"And stay where?"

"At our apartment, if you'd like."

"Couldn't I just stay here?"

"All by yourself?"

"Why, you think I'm going to *steal* something?"

"Not at all. But after last night I thought you might be frightened."

"No, like, I'm totally over that," she assured me. "Plus Dwayne's coming tomorrow, right?"

"Right," I acknowledged, thinking maybe he had a little to do with why she wanted to stay. Briefly, I felt a pang of something—I didn't know what, and I didn't want to know what. "Our number in the city is right by the phone. There's a ton of food in the house but if you need anything the key to the Rover is hanging behind the kitchen door. There's also Thor's bike."

"No way. That thing scares me shitless." She smiled at me, a big smile. "Have a great time in New York, Hoagy.

And thanks for everything. I mean it." And then she turned her attention back to Granny and a man named Jed.

I wasn't there anymore.

I was dismissed.

It had been a while since I'd been up to Columbia, that fortified stronghold of red brick and so-called free thought up in Morningside Heights, hard on the edge of Harlem. The last time was three years before when the journalism school asked me to participate in a spirited panel discussion on the wonderful world of freelancing. I was the designated ghost. The fifty or so students who attended were keenly interested in what the woman from *Vanity Fair* had to say. None of them were interested in what I had to say, largely because none of them thought that ghosting was anything they'd ever have to do. I didn't blame them. I never thought I'd have to do it either.

I got there around lunchtime. Students toting backpacks crammed with books and laptops were tromping about in rumpled flannel shirts, khakis and unlaced boots. It was a bright, clear day. Not too cold. Many sat on the steps of Low Library eating their lunches in the sunshine. They seemed carefree and happy. I envied them this. I couldn't even remember what it felt like.

Tyler Kampmann's dorm, Furnald Hall, was located just inside the big gate at Broadway and West 116th Street. It was a coed dorm. An amiable old geezer at the counter just inside the door sorted the mail and served as a receptionist. A uniformed security guard backed him up. There was no getting by either of them without a student ID card, not unless you were the guest of one of the residents—and one of them had to sign you in. I got Tyler's room number, 461, from the old guy and tried phoning up, but Tyler wasn't in his room. I thanked the man anyway. He seemed surprised. Politeness tends to surprise people these days.

I told the woman at the registrar's office I was Tyler's uncle and that there was a family emergency. She gave Lulu a doubtful once-over, but she bought my story. Just one of the many advantages of having an above-average wardrobe. Tyler was in an English lit class from noon until one-thirty. I found the building and waited outside on a bench while Lulu growled at the pigeons. To my surprise, I found I was thinking about how appealing it was to be back on a campus again. I hadn't particularly enjoyed the academic life when I was a part of it. I believe the phrase *intellectual masturbation* came up a lot, as it were. But now that I'm older I can see the ivory tower's rewards. It's a place where you can talk about the way the world ought to be and not get laughed at. It's a place where you can hide out from the world the way it is and get paid for it. I don't knock such places anymore.

At one-thirty a couple of dozen kids came trudging slowly out, more than a few of them yawning and rubbing their eyes as if they'd just awakened from a long, deep sleep. I tried to guess which one would be Tyler. Knowing Clethra, I started with the grungiest guy and worked my way down the food chain from there. Struck out three times—until a pale, chubby kid with curly black hair and bloodshot eyes told me Tyler hadn't come to class today.

"I don't think he's feeling too together, man," he explained, after I told him I was Tyler's uncle. His name was Ian Gardner and he lived right across the hall from Tyler. "He bailed on all his classes today."

"Are you sure he's on campus?" I was thinking maybe he'd run off to a warm beach with a cool blonde, his pockets stuffed with tabloid loot.

"Oh, yeah. He's here. I pounded on his door this morn-

ing to see if he was coming to French with me. He said no
way."

"What time was that?"

"Just before nine. Knowing Ty, he's probably still in the
sack."

"He's not," I said. "Or if he is he's not answering his
phone."

"Probably just stuck it in his dresser under twelve pairs
of shorts." Ian grinned at me goofily. "We got, like, major
trashed on champagne last night. He just came into some
righteous family bucks and . . . Jeez, what am I saying?
You'd know all about that, huh?"

"Yes, I would."

"I'm heading back to Furnald right now. I can tell him
you're here, you want."

"May I come with you? It's rather important."

We walked back to Furnald together. He signed Lulu
and me in as his guests and we went upstairs. The fourth-
floor hallway was narrow and it was dingy. It smelled of
Right Guard, dirty socks and musty bedding.

"Yo, Kampmann!" Ian bellowed, pounding on Tyler's
door with his open palm. "Get your butt outta bed, cuz!
Uncle's here to see you!" When there was no answer he
pounded on it louder. "C'mon, Kampmann! You got family here!" He yelled this loud enough for a couple of guys
down the hall to poke their heads out of their doors. But
still there was no answer.

"Guess he went out," Ian apologized to me. "Want to
leave him a note?"

It was an old building and it had settled. There was at
least an inch of space between the bottom of the door and
the carpet. Lulu was snuffling at it intently, her large black
nose aquiver—until she stiffened and let out that forlorn
moan I've come to know and loathe. Right away she

started off down the hallway with her tail between her legs.

I told her to stay put. And told Ian to call campus security.

"What for?" he wondered, baffled. "What's the problem?"

"We have to get that door open right away."

"No problem, man," he said calmly. "Got me a key." He unlocked the door to his own room, 460, fished it out of his desk and came back and used it to unlock Tyler's door.

Tyler's bed was unmade, his books and sneakers and dirty clothes strewn about haphazardly. Typical male dorm room, right down to the pyramid of beer cans next to the closet. Typical except for the corpse on the floor. Tyler Kampmann had been a small, slender boy with blond hair. The eyes that bulged out of his head were baby blue. The welts around his throat were purple.

Ian ran down the hall at once to be sick. I asked the boy next door if I could use his phone, since I didn't want to touch Tyler's. He said sure thing. I used it to call Romaine Very.

Eight

I WAITED FOR HIM outside on the steps with Lulu. There was already such a crowd up there in room 461—the campus police, NYPD, EMS people, medical examiner's people. I didn't want to get in their way. Or get asked what the hell I'd been doing around campus pretending to be the victim's uncle. A pair of truly ill-looking university administrators arrived while I sat out there. A murder on campus is their worst nightmare. Expensive Ivy League school, none too choice neighborhood . . . it doesn't get any worse. The New York press corps showed up as well, reporters and cameramen crowding the entrance to Furnald Hall in desperate search of somebody to talk to or shoot or both. Everywhere I went these days, it seemed, the press showed up. I was beginning to feel like Princess Di.

Very came strutting out about a half hour later. The press he ignored. Me he made right for. I can't honestly say Detective Lieutenant Romaine Very and I are friends. I can't honestly say that because he doesn't like me. We'd been around the bases twice before, most recently when I ghosted the memoirs of Lyle Hudnut, the top-rated TV comic.

"Wish I could say I was glad to see you again, dude," Very said, his jaw working on a piece of gum.

"I wish you could as well, Lieutenant."

He started to say something else, stopped, and stood there a moment with his eyes shut and his lips moving silently as if he were, well, talking to himself. Very was in his late twenties, short and muscular and ultra-street, with soft brown eyes, wavy black hair, an earring and a degree in romance languages from this very college. He had on a hooded blue sweatshirt, matching sweatpants and a pair of black Chuck Taylor high-tops. He could have easily passed for a student except for the bulge under his sweatshirt where his gun was. For as long as I'd known him, Romaine Very had had this serious problem with his intensity, as in he had too much of it. Often, he'd vent it by nodding his head rhythmically, as if he heard his own hip-hop beat. But he wasn't doing that right now. No, there was something decidedly odd about Romaine Very's behavior right now.

He was smiling at me. Blissfully.

"My alma mater," he proclaimed happily as he flopped down on the step next to me. "Spent some of the worst fucking years of my life here." He reached over and patted Lulu, still smiling at me in this most peculiar way. "How's fatherhood treating you, dude?"

"Shabbily, if the past two days are any indication." I peered at him curiously. "How did he die?"

"Strangled, bare hands. No apparent motive. Had a hundred bucks in cash still on him."

"Any idea when?"

"Not yet."

"Well, we do know he was alive a few minutes before nine."

Very chuckled at me, a forced chuckle that went on just a little too long. "And how do we know that?" he asked calmly.

"Ian says so," I replied, continuing to peer at him. Clearly, this was a new Very, a warmer, fuzzier Very. It was downright creepy. "Ian spoke to him."

"I see." Very closed his eyes and clasped his hands together. Now he looked like he was asking Santa to please, *please* bring him a new bicycle. "Would you care to tell me why you were impersonating a member of the victim's family?"

"He was somewhat connected to a project I'm working on."

"Now that particular response doesn't surprise me," he conceded. "But I don't recall reading nothing about it. Usually do."

"I'm on this one unofficially. Strictly as a favor for a friend. Make that former friend."

"Not a friend anymore?"

"Not among the living anymore."

Very took a deep breath and held it in for several seconds, then let it out. He did this three times, in and out, as if he were trying to blow up a life raft. Possibly his own. "Okay, sure. We're talking Thor Gibbs, am I right? That's why his body was found at your ex-wife's farm yesterday."

"That's correct."

"And you're helping out sweet little Clethra. She's your celebrity."

"That's correct."

"I never knew you were friends with Thor Gibbs."

"There's a lot about me you don't know, Lieutenant."

"So true," he admitted. "I gotta try harder, on account of you're a bright, sensitive guy. I should make more of an effort to relate to you."

Lulu and I exchanged a look. "Stop this, Lieutenant. You're starting to frighten me."

"I'm serious, dude."

"I know you are. That's what's frightening me."

"Wanna tell me about it?" he asked. "What's going down?"

"A whole lot of crosstown traffic, Lieutenant. I seem to be stuck in it."

"Let's start with Tyler, okay?" Very suggested patiently. This from a man who'd given himself an ulcer before he was twenty-six. "How did he fit into this?"

I told him how. I told him how he was Clethra's ex-honey and that she believed he was the one who'd peddled the striptease video to *Hard Copy*.

"That plays," Very said. "We just found a two-day-old bank deposit slip in his desk like you wouldn't believe."

"Oh, I'd believe it," I said. "I also believe he knew something, Lieutenant. Something about Clethra and Thor's love affair. I don't know what—she got most evasive when I pressed her on it. That's why I came here. Only I was too late. Whatever Tyler knew died with him. Possibly, that's why he was killed."

"Or possibly," Very countered, "somebody was just paying him back for peddling that tape."

"Possibly."

"Like who, dude? Who we looking at in the way of suspects?"

I gave him the big three—Ruth, Barry and Marco—and how they figured in. "All three of them were in Connecticut yesterday when Thor was killed. All three of them are here in the city today. They have to be considered our prime candidates. Except for . . ." I stopped short, remembering what had—or I should say had not—occurred yesterday when we were out in Barry's yard.

"Except for what, dude?"

"Nothing, Lieutenant."

"Who's handling the investigation out there?"

"Fellow called Chick Munger. He's a lieutenant with the Major Crime Squad, Central District. But you'll want to deal with Resident Trooper Slawski."

"Why would I want to do that?"

"Because we don't like Munger."

Very squeezed out that strange chuckle again. "You never learn, do you, dude?"

"I try to, Lieutenant. I just never seem to get anywhere."

"Check, lemme explain it to you then, okay?" Now he sounded like he was addressing a kindergarten class on the subject of what Mr. Policeman does. "I ain't interested in getting mixed up in some other department's political bullshit. And I really, really ain't interested in playing any of your head games."

"I'm not playing games, Lieutenant. Head or otherwise."

"All I want," he went on, "is a nice, orderly joint investigation. Two departments working hand in hand in a cooperative and professional manner. Because if we don't then the FBI will swoop in and take a big dump all over us, which they may do anyway with all of the pub this is generating. They sure as hell won't give us much time, bet on it."

The university administrators came back outside now to face the press. They looked even sicker than they had before.

"Tell me, Lieutenant," I said. "Did any of Tyler's neighbors on the fourth floor hear anything?"

"We're checking on that. Some of 'em are still in class."

"What about the security guard down in the lobby?"

"According to him, the victim had no guests this morning. And he don't remember anybody asking about him—except for you, of course."

"Was someone on duty all night?"

"All night," he affirmed. "Same story. No one came to see him."

I pondered this, frowning. "But how is that possible?"

"Dunno how it's possible, dude," he responded cheerfully. "We're checking on that, too."

I stared at him. "You know, you're acting really, really unusual, Lieutenant."

He showed me that same tranquil, creepy smile. "You noticed, huh?"

"Hard not to."

"I've made a major change in my life since the last time I saw you, dude."

"Let me guess—you met a nice girl."

"Nope."

"A nice boy?"

"Get outta here."

"Wait, don't tell me . . ." I lowered my voice. "They've put you on Prozac."

"No way. It's Yoga—an hour in the morning, an hour at bedtime. And I ain't just talking about exercise, although I am in the best shape I ever been in in my whole life."

"You do look fabulous. Lulu said so first thing she saw you."

"I'm talking mind-set, dude," he explained, tapping his forehead with his index finger. "I'm talking progressive relaxation techniques designed to reduce your brain wave activities."

Lulu and I exchanged a puzzled look.

"Check it out," he elaborated. "The reason I seem different to you is that I'm now in total control of my own responses, okay? I have choices. I *choose* to be healthy. I *choose* to be relaxed. I am no longer a slave to competition. I no longer get upset about shit I can't control."

"Healthy attitude in your line of work."

"You got that right. And here's the best part: I don't beat up on myself no more. I've pulled all of that shit over to the curb. I accept that I'm not perfect. I accept that I'm human. I'm learning, I'm growing, I'm chillin'." Mr. Serenity jumped to his feet, limber and supple as a gymnast. "Of course, I still haven't met the ultimate test."

"What's that, Lieutenant?"

"You, dude."

"Careful, I flatter easy."

"Dude, you don't do nothing easy. But this time I'm not going to let you get to me." They were bringing Tyler's body out the door now, the cameramen pushing and shoving for position. Very watched them a moment, jaw working his gum, before he turned back to me. And smiled. And said, "Stay with me, dude."

"Why, darling, what on earth brings you to town?"

"Nothing major. Just thought I'd come in and find another dead body. Hope you don't mind."

She was sprawled on the Stickley leather settee in the living room working her way through a pile of manuscripts and a pot of Lemon Zinger. Tracy was asleep in the nursery. Pam was out shopping. "Another dead body?" She whipped off her reading glasses, forever self-conscious about them. "Whose?"

"Tyler Kampmann, Clethra's ex-boyfriend."

"Was it awful, darling?"

"It wasn't pretty. Actually, Lulu's the one who found him. She could use a hug."

"Oh, my poor, brave sweetness," Merilee cried, patting the settee next to her.

Lulu needed no further encouragement. She dove into

Merilee's lap, whimpering, tail thumping, starved for her mommy's undivided attention.

"Mercy," Merilee fretted, stroking her. "The men in Clethra's life don't seem to be faring too well these days, do they?"

"Why should they be different than anyone else?"

I sat wearily in the chair opposite her. Merilee extricated herself from Lulu and got another cup and poured me some tea.

I thanked her, sipping it. "Anything good?" I asked, meaning the pile of manuscripts.

"A remake of *The Third Man* with Keanu Reeves and Snoop Doggy Dogg that may not be too terrible. They're moving it from Vienna to Telluride."

"Why does *everything* these days have to be a god-damned remake of something else?" I wondered. "Why don't they do anything original anymore?"

"Because, darling," she replied, "that would mean someone would have to come up with an original thought. Not likely. And someone else would have to be willing to stake their entire career on it. Even less likely."

"I suppose I'm being terribly retro. Sorry."

"Don't apologize, darling. That's one of the things I adore about you." Merilee sat back down, one leg folded underneath her. Women often sit that way, just as women often try on each other's shoes and sample food off each other's plates. Men never do any of these things. Someone ought to come up with an explanation for that sometime. "Did she come in with you?" she wondered, meaning Clethra.

"I left her at the house."

"Alone?"

"She'll be fine. There's a large trooper watching over her. And she has the Land Rover if she needs to . . ."

She narrowed her eyes at me. "Needs to what, darling?"

"Nothing. Never mind."

Could she have done it—driven in to the city right after me and strangled Tyler? She sure had the motive. And who better to slip into his coed dorm unnoticed. Hell, she probably still had her Barnard student ID card. But was she strong enough to kill Tyler with her bare hands?

I finished my tea and got to my feet. "Have you made plans for tonight?"

"Sigourney's coming over for soup. Why?"

"Cancel her. This is our night. We three are painting the town, just like old times."

"Oh, excellent," she exclaimed happily.

Lulu seemed pleased, too. She jumped down and began circling the settee at Warp Factor 9, snarfling excitedly.

"Hoagy?" She said it softly, gazing at me over her teacup.

"Yes, Merilee?"

"What do you think is going on here?"

"A love story."

"Why do you say that?"

"Because it's always a love story, Merilee. The trick is figuring out which kind."

"Which kind of love story?"

"Which kind of love."

My study was now Tracy's nursery. I used the phone in our bedroom, which was where my desk had ended up. Clethra answered on the second ring, sounding shaken and scared. She'd already heard the news from Barry, who got it from Ruth, who had been visited by Very, who still moved fast, even in his newly chilled state.

"God, poor Tyler," she wailed mournfully. "D-Do they know who did it?"

"Not yet."

"What's *happening* to me, Hoagy? Why is this *happening*?"

"I wish I knew, Clethra. But I don't. What did you do today?"

"Nothing much."

"Go anywhere?"

"Not really."

"Are the police still there?"

"Trooper Slawski's here. Him and a couple of others."

"Would you ask him to call me when he gets a chance?"

"Okay." She was silent a moment. "Why Tyler, Hoagy?"

"You tell me," I snapped.

"W-What do you mean?"

"I mean you haven't exactly been honest with me, have you?" I said, getting rough with her and hating myself for it. It's damned cruel to use someone's grief to pry them open. But sometimes in my line I have to. That's one of the reasons I don't like my line. One of many.

"I have so!" she cried. "Don't you *believe* me?"

"Why the hell should I? You've done nothing but lie to me."

"That's not true! Why are you *talking* to me this way?"

"You lied to me about you and Thor. First you said he was your lover, then you said he wasn't. Now he's dead. You told me Tyler didn't know anything about you two. And now *he's* dead. I'm sick of this, Clethra. I'm sick of having to peel you like a Vidalia onion. I'm sick of finding dead people."

"But Tyler didn't know anything!" she sobbed. "I *swear* he didn't. He knew shit about me and Thor!"

Briefly, I stopped breathing. Not that it was anything she'd said. It was how she'd said it. All a matter of the emphasis a single word. "Okay, Clethra," I said, slowly and carefully. "Then did he know something about you and someone *other* than Thor?"

She was silent again. "Well, maybe," she admitted

grudgingly. "But, like, I can't believe anybody would give a shit."

"Who was he, Clethra?"

"I mean, not enough to *kill* Tyler. I mean, like, why bother?"

"Who was he, Clethra?"

She let out a huge sigh. Or maybe it was a sob. And then she told me.

I caught up with him on Madison Avenue right around the corner from his school. The Dalton School was on East Eighty-ninth Street, and was the private academy of choice for the children of New York City's social and cultural cream. Classes had just let out for the day. He was scuffling along all by himself in a blue blazer, white oxford cloth button-down shirt and khakis, his shoulders hunched, his nose buried in a sci-fi paperback.

He noticed the Jag right away when I honked. Hard not to. I said to get in. He got in, squeezing his geeky frame around Lulu, who ended up on the floor at his feet, immensely put out.

"How was school today, Arvin?"

"Okay," he replied sullenly. His body might have been right there next to mine, but his voice was two or three light-years away.

"Surprised you didn't take a couple of days off."

He said nothing. The eyes behind his thick, wire-rimmed glasses were vacant and lusterless. He had withdrawn into a place where nobody could hurt him.

"It's okay to be upset, you know," I told him. "It's even okay to cry."

Again he said nothing.

I left it alone. Worked us over to Fifth and parked there. We strolled into Central Park. There were a lot of rollerbladers and dog-walkers out. The leaves were falling from the trees in huge bunches. I bought us two Italian ices from a vendor. We ate them while we walked. Lulu chased squirrels, which is one of her favorite things in the world to do—squirrels being just about the only members of the animal kingdom she can scare.

"Someone murdered Tyler Kampmann today, Arvin," I said, watching his face for a reaction.

It wasn't surprise. It was a satisfied smile. "Good," he said.

I frowned at him. "Good?"

"T-Tyler was a schmuck," he sputtered, Adam's apple bobbing up and down inside his pimply throat. "He treated Clethra like shit and then he sold that videotape of her for all that money. He got what he deserved, you ask me."

"Have any idea who did it?"

"Who, me?" His voice shot up several octaves, way up into the land of the Pigeon Sisters. "W-Why would . . . ?" Back down it came, into Barry White country. "Why would *I* have any idea?"

"Well, he did sort of take Clethra away from you, didn't he?"

Arvin's eyes widened in shock, as if he'd just been shot in the back by a Special Forces sniper stationed on the roof of the Metropolitan Museum. He made a huge, painful effort to swallow and failed, gagging. Ashen, he stumbled toward a bench and flopped down onto it. "She *told* you?"

I sat next to him. "Let's say I figured it out."

"How?"

"Everyone ought to be good at something." Me, I was good at having a dirty mind. "Care to tell me about it, Arvin?"

"Do I have to?" he wondered plaintively.

"You don't have to do anything," I said to him, crossing my legs. "But I'm trying to help her. As well as stop whoever is doing all of this. Whatever you can tell me might be important."

"Well, okay . . . Only, it sounds a whole lot worse than . . . What I mean is we love each other, okay?"

"Like brother and sister?"

He gazed at me earnestly. "Do you have a sister, Hoagy?"

"No, I don't."

"Clethra and me," he said, "we're as close as two people can possibly be. Whatever happened to her while we were growing up, she always shared it with me. Personal stuff. Stuff no one else knows. And same here. I-I tell her everything. We spent a lot of time alone together, see. Thor and Mom were always away on speaking tours, and Clethra was old enough we really didn't need anyone to stay with us. We're *there* for each other. Know what I mean?"

"Yes, I do."

He hesitated, fidgeting uncomfortably on the bench. He wasn't pale anymore. He was bright red. "When we were real little we'd go in Mom's closet and I'd show her m-my thing. And she'd show me hers. And . . . as we got older, we stayed really open with each other about what was happening to us. Our bodies, I mean. Like, she learned about boys from me and I learned about g-girls from . . ." He stopped short, gulping for air. "Is that weird?"

"Not really."

"Sometimes, when it was just the two of us, we'd sleep in the same b-bed together. Clethra doesn't like to sleep alone. She sometimes gets frightened."

"I know."

He looked at me sharply. "How do you know that?"

"She told me," I replied. "Go on, Arvin."

"One night . . ." His knees were jiggling almost convulsively now. His breathing was jagged. "I w-was eleven, she was fifteen . . . We discovered if I put my . . . if I did *things* to her that she would . . . that she . . ." He took a deep breath, glancing at me furtively. "I even used my tongue sometimes," he blurted out.

"Did she do things for you?"

"When I was old enough."

"How?"

"How?" he echoed, puzzled.

"How did she give you pleasure?"

"With her hand."

"Did the two of you ever go all the way together?"

"Oh, no," he gasped, appalled. "Never. Not ever. I-I never have. Not with anyone. A lot of the guys in my class have. Or they say they have. But not me. And Clethra, she's too old for that stuff now. She's more interested in, y'know, other guys."

"Bother you much?"

"Does what bother me much?"

"Do you miss being with her that way?"

"Well, sure," he admitted. "She says she still loves me and someday I'll meet a girl my own age and everything, but I miss her bad. And I don't like other girls. They're so vain and shallow and dorky."

"Nobody's perfect."

"Clethra is," he said insistently. "Clethra's perfect."

"Sorry. My mistake."

He sat there staring at me miserably. "Did she tell Tyler about her and me?"

"She did."

"She must have been stoned," he said feebly. "She gets real blabby when she's stoned. Otherwise she never would have . . . I-I mean, that was our secret."

And one helluva juicy little secret it was, too. Enterprising Tyler could have cleared another half million for this tale of forbidden love, easy. True, it would have been a little tough on Clethra and the poor kid. But so what? He'd be a made man—a millionaire by his twenty-first birthday, every college student's dream these days. Only, Tyler hadn't made it to his twenty-first birthday. And I had a pretty good idea why.

"Arvin, who else knew about Clethra and you? Did Thor know?" Thor, who'd taken Clethra away from him just as Tyler had. And was dead, too. "Did your mom know?"

"No one knew," Arvin answered bitterly. "Not unless she told them."

We sat there in silence. Lulu came strutting back to us, all rough and tough after her latest triumph over the rodent kingdom. She sat between my feet. I patted her on the head.

"Hoagy?"

"Yes, Arvin?"

"Is it wrong what we did?"

I sighed inwardly. "I don't know very much about right and wrong. I used to think I did, but I don't anymore."

"Are you gonna tell on us?"

"Not unless I have to."

"But you would if you had to?" he persisted.

"I won't have to."

"What if Clethra wants to put it in her b-book?"

"Then I'll have something to say about it. See, if somebody gets hurt—in this case, it would be you—that *is* wrong." I patted his jiggling knee. "That much I do know, Arvin."

"It was a secret," he said, his voice rising. "I can't believe she . . . It was our . . ." He broke off, his scrawny chest heaving, his eyes filling with tears. It was finally happening. He was finally letting go.

I reached for my linen handkerchief, only I wasn't fast enough. By the time I'd gotten it out of my pocket he didn't need it anymore. He'd fought back those tears and he'd conquered them. Arvin Gibbs was one tough customer, all right. Particularly on himself. He would not give in. He would not cry.

We were dressing for dinner when Slawski called.

"Mr. Hoag, this is Resident State Trooper Tyrone Slawski calling from Lyme, Connecticut," he barked into my ear. "Detective Lieutenant Romaine Very of the New York Police Department is presently on the line along with myself. Per your suggestion, Detective Lieutenant Very called me earlier today so as to interface on the multiple victim scenario as well as to establish lines of mutual interdepartmental communication."

"Oh, good," I said. "I knew you two would hit it off." Just as I knew Very would try Munger first and hate him.

"If you will please hold on a moment," Slawski continued, ignoring this, "I will expedite a conference call configuration so the three of us may converse in a simultaneous manner."

The line went dead.

I sat down on the edge of the bed and waited. I was in no hurry. Merilee was still in the bathtub devouring her new issue of *People* magazine. Thor had made the cover, an old *Life* magazine photo of him on skis alongside Papa Hemingway in Ketchum, both of them looking virile and invincible. The headline read: LAST CHAPTER FOR THE LAST MAN'S MAN.

After a moment I heard Very say, "Hello?" And Slawski say, "Hello?" I chimed in a greeting, just to hold up my end. All three of us could hear each other perfectly, even though Mr. Serenity and I were in New York and Slawski was in Lyme. And to think they say the world is going straight to hell. Well, *they* don't say it, but *I* do.

"Lieutenant, I would like to bring both yourself and Mr.

Hoag up-to-date on the preliminary findings of the state medical examiner," Slawski began, "which I have, I am pleased to report, managed to obtain through a former teammate who is associated with the laboratory." Translation: Munger was shutting him out. "The deceased, Mr. Thorvin Gibbs, suffered extensive shattering of the parietal and occipital regions of the skull, which were driven downward with great force into the corresponding lobes of the cerebrum . . . As we deduced from the visual evidence, the weapon was the six-pound sledgehammer recovered at the scene. There appear to have been three blows, one blow delivered with greater verticality than the others, which may indicate the victim was down on the ground when it was delivered . . . Blood and hair found on the sledge match those of the deceased. Blood samples found in the woodshed also match the victim's."

"Anyone else's blood found there?" It was Very who asked this.

"No sir. Just the victim's."

"Do the blows tell us anything about the killer's height or weight?" My question.

"At present, they won't commit to anything more precise than average height and weight, most likely right-handed. A weighted sledge swung high overhead makes a pulverizing wound. We're talking massive trauma. Serious lab work may tell us more, but that will take several days."

"Still," I put in, "his killer would have to be someone strong, don't you think?"

"Fairly strong," Slawski conceded.

"Could a woman have done it?"

"I seen it happen, dude," Very said. "Domestic dispute in Hell's Kitchen couple of years ago. Woman did her boyfriend with one. Guy was big as a fridge. She couldn't have weighed more than ninety pounds, but she was a natural. Mechanics of her swing were perfect, is what I'm saying.

Generated as much head speed at the point of impact as
Frank Thomas taking the Rocket Man downtown."

"A woman could not have hoisted the victim into that
cart," Slawski pointed out.

"True," Very allowed.

"How about a boy?" I asked.

"Depend on the boy," Very replied. "Why, you got
something on Arvin?"

"Do they know what time Thor was killed, Trooper?"

"Not precisely, what with him being in that cold pond
water. They estimate between eleven and eleven-thirty."

"Was there a struggle?"

"No preliminary evidence of one. Victim's hands
showed residual bruising consistent with the fight at Slim
Jim's on Saturday. But he had no fresh scratches, nothing
under his nails." Slawski cleared his throat uneasily. "Mr.
Hoag, there was one other finding of possible signifi-
cance . . ." I heard a slow intake of breath. ". . . to do
with the victim's pancreas."

"What about it?"

"He had a malignancy. Man was terminal. What I mean
is, he had six, maybe twelve months to live. His estranged
wife says she knew nothing about it. Neither did his doctor, who last saw him two years ago, at which time he was
pronounced in perfect health. Did you know, Mr. Hoag?"

I didn't answer him right away. I couldn't. For some
reason, learning this about Thor had made him come back
to life for me again. Fragile, painful life. "I did not," I
replied quietly. "I wonder if he did."

"Dude's got six months to live, he *knows*," Very declared.

"Not necessarily, Lieutenant," I countered. "They call
pancreatic cancer the silent killer—people often don't
know they have it until it's way too late." Still, if Thor had
known, it explained a lot. Such as why he was pushing

himself and everyone around him so hard. Did it explain Clethra, too? Did it explain why he'd run off with her?

Slawski was talking again: "There were no fingerprints on the weapon. His attacker wore gloves. A thread got caught in the handle of the garden cart. Common cotton work gloves, available anywhere. No prints on the garden pruners either. Traces of the victim's blood and tissue were found on the blades."

"Was the penis severed post-mortem or ante-mortem?" That was Very speaking. I don't use words like ante-mortem. Or at least I try not to.

"Post," answered Slawski.

"Is there any way of knowing if the same person committed both acts?" That was me.

"At present, there is no evidence to support the theory that multiple perpetrators were involved."

Very said, "What about shoe prints?"

"Investigators are still on mud detail," said Slawski. "But I ain't optimistic. They got dog and cat prints, ducks, raccoon, deer. They got the garden cart coming and going, the baby buggy. They got a light but steady rain falling before they sealed the area. They do got a few partials so far, which they'll be looking to match up with Mr. Hoag, Miss Nash, their hired man and so forth. But mostly what they got there is a real mess."

"I apologize, Trooper," I snapped. "Next time someone dies there I'll make sure I drag a rake across it beforehand."

"Chill, dude," Very cautioned me.

"I wasn't casting any aspersions," Slawski said crisply.

"I know you weren't," I said, running my hand through what was left of my hair. "I was out of line. Anything else?"

"Yessir," he replied. "Lieutenant Munger has officially eliminated the crew from Slim Jim's. Kirk Bennett and his posse were out on a charter boat catching blues at the time of the homicide. Left New London at six in the morning, came back at two in the afternoon. Got dozens of people can vouch for 'em. So the lieutenant won't be stumbling down that particular alley no more." Slawski didn't say how unhappy this particular development made him. He didn't have to. "We can cross off your hired man, too."

"You've been checking out Dwayne?" I asked, somewhat surprised.

"We had to," Slawski said. "Matter of routine. But you can set your mind at ease—he was helping his mom around the house all morning. Nice lady. Still think she got a bum rap." He coughed and went silent after that.

"It doesn't sound as if you have very much to go on, Trooper," I concluded.

"We're still in the preliminary stages. We have a great deal of evidence to compile. Numerous alternative leads to pursue . . ."

I tried it again, louder this time. "It doesn't sound as if you have much to go on, Trooper."

"We got shit," he admitted. "And that's no lie. Lieutenant Munger is requesting that Ruth Feingold, Barry Feingold and Marco Paolo return later this week for formal questioning."

"What the hell kind of name is Marco Paolo?" Very wondered.

"A fake one," I told him.

"Her boy Arvin's coming too," Slawski added. "You're welcome to sit in, Lieutenant Very."

"I'm there," Very said.

"I didn't know you ever left the city, Lieutenant."

"Oh, sure. I'm cool as long as I'm safely home on the streets by nightfall. Check, that Ruth Feingold practically shot my ears off this afternoon. She's some kind of pistol."

"I'm down to that," Slawski agreed.

"Just us three gees spitballing, though, I'm liking Barry for both killings. Solid motive for taking out Gibbs—father protecting his daughter—plus he's super-vague about his whereabouts when it went down."

"And his motive for killing Tyler?" I asked.

"Dude trashed his daughter. Payback time."

"I understand you have your own medical examiner's preliminary findings, Lieutenant," said Slawski.

"You understand right."

"That was fast," I said.

"We're talking high-profile case here. Rich kid dies in his room at Columbia he goes right to the head of the line. Not that I'm gonna dish *you* word one, dude," he said to me, as laid-back as can be. "Not until you give me some. First you gotta give me some."

"Why, Lieutenant, whatever do you—?"

"With this guy you gotta trade," he explained to Slawski. To me he said, "Gimme."

"As you wish." I gave him Barry's ex-lover, the one who was his supposed alibi for when Thor was killed. Which means I also gave him the HIV angle. Very promised he'd be discreet. I knew I could count on it. I did not give him Arvin and Clethra and what Tyler knew about the two of them. It was Barry he liked for it. I gave him Barry. "Satisfied?" I asked him.

"For now," he replied, with that new and unnerving chuckle of his. "Okay, I got me a strangler with an average-sized pair of hands—"

"Average for a man or for a woman?" I broke in.

"Ruth could have done it, if that's what you're tripping on. Victim was a twerp—five-feet-six, a hundred and thirty pounds, almost no muscle tone. Ruth outweighed him by a good hundred pounds, and she's got a helluva grip on her. I made sure—I shook her hand."

"She's no shrinking violet," I concurred, wondering

again about my teenaged celebrity. Could she have strangled Tyler with those soft, pudgy little hands of hers?
"Trooper, did the man guarding the farm today mention
anything about Clethra going out?"

"He said she didn't. Why?"

"Just curious. Please continue, Lieutenant."

"Time of death," Very went on, "was somewhere between seven-thirty and eight o'clock this morning. Our
three prime suspects all claim they were home at the time
. . . Ruth was home alone working on a speech."

"Arvin had left for school?" I asked.

"Correct. He left the house at seven-twenty, arrived at
the Dalton School by subway in time for class at eight
. . . Barry and Marco swear they were still in bed asleep."

"Is it possible one of them was and one of them
wasn't?" Slawski asked.

"Very," I said.

"Yeah, what is it, dude?" he asked.

"I'm saying it's very possible," I explained wearily.

"Mucho possible," he agreed. "It's also possible, we end
up with nothing but *bupkes,* we can maybe pry them two
lovebirds apart. But as of this minute, they're sticking together."

"Wait a minute, Lieutenant," I pointed out, "Tyler
Kampmann couldn't have been murdered between seven-
thirty and eight o'clock."

"Why not?" A testy little edge crept back into his voice
for the first time. It made me downright nostalgic for the
old Very.

"Ian from across the hall spoke to him at a few minutes
before nine," I replied.

Right away Very started breathing in and out, in and
out. "Ian must be mistaken," he said gently.

"I don't see how he could be, Lieutenant," I argued.
"He was on his way to a nine o'clock class. He pounded

on Tyler's door to see if Tyler was coming. Tyler said no. They'd been out partying late."

Very stayed calm. "Okay, I can't explain it, dude," he conceded blandly. Damn, it was strange. "Coroner might be off. It happens."

"Did anyone else on Tyler's floor see or hear anything?"

"No one saw him all morning. And no one saw anyone who didn't belong there. Security guard downstairs swears no one could have sneaked by him."

Slawski sniffed. "Man's bound to swear that. Job's on the line."

"Agreed," said Very. "I'm going back up there to show him a photo of Ruth. Barry and Marco, too. You never know."

"I'd show him a picture of Clethra as well," I suggested.

"Why?"

"You never know." I sat there on the edge of the bed, mulling it all over. Merilee was running the shower now, her bath completed. "Is it possible that these two murders aren't related at all?"

"Possible," Very admitted. "But not likely."

"But why mutilate Thor and not Tyler?"

"Matter of being practical," he offered. "Small dorm room, crowded floor. Perp had to make it quick and quiet."

"Okay, but why go to the trouble of hiding one body and not the other?"

"Same reason, dude. Where the hell you gonna hide a dead guy in an eight-by-ten room?"

"Good answer, Lieutenant."

"Thanks. Does Lieutenant Munger have any ideas, Trooper?"

"If he does he ain't sharing 'em with me."

"Or me," Very said. "All I can get out of him is attitude. What's the gee's problem, anyway?"

"I just assumed he had a certain personal difficulty with African-American individuals," Slawski answered stiffly.

"Could be," Very suggested, "he's just an all-around schmuck."

"I'm down to that," Slawski agreed.

"Dude?"

"Yes, Lieutenant?"

"Anyone else's photo I should be showing to the security guard?"

"Arvin."

"You got some reason to believe the kid's involved?"

"I've got no reason to believe he isn't."

"What aren't you telling me, dude?" he persisted, his voice growing heavy with apprehension.

"Nothing that I can share with you at the present time."

"You're trying to destroy me, aren't you? You're purposely trying to destroy me!"

"Why, Lieutenant, whatever do you—?"

"I *knew* this was gonna happen," he fumed. "The second I laid eyes on you!" He was getting good and agitated now. He almost sounded like his old, normal self. "I *knew* it!"

"Careful, Lieutenant. Think of your brain waves."

"What seems to be the difficulty here?" Slawski wondered.

"The problem is this gee's all the time getting in my face!" Very roared.

"I heard that. He the Piffle Man."

"He *tells* me my business. He *withholds* key information from me—"

"Uh-huh," Slawski chimed in. "That's right."

"He stirs up every single person he comes in contact with—"

"You the man." Slawski egging him on. "Uh-huh!"

"And *then,* just when he's managed to turn a neat, orderly investigation into a rat's nest of nutsiness and hysteria, he pulls some bonehead play that just about gets everybody killed. And guess who he leaves to pick up the pieces? *Me! Always me!*" Very stopped short, breathing heavily into the phone, in and out, in and out. "But he doesn't get under my skin anymore," he insisted, his voice as soft and sweet as warm maple syrup. "That was the old me."

"I surely would like to know how you manage it, Lieutenant," Slawski said. "On account of, dig, I could use me some of that."

This seemed like a really good time for me to hang up. I left the two of them to hash over the details, pleased that they were starting to bond.

And even more puzzled than I had been. Sometimes, as more information comes to light, the picture becomes clearer. This wasn't one of those times. Thor had been a dying man. Had he known about it? Is that why he'd shown up on my doorstep? And what about Marco? For some reason Barry's volatile lover kept nagging at me. Was there something about Marco I was overlooking? Some personal stake he had in Thor's affair with Clethra? Some connection between him and Tyler? What was I missing?

The phone rang not ten seconds after I'd hung up.

"The police," Ruth Feingold blustered, "think I killed them both."

"The police," I said, "don't know what to think."

"Where's Clethra?" she demanded. "And don't you dare lie to me."

"In Connecticut."

"What, alone?"

"She wanted some time to herself."

"I see," she said harshly.

"She's got a lot on her mind, Ruth. Don't crowd her or you'll drive her further away."

"What the hell do you know about teenagers?"

"Plenty. I still am one."

That silenced her for a moment. No small feat. "Hoagy, did Thor . . . did he say anything to you about his health?"

"Not a word."

"Maybe this explains some of his . . ." She trailed off, groping around in the eternal dark for some comfort. "How he behaved. Maybe it had already gotten to his brain. That can happen."

"It can," I agreed. Who was I to take this crumb of solace away from her?

"I always used to joke about how he was the living embodiment of the dead white male. And now . . ." She let out a sob. "The poor bastard."

"Just give Clethra some time to sort through things, Ruth. She'll come back to you. She's a good kid."

"She's a bitch," Ruth snarled. "It runs in the family." And with that she hung up.

Merilee came padding in from the bath in her silk dressing gown. "Darling, I didn't mean to eavesdrop, but I could have sworn I just heard you say Clethra was a good kid."

"You must be imagining things." I glanced up at her standing there, all dewy and fragrant, her cheeks flushed. Tired as always, to be sure. But she'd never seemed lovelier to me than she did at that moment. "Clethra slept in our bed last night."

"Did she?" she said mildly. "And where did you sleep?"

"In our bed. She came up in the middle of the night. She was frightened. She had a claw hammer."

"Oh, that old ploy." Merilee went over to her dressing table and began pawing noisily through her jewelry box. "What *did* I do with my diamond earrings?"

"I calmed her down."

"Have you seen my diamond earrings, darling?"

"No, Merilee, I haven't seen your diamond earrings." I tugged at my ear. "Nothing happened, of course."

She treated me to her up-from-under look, the one that turns the lower half of my body into ooze. "Of course."

"You do believe me, don't you, Merilee?"

"Darling, if I can't believe in you after all these years who can I believe in?"

"Maybe Neil Young, but I can't think of anyone else." I got to my feet and went over to her. "Thor was dying of cancer."

"I wondered."

I frowned at her, puzzled. "You wondered?"

"To me, the man was positively begging for it. Running off with his own stepdaughter that way. Picking that fight with those hairy mastodons at Slim Jim's. Rather surprising, really. Don't you think?"

"What is?"

"That with all of his macho posturing Thor Gibbs didn't have the nerve to commit suicide."

I considered this. "Unless that's precisely what he did do, Merilee."

We dressed. The tux for me. Starched white broadcloth shirt with ten-pleat bib front and wing collar, black silk bow tie, Grandfather's pearl studs and cuff links, something greasy in what was left of my hair. Just kidding about the hair, actually. I have a lush, rampant growth of hair. It's just that very little of it happens to be on my head anymore. Merilee went with the black velvet Ralph Lauren, the bare-shouldered one that makes her look as willowy as a schoolgirl. Diamond necklace and earrings—yes, she found them. Her long, golden hair up, a bit of color on her lips. She looked positively radiant.

"Where are we going?" she demanded eagerly. She hates secrets more than just about anything else, except possibly Velcro.

"You'll find out soon enough."

"But I must tell Pam where we'll be, darling. We can't just be footloose and fancy-free anymore, you know. We have Tracy. We have responsibilities. We have—"

"I've written it all down for her," I said to her soothingly. "Besides, we can pretend, can't we?"

She straightened my tie and kissed me lightly on the mouth. "We can do more than pretend."

I unstraightened the tie and kissed her back, not so lightly. Until she lunged for her grandmother's white silk shawl and escaped for the kitchen, swaying on her three-inch heels in a most beguiling manner.

Pam was rolling out dough for our breakfast scones, all cheerful and pink-cheeked, Tracy watching her solemnly from her bassinet. Lulu was waiting for us anxiously in the doorway wearing the black silk top hat Merilee had had made for her that year she did the Cole Porter musical. A chin strap holds it in place.

"I understand he's given you our numbers," Merilee said to Pam dubiously.

"Yes, yes," Pam reassured her. "Now please do relax and enjoy yourself. I have minded dozens of babies and I haven't lost one yet. Several, in fact, have gone on to serve in high government positions.

Merilee and I exchanged a look.

I said, "I'm really sorry you said that, Pam."

Merilee said, "Now you have me truly frightened."

"Don't be," Pam commanded her.

Merilee bent down and kissed Tracy, lingering over her tearfully. Until finally she gathered herself and exclaimed, "I can't believe we're actually going out on a date."

"Believe it."

She hesitated, glancing at the sheet I'd left by the phone for Pam. "Perhaps I'd better just have one quick little look at the phone numbers where we'll—"

"Let's go, Merilee," I growled, grabbing her by the arm.

"Yes, dear. Gosh, you're a brute."

Our limousine was waiting for us downstairs at the awning, turning some heads. It was a spotless 1933 Rolls Phantom II, black and yellow. The uniformed driver, Jimmy Piper, was a retired Scottish race car driver who operated three such vintage limos around town. And had himself a soft spot for Pam's hot cross buns, as it were. A tub of caviar, toast points and a chilled bottle of Dom Perignon awaited us in the backseat.

The champagne was gone by the time we finished crossing Central Park.

Lulu ate most of the caviar.

First stop was the Post House on East Sixty-third Street, a rousing and boisterous chophouse that served the finest —not to mention largest—cuts of meat in New York City. Chalkboards announced the daily specials, few if any of them recommended as a regular part of one's daily food pyramid. Not the most romantic dining spot in town, I'll grant you. But Merilee Nash, in case you didn't know it, happens to be one of Gotham's preeminent carnivores. When Rusty's held a celebrity rib-eating fund-raiser for the Special Olympics she put away more baby back ribs than four out of the five Knick starters. Only Charles Oakley could outeat her.

When Merilee eats out she eats meat. Period.

She turned more than a few heads when we came down the steps from the bar and crossed the dining room to our table. She generally does. Another bottle of Dom Perignon, properly chilled, awaited us. We drank it while we ordered. Caesar salads for starters, mammoth grilled veal chops, blood rare, and nothing but sin on the side—double orders of onion rings, hashed browns and creamed spinach. Merilee tore into her food like a starved, feral animal, pausing only occasionally to wash it down with the not

terrible Cotes du Rhone I'd found on the wine list. Lulu
went for the pan-fried trout, her tail thumping while she
ate. It was the happiest I'd seen her in months. Six months
and eleven days, to be exact.

Rob Reiner and Bill Goldman were there polishing off
steaks at Goldman's usual table. Merilee did that thriller
with them a few years back, the one she was nominated
for, and the three of them have remained friends. Highly
unusual in that business. They sent us over another bottle
of the wine. We raised our glasses to them and sent them
back two slabs of chocolate cake, though in Rob's case the
fresh melon in season might have been a kinder selection.

After Merilee had cleaned her plate she dabbed genteelly
at her mouth with her napkin and sat back, green eyes
gleaming. "It feels so good to be out and about again,
darling," she purred. "Doesn't it?"

"It does."

She gazed across the table at me. "I just have one word
for you, mister."

"What is it?" I asked, gazing back at her.

"Cheesecake."

"And a lovely word it is, Merilee. Only—"

She stiffened. "Only what?"

"We're not having dessert here. The evening is young
and so are we. Or at least we were at some vague point in
the not too distant past."

She reached across the table and took my hand, her grip
steely. She'd ingested a lot of protein. "Where to, darling?"

Where to was the Hotel Carlyle. Not the Cafe, where
Bobby Short held court. To the penthouse, where one of
the apartments was undergoing renovation that season. I
had rented its rooftop terrace for the evening, complete
with its view of most of the East Side. A uniformed waiter
met us at the elevator with more chilled Dom Perignon.

And out on the terrace, in the cool of a sparkling autumn night, the Brad Kerr Trio was playing *Don't Get Around Much Anymore*. Brad was a young piano player from East St. Louis, half black, half Asian and all blind. No one who liked Harry Connick, Jr., had the slightest idea who he was. And that was how he liked it. He was a true keeper of the flame. Two ancient Ellington sidemen backed him on bass and drums. They knew he was the real thing.

Merilee let out a small gasp of glee when they segued into *Georgia on My Mind*. Because this was our song, the one we danced to that first night in the Polish seamen's club on First Avenue and Ninth Street, when we drank up peppery vodka and each other. When we knew. Just as we still knew.

She slipped into my arms. We danced.

"Darling," she said huskily, "you very seldom disappoint me."

"Name one time I have."

"That opening night party for the Albee play, when I caught you and those other men laughing heartily at Sharon Stone's jokes."

"Sharon happens to be a very amusing woman."

"I see. And what else does she happen to be?"

"Ssh."

We danced, the city at our feet, the waiter refilling our glasses. Lulu curled up on a cushioned wicker settee and watched us, drowsing contentedly under her top hat. We danced.

"About your brother Philip . . ." I said, after a while.

"Did you say Philip?" She was somewhat startled. I seldom mentioned him. *She* seldom mentioned him. Merilee's brother was a lazy, useless sort of person. Had something to do with operating ski lodges somewhere out in Colorado or Utah. "What about him?"

"Did you two ever play doctor when you were growing up?"

"Naturally." She drew herself up a bit. "It's normal and healthy for children to be curious about each other's bodies."

"How old were you when you stopped playing?"

"Merciful heavens, Hoagy, I don't remember. I was five or six, I suppose. He was perhaps eight. Why on earth are you—?"

"And is that normal as well?"

"Darling, I really wouldn't know. And if this is your idea of romantic patter I'm sorry to inform you that you've slipped rather dramatically."

"Clethra and Arvin continued playing it well on into their teens. They slept in the same bed. They even gave each other pleasure."

"Reeeeally?!" She coughed, then lowered her voice discreetly. "Honestly, that's quite . . . Well, we're approaching the 'I' word, are we not?"

"He loves her, Merilee. Truly and completely loves her."

"Does she feel the same way?"

"She's moved on."

Merilee shook her head. "Poor little Arvin."

"He's fourteen."

"Meaning what?"

"Meaning he's not so little."

"You don't think that boy could have killed his own father, do you?"

"People kill their own fathers all the time," I replied, with perhaps just a bit too much personal conviction.

She raised an eyebrow at me. "But how could he have gotten to the farm from Debbie's Diner? He can't drive."

"Clethra can."

"You're suggesting the two of them together killed Thor?"

"You have to consider all the possibilities. Speaking of my father . . ."

"We weren't, actually," she pointed out tactfully. "But if you'd care to . . ."

"I believe I've figured out why his . . . condition has been so hard for me to deal with."

"Yes, dear?" she said encouragingly.

"For a man," I began, "your father is your very first hero. He's your idol, your Errol Flynn. And you never outgrow worshiping him—even though you want to, even though you think you have. So when it's his time to go, you want him to go out like a hero. Shoulders back, head high, laughing in the face of death. You don't want him to be weak and frightened. You don't want him to be needy. Because that shatters him in your eyes. And because . . . it makes you wonder if the same goddamned thing is going to happen to you when it's your turn to go."

Merilee's brow creased, which is what it does when she's trying not to cry. "Darling, what is it you want from that man?"

"I don't want anything from him."

"Horseradish. You want him to admit he was wrong about you."

"I don't want anything from him," I insisted. "It would be nice if he read *one* of my novels before he died, but I've pretty much given up hope of that."

"He's not going to admit he was wrong, Hoagy. Just as he's not going to admit he needs your help now. Don't you know why?"

"Of course I do. Because he's a mean, stubborn son of a bitch."

Angrily, she shook her head at me. "Because he doesn't want to admit to you that he's *not* your Errol Flynn. That he *is* scared and confused and can't handle things anymore. He can't admit it, Hoagy. He won't admit it. So it's up to you to take control. You're in charge now."

"You seem to be confusing me with Speaker Newt."

"You have to, darling. Whether you like it or not. Whether you like *him* or not. You're the grown-up now. He's the child. That's the way it happens. It's all a part of nature."

"Nature sucks."

"You've been hanging around with Clethra too much," she observed, her eyes twinkling at me.

"I'm not happy about this, Merilee."

"What's to be happy about? We're getting old."

"I'm starting to figure that out, too."

"What are you going to do about it?"

"I was thinking about having my teeth bleached."

"What about your father?"

"You're absolutely right. His teeth could use a bleaching, too."

"Hoagy . . ."

"And he and I need to have a talk."

She took my face in her hands. "I'm terribly proud of you, mister."

I kissed her. "I'd go right down the drain without you, Merilee."

She nodded. "It's true, you would."

"You weren't supposed to agree with me."

"I wasn't supposed to get my mother's thighs either." She stifled a weary yawn. "Thank you for tonight, darling. I needed it so."

She put her head on my shoulder and we danced, swaying gently to *Stardust* there on the roof of the Carlyle in the New York City night, hardly moving at all. In fact, by the time the band took a short break, Merilee wasn't moving, period. She'd fallen fast asleep right there in my arms.

The poor woman was so exhausted she'd actually fallen asleep standing up.

Which made it official. Merilee Nash, international star of stage and screen and the one great love of my life, *had* become a farm animal.

"I'm so embarrassed."

"Don't be."

"But it was our big night out and I fell asleep. You must hate me."

"Forget about it, Merilee. I've done it myself."

"And I've hated you for it."

It was four in the morning and she was seated at the kitchen table with Tracy, who had just finished an early breakfast and was now giving grave consideration to a burp. Merilee was raiding Pam's scones and looking ultra-sheepish.

I reached for a scone myself and sat, munching on it. Pam's scones were superior. The currants made all the difference. "Besides, it was quite late."

"Hoagy, it was a quarter to eleven."

"Was it? Well, in the country that's late."

"I'm so embarrassed."

"You shouldn't be, Merilee. You've never looked or sounded lovelier."

She stared at me in horror. "I *snored?*"

"Not to worry. I don't believe the musicians noticed. It was so soft and gentle. More like a purr, really. And my shoulder muffled quite a bit of it. Of course, they did notice when I carried you to the elevator . . ."

"Why, what did I—?"

"Your mouth, after all, was agape."

"My mouth was what?"

"And then there was the matter of that drool on your chin. But that was, you know, cute."

"Cute, Hoagy? *Cute?*" She sighed grandly, tragically. "Oh, God, what's happening to us? Are we turning into a boring, old married couple?"

"We can't possibly be. We're not married, remember?"

"That's right, we're not. Whew, that's a relief."

"I'll say."

Tracy was nodding off now—like mother, like daughter. Merilee carried her into the nursery and put her down. I poured myself a glass of milk and washed down another scone with it.

Merilee returned, running her fingers through my hair. "I'm sorry, darling. I was just so sleepy."

I took her in my arms and kissed her. "Are you sleepy now?"

She gave me her up-from-under look. "As it happens, I'm not."

"Good, neither am I." I smiled at her. "Let's go to bed."

Nine

TYLER KAMPMANN'S death made page one of all three New York City newspapers next morning. Not because they tied it in to Thor's murder. They still didn't have it that Tyler used to date the girl who ran off with Thor Gibbs. No, it was front-page news simply because it's still front-page news when a student at a prestigious Ivy League university is found murdered in his dorm room. I can't speak for the future.

Actually, I can. But I'd rather not.

Not that it was going to take the press long to connect Tyler. The folks at *Hard Copy* had to know he was Clethra's ex-boyfriend—they'd bought the videotape from him. They'd break it on that evening's broadcast, no question. The so-called legitimate press would then pick it up from them. People keep wondering how come the cash press keeps outscooping the competition. It's simple—they get what they pay for. Good, dishonest American value. Nothing more or less.

Robbery, according to Detective Lieutenant Romaine Very of the NYPD, had been ruled out. He had told them about the cash found on Tyler's body. He had not mentioned the hefty bank deposit slip or the tall, dashing, bogus uncle who'd found the body. They had it that Tyler's neighbor, Ian Gardner, found him. Very didn't believe in being straight with the press. Very hated the press. Afer numerous celebrity blowouts of my own, I couldn't blame him. That's not to say I hate the press. I just wish they'd go after real news with the same lunatic zeal they go after Julia Roberts.

We slept late that morning. Or at least we stayed in bed together an awfully long time. I'll let you use your imagination here. I'm sure it will be far more feverish and lurid than the reality of what goes on between two middle-aged white people who have been having sex together off and on since the days when Mickey Rourke was considered a promising young acting talent.

Merilee luxuriated there under the covers while I showered and dressed. She was still there when I left, looking slightly debauched and more than slightly pleased with herself.

I got back out to the country about one, top up, Lulu napping in the seat next to me. It was a brisk, slate-gray day with a gusty wind that buffeted the Jag like a tall-masted schooner at sea and made little maelstroms of the downed leaves, its cold bite hinting at November and the long, cold winter that waited on the other side of it. Lulu stirred when we got off the highway and started our way up narrow Route 156 for home. The cows were grazing alongside the road at Tiffany Farms near Reynolds' general store. She barked at them gleefully. That's another one of her biggest thrills in life—barking at cows.

The press vans still lined Joshua Town Road. One of our besieged neighbors went hurtling past them, looking like he was on his way out to buy sandbags and razor wire. Me he glowered at—I had caused an invasion of noisy outsiders. You don't do that in Lyme. It's the worst offense there is, worse than selling out to a developer. The trooper at the foot of our drive let me in.

The ducks were back, the natural spring slowly filling their pond back up again. And Dwayne was back, too, hard at work on the foundation of the carriage barn. Had himself a helper now. Clethra, a red bandanna tied over her head, was sighting through his transit and calling out elevations to him as he moved his tape measure from spot to spot. Death metal thumped on the stereo of his pickup. Both of them waved when I pulled up.

Dwayne went and turned down the music. "Borrowed your house guest, Mr. H. Hope ya don't mind."

"Not as long as you're paying her out of your own pocket."

"I got, like, bored watching television," Clethra explained.

"I can't tell you how glad I am to hear that."

"Um, my mom called a little while ago," she mentioned, glancing uneasily over in Dwayne's direction.

He got busy in the barn, discreetly out of earshot.

She lit a cigarette and drew on it, poking at the gravel with her steel-toed boot. "They're coming back out to Barry's place sometime later today. Like, to talk to the police and take care of Thor's body and stuff."

"I can run over there with you. If you want to see her, I mean."

"I don't," she declared, her chin stuck out defiantly.

"What about Arvin?"

"What about him?"

"Don't you want to see him?"

"Not really. I need to take care of *me* right now. I mean, there's just been too much bad shit going down, y'know?"

"Yes, I do."

She tilted her head at me quizzically. "And you're cool with that?"

"Why wouldn't I be?"

"You don't think I'm being, like, selfish?"

"I think you're trying to survive."

"Will I?" she asked me pleadingly.

"I hope so."

"Do you really?"

"I hope we all do, Clethra. I'm extremely retro that way."

I headed for the house, leaving her staring after me. I get a lot of that from my celebrities. I get a lot of that from everybody.

There were three more faxes from her editor. I threw them in the trash unread, put down food and water for Lulu and made myself a sandwich out of homemade peanut butter and Merilee's wild blackberry jam. I put on a pot of coffee. I was pouring it when Chick Munger eased his unmarked cruiser up the drive and got out. I doubted the lieutenant's timing was a coincidence. He must have told the trooper on the driveway to contact him when I showed.

He came into the house without knocking and sat down at the kitchen table across from me, smelling of Vitalis, the tremor in his left eye so bad it looked as if it were transmitting Morse code . . . *Dot-dot* . . . *Dash* . . . *Dot* . . . He wore that same shiny three-piece suit and a tie that looked way too much like a Spanish omelet. He had cut himself shaving that morning—there was a spot of dried blood on his chin. The way his hands were shaking, he was lucky he hadn't cut his throat. I offered him coffee. He took it black, slurping it loudly from his cup. I ate. He watched me. Lulu watched him watch me, her lip curled. She didn't like him. She has very good instincts that way.

"How's your investigation going, Lieutenant?"

"It's not," Munger grunted.

"What brings you out?"

"Came by to get shoe prints from you," he answered in his nasal New Britain accent. "So's we can get a reading vis-à-vis that mud."

"Slawski told me he wasn't very optimistic about it."

"Slawski told you a lot," he said sourly.

"What else is on your mind, Lieutenant? Surely you didn't come all the way out here personally just for an errand like that."

Munger eyed me shrewdly, or what I'm sure he thought was shrewdly. "Maybe the reason we're not getting nowhere, Hoag, is we're pointed in the wrong direction."

I chewed on my sandwich, not liking where this was going.

"Kinda funny," he went on, "how you was around when Gibbs got knocked off, and then, boomp, you was there in New York, too, when this other kid gets it."

"Boomp?"

"Kinda funny," he repeated.

"I was on my way in to the city when Tyler Kampmann was strangled," I pointed out. "And I was visiting my parents in Essex when Thor was attacked."

"Details." He waved me off with a trembly hand. "Smart cookie like you can figure your way around 'em."

Lulu started coughing violently.

Munger scowled. "What's her problem?"

"It's just been a long time since anyone's called me a smart cookie."

"You better be, pal," he warned, sneering at me, "on account of you're our prime suspect from now on, far as I'm concerned. And I don't care what Slawski thinks."

"Yes, you've made that rather clear."

"And I *sure* as hell don't care what that pomegranate from New York City, that Romaine whatever—"

"It's Very."

"It's very *what?*"

"That's his name."

"Well, I don't care what he says neither."

"Why, what does he say?"

"That you're okay."

"Very said that? I'm touched."

Munger slurped some more of his coffee, sucking down a whole lot of air with it, rather like an old toothless geezer sitting on a park bench with a runny nose and nowhere to go. "I don't like the whole idea of you being in contact with Slawski, y'hear? I want ya to stop calling him. This is *my* investigation, not his. I'm the primary detective vis-à-vis this case."

I finished my sandwich and poured myself more coffee. "Okay, let's say I did kill Thor Gibbs."

"Let's say you did," he agreed.

"Why did I do it? What's my motive?"

Munger held his hands out to me, palms up. "You tell me."

"No, no. Please continue, Lieutenant. You're doing so much better than I ever could."

"Okay." Munger stuck out his lower lip, flicking at it with his thumb as if he were about to count out a wad of bill. "The oldest one working—the girl."

"What about her?"

"Helluva pair of tits on her, huh? Guy might do just about anything for a chance to bury his teeth into 'em. Bet she's got some kind of little lemon squeezer on her, too. Sweet and juicy and—"

"Are you trying to get a rise out of me or a rise out of yourself?"

"Don't dick me, Hoag," he snarled, turning mean. "Trooper on duty the other night saw Clethra Feingold sneak in here in the wee hours wearing almost nothing. Saw a light go on upstairs in the master bedroom. Saw it go out. And he didn't see her come out again until morning."

"So?"

He leered at me. "So your wife—"

"Ex-wife."

"Your *ex*-wife was in New York. Just you and the girl here all alone in this great big house. Old man Gibbs out of the way. Nice and tidy, y'ask me."

"Are you insinuating there's something going on between the two of us?"

"I ain't insinuating it, Hoag. I'm *saying* it—you're slipping it to her. The man showed up here with her. You wanted her. So you killed him for her."

I tugged at my ear. "I see. And why did I kill Tyler Kampmann?"

"I'm still working on that," Munger said threateningly.

"You keep right on working, Lieutenant," I said. "And while you're at it I suggest you go home and wash your mind out with strong soap. I'd try Lava. I believe they still make it."

"You're the one needs to come clean, Hoag. You'll feel a lot better, y'know."

"I feel fine," I assured him, "aside from the pesky little fact that I've just lost a dear friend due to a close encounter with a sledgehammer. I am a family friend. I am Clethra's collaborator. Period. There's only one woman in my life, and her name is Merilee Nash."

"No chance," he scoffed. "You showbiz types hop in and out of bed with babes by the dozen. Blondes—"

"I'm a writer, Lieutenant, not the lead singer of a rock 'n' roll band."

234 / David Handler

"—brunettes, redheads—you bang 'em all. Younger the better."

"I really wish I had this on tape."

He narrowed his eyes at me. "We can make this official, that's what you want."

"What I want, Lieutenant, is for you to leave. Unless you have some specific questions regarding this murder investigation, I'm going to ask you politely to get the hell out of here. And if you don't I shall cease being polite and sic my dog on you."

He snorted at her derisively. "What's she gonna do, lick me to death?"

"It's been known to happen, vis-à-vis her breath."

Munger didn't budge for a moment. Just sat there, his left eye twitching at me. Until, abruptly, he shoved his chair back and stood. "I ain't kidding around, Hoag!" he warned me, waving his finger under my nose.

"Nor am I, Lieutenant," I said, resisting the urge to bite it off. "Now get out."

We stared at each other in charged silence. My fists, I discovered, were clenched. The man made me angrier than anyone I'd met in a long time. I felt like hitting him. He wanted me to hit him. Sure he did. Then he could haul me in and show everybody he was doing something—aside from peeing down his own leg.

But I didn't hit Chick Munger.

He moseyed out the door, taking his sweet time, then got back in his car and drove away. He never did ask me for any of my shoes.

I changed into the heavy oiled wool sweater from the Aran Islands and my leather jacket. Outside, the kids were sitting on Dwayne's tailgate eyeballing me with newfound respect.

"Whoa, Mr. H," Dwayne marveled. "Did you piss that

fucker off or what? Looked like he was ready to have a heart attack."

"I sincerely wish he had."

"Cool," exclaimed Clethra. "Like, what'd you do?"

"Would you two mind keeping an eye on Lulu for a while?" I asked, marching grimly and determinedly toward Thor's Norton Commando. "I have to run a certain personal errand of an unpleasant nature."

"No problem, Mr. H."

I climbed aboard and kick-started it. Or tried to. It didn't catch until the third try, the exhaust billowing thickly. It had been sitting for a few days, and the nights were cold.

Dwayne came shambling over to check it out, his rough, veiny hands stuffed into the back pockets of his jeans. "Totally awesome machine."

"That it is." I fished my aviator shades out of my jacket pocket and put them on. I revved the engine. "I suppose Ruth will be selling it, unless she wants to keep it for Arvin, which I rather doubt." I revved it some more. "If you want to make an offer I'll let her know."

"No way," he said, with that lopsided grin of his. "Couldn't handle somethin' this fine on my paycheck, man."

Clethra hopped from the tailgate of the truck and started toward the house, dusting off her bottom as she went along. We watched her. Or at least Dwayne did. I was watching him watching her. There was naked desire on that scarred young face of his. There was hunger.

"Thanks, by the way."

He frowned at me. "For what?"

"Keeping her busy. She's got a lot on her mind. Do her good to be out and about, instead of sitting inside brooding."

Dwayne ducked his head bashfully. "We been talking a

lot about her plans. Y'know, like whether or not she should be moving back in with her ol' lady or going back to school or what."

"Any idea what her plans are?"

He shook his head, his eyes still on the ground.

"What do you think she should do?"

"What do *I* think?" Dwayne tugged at his goatee. I suppose he was seldom asked his opinion by anyone about much of anything. "School's probably the best place for her. I don't think she's ready to handle real life."

"If this is real life I don't think anybody is."

"She could take classes just about anywhere though, right?" he ventured hopefully. "She wouldn't have to go back to New York, would she?"

"She's in a rather delicate frame of mind right now, Dwayne," I cautioned.

His eyes met mine. A rare thing. There was hurt in them. "Jeez, Mr. H, you don't really think I'd try to get with a girl whose old man just got killed, do you? I mean, for sure, I think she's pretty outrageous. But I'm not that kind of snake."

"I know you're not."

He thought it over for a moment, and decided not to be offended. "She sure has a lot of respect for you, Mr. H."

"Only because she doesn't know me very well."

He grinned at me and started back toward the barn to his work. I eased the Norton down the drive and bulldozed my way through the swarming press corps, then zoomed it the hell out of there. The narrow, twisting country roads were made for a motorcycle. I let it out, enjoying the speed and the cold wind in my hair. I took the bridge at East Haddam and then tore down Route 9 to Essex. Made a huge racket when I pulled into the Exit Meadows parking lot, greatly alarming the three Q-Tips who were using the putting green. Maybe that was why I took the bike in the first place. Maybe there was no maybe to it.

It was too chilly for them to be out on the terrace that day. They were in the living room. I stood out there a moment looking at the pair of them through the sliding glass door. He was dozing in his wheelchair, the *Times* crossword puzzle folded in his lap. She was doing needlepoint. They could have been a Diane Arbus photograph: *Two Connecticut Yankees Waiting to Die.*

Eventually, she saw me there and let me in, gasping with delight. "Look who it is, Monty! My, my, what a lovely surprise."

He sat there scowling at me, frail and shrunken. "What . . . happened t-to your hair?"

"Wind got to it," I said, brushing it back with my fingers.

"Look thoroughly dis-disreputable," he muttered, stumbling impatiently over the words. "Like a hippie or y-yippie or . . . Gonna g-get us thrown out of here. Any idea how long the . . . w-waiting list is here?"

"Coffee, darling?" said Mother. "Shall I make some?"

"That would be nice." I sat.

She flashed me a grateful smile and went into their little kitchen to fix it. I knew she wouldn't come out for at least twenty minutes, and she knew I knew.

He and I sat there in silence, staring at the TV.

"Shall I turn it on?" I asked.

No answer. Only another long silence.

Until he said, "What are you . . . w-working on these days, Stewart?"

"Working on?" This one caught me short. He hadn't asked me about my work since, well, never. I said it again. "Working on?"

"Working . . . on." He stared at me with that drooping, lifeless eye of his, waiting for a response. He seemed much more alert than last time. He'd even called me Stewart.

I told him. Told him about how I was trying to write another novel but it wasn't going very well—so I was helping a friend's stepdaughter tell her story, although my friend had died, as had the girl's ex-boyfriend. I told him about Thor and Clethra and Ruth, about Arvin, Barry and Marco, Tyler. I told him about everything that had happened. I don't know why I did. Maybe because it was easier than talking about something else. Like us, for instance. Maybe because he asked me.

He listened intently, nodding and moistening his chalky lips from time to time. For a while, he shut his eyes. I thought he'd drifted off, but he hadn't. He was just concentrating. "Police people . . . c-can't get to the . . . bottom of it, you say?"

"Two police departments are stymied so far."

"Want . . . an old m-man's advice?"

"Any particular old man?"

"Mothers," he declared firmly. "They always p-protect their young."

"You think it's Ruth?"

"Strongest b-bond there is. Stronger than . . . anything. But y-you don't need me to tell y-you that," he said, his voice quavering weakly. "Already know it."

"Do I?"

"Wrote . . . it."

Briefly, I stopped breathing. "Did I?"

"That scene in your f-first novel," he recalled, his lips pulling back from his teeth in a horsy grimace. "When the . . . the s-son tells the f-father he wants out of the business. The father w-wants to lash out at him, hurt him l-like . . . he's just b-been hurt himself. A-And the mother, she . . . What was it she s-says? 'We are not a business, Harrison . . . We are a f-family. If you hurt that boy . . .

you hurt me. If y-you hurt me, you hurt us. And if you hurt us, you only h-hurt yourself.' " He nodded. "D-Damned fine piece of . . . writing, Stewart. Not a day g-goes by I don't think about it. About how . . . the father d-didn't heed her advice. That . . . that was his big mistake."

I swallowed hard, gaping at him. So he *had* read it. He'd even memorized the damned thing. But he'd never told me. All these years he'd never told me. Why the hell hadn't he told me? I glanced up at Mother, who was standing in the kitchen doorway, smiling at me encouragingly, her eyes filled with tears. I glanced back at him. He'd gone back to staring at the silent TV. He was done. It wasn't an apology. But it was probably the closest he would ever get to one. I sat there, letting it sink in. And then I did something I'm not very proud of.

I bolted. Grabbed my jacket and ran. Didn't so much as say goodbye. Just sprinted to the Norton and jumped on. I didn't start it up. I sat there. I just sat there.

Until she caught up with me. A cardigan sweater was thrown over her shoulders. "That was not easy for him, Stewart. It may have been the single hardest thing he's ever had to do in his life."

"I know that, Mother."

"The rest is up to you."

"I know that, too."

"You're not willing, are you?"

"Willing?"

"To forgive him."

"I'm not a forgiving person. A trait I happen to come by genetically."

"I am not impressed by your attitude, Stewart," she said sternly.

"I haven't heard that one in a while."

"Possibly that's part of your problem."

"Who says I have a problem?"

She wrinkled her nose at the Norton in disapproval, as if it smelled bad. She'd been doing that for as long as I could remember. Her dead cat look, I called it. "Where on earth did you get this contraption?"

"A friend loaned it to me. Sort of."

"Where's your helmet?"

"Haven't got one."

"Stewart, Stewart, Stewart . . ." She shook her head at me. "You have responsibilities now. You're a father."

"You'll recall that—"

"Stop, I know exactly what you're going to say next."

"How can you when I don't?"

"Because I'm your mother. I know you better than you know yourself."

"You poor woman. That should qualify you for federal disaster relief. What was I going to say?"

"That Tracy wasn't entirely your idea."

"Actually, Tracy wasn't my idea at all."

"Well, that's just tough," she snapped. "Life is a matter of embracing the future, not rejecting it. Do you want her to end up forty years from now feeling toward you the same way you feel toward your father?"

"God, no." I peered at her curiously. "Why would she?"

"Ask yourself that sometime."

"Mother, do you . . . ?"

"Do I what?"

"Do you remember when he used to come downstairs in the middle of the night for a glass of milk?"

She furrowed her brow thoughtfully, one index finger raised under her chin. The thing with the finger she'd done for as long as I could remember, too, though I had no name for it. "Monty? Are you sure?"

"Oh, yeah. I'm sure."

"No, I don't remember it, Stewart. But I was always a

very sound sleeper. Not so much anymore. Too many aches and pains."

I sat there twirling Thor's bracelet a moment. "I'll come back when I can, Mother," I told her quietly. "Will that be okay?"

"I suppose it will have to be," she replied stiffly.

She bent down and kissed my cheek. Then she headed back inside, limping a little. She seemed to be favoring her left hip. I hadn't noticed that before. I wondered how long she'd been doing it.

"It's pretty down here."

"It is."

"Peaceful."

"It certainly used to be."

We were seated on two of the weathered teak Adirondack chairs that were grouped down by the salt marsh. I was drinking a Cream Stout, Clethra a vodka and Diet Coke. The ospreys were hunting in the shallows. And the sun, which had only just broken through the clouds, was setting over Whalebone Cove, bathing the water and the golden autumn leaves and us in an orange-amber glow. Lulu lay at my feet in the grass. Sadie, the barn cat, was crouched nearby stalking a mole. It was calm and quiet down there, so quiet you couldn't hear the press vans out on the road. Almost.

"He had cancer, Clethra," I said, wondering when the last time was she got some good news. "He would have been dead in six months."

She didn't react at all. Just stubbed out her cigarette on the ribbed sole of one of her Doc Maartens, staring out at the water. "I guess that means his sailing expedition was bullshit."

"That's certainly one word for it." I sipped my stout. "You didn't know?"

"He never talked personal with me," she said with glum resignation.

"What did he talk about?"

"His philosophies of life, mostly," she replied, hugging her knees with her arms. "Like about how life is a grand adventure, shit like that. He was real inspirational."

"You didn't know him at all, did you?" I said, not unkindly.

"I grew up in the same house with him."

"Like I said, you didn't know him at all."

"He just never really talked much about himself. He was more into trying to get me to think about things and question . . ." She stopped, gazing at me imploringly. "Geez, y'think that's why he never fucked me? On account of he was sick?"

"Possibly. What about Arvin?"

"What about him?" she demanded.

"Did Thor ever talk to him about things?"

"No way. As far as he was concerned, anything Arvy needed to know he could find in *The Thinking Man's Diet*. Like, that's totally why he wrote it. So he wouldn't have to do the face time thing with him. Which totally bites, don't you think? People living in the same house and not communicating, I mean."

"Have you been talking to my mother?"

"Have I *what?*"

"Never mind."

"It's like he gave us gifts or something, okay? Like he gave Arvy that book. Like he gave me . . . I don't know what he gave me. Nothing, I guess."

"I wouldn't be so sure. He gave you notoriety. Which in today's world translates into a career. If you want it."

"I don't know what I want."

"Don't let that worry you. No one does."

She sipped her drink, studying me over her glass. "How come you got so mad at that cop Munger this afternoon?"

"How come you ask so many questions?"

"Because *you* do." She was a quick learner. I had to give her that. "How come?"

"He accused me of killing Thor so I could have you for myself. He thinks we're doing the wild thing, you and me."

"Oh." She pondered this. "That would never actually happen, would it?"

"No, it wouldn't. Actually or otherwise."

"No way," she agreed, nodding. "I like you way too much to do that to you."

"Meaning what?"

"Meaning I'm bad news when it comes to guys. Like, I totally fuck 'em up—Arvy's a mess, Thor's dead, Tyler's dead . . ." She sighed mournfully. "Is there something really, really wrong with me, Hoagy?"

I drank the last of my stout. "No, Clethra, there's nothing wrong with you. But there's something terribly wrong with someone else."

We sat there in silence. The orange glow in the sky changed to purple.

"Can I ask you something else, Hoagy?" she wondered, chewing fretfully on her plump lower lip.

"You can ask me anything."

But before she could we heard car doors slam up at the house. Footsteps crunched on the gravel. I could see Slawski up there knocking on the kitchen door. Slawski and somebody else. I waved to them. They spotted us and came on down across the pasture toward us.

The someone else was Very. He wore a tweed jacket and trail pants, and moved most gingerly across the mown stubble, as if he were trying to cross the slippery deck of a ship in roiling seas. The man was not used to walking on anything that wasn't pavement.

"Welcome to God's country, Lieutenant," I called to him.

"Check, dude, I didn't know you lived in one of *these* places," he exclaimed, somewhat wide-eyed.

"*These* places, Lieutenant?"

"Y'know, where nobody ever raises their voices and everybody is blond and thin and named Wippy or Weezy and they all play tennis and sail and go to the dump Saturday morning in their twelve-year-old station wagons."

"We don't call it the dump," I informed him politely. "We call it the landfill."

"I love this!" Very gushed, gazing around at the trees. "But school me, dude. Are there bats?"

"There are." At my feet, Lulu let out a moan of consternation. "But we don't let them worry us. Say hello to Clethra Feingold, Lieutenant."

"Evening, Clethra. I dig your ring," he said, meaning the one in her nose.

She just stared. At the soft dark eyes. At the wavy black hair. At the shoulders bulging in the tweed jacket. Very had magical powers over certain types of women. Clethra's type, evidently.

"This must be quite some ordeal for you," he suggested kindly, smiling at her.

"I'm okay," she said, with a careless toss of her head.

"Get your gents a beer?" I offered.

Slawski said no. He was on duty—uniform, silly hat, the works. Very said he wouldn't mind one. I started to get up.

Clethra stopped me. "I'll get it." And off she scampered to the house, seemingly eager to let Very check out her ripe little butt. She was certainly wiggling it hard enough.

But he wasn't having any. Not so much as a peek. He sat

in one of the chairs. Slawski stood, his arms crossed, posture perfect.

"Where's Klaus?" I asked him.

"In my ride."

"He's welcome to join us."

"He's trained to remain there."

"He doesn't have much fun, does he?"

Slawski squared his jaw at me. "He's a professional."

"Speaking of which, I saw your close personal friend Chick Munger this afternoon."

The resident trooper took off his hat and examined the brim, turning it in his huge hands. He said nothing.

"Chick seems to think I'm his prime suspect," I went on. "I'm afraid it got rather ugly between us."

"I'm not excusing the man," Very said tactfully, "but he's under a lot of pressure to deliver. I been there, believe me."

"He called you a pomegranate, Lieutenant."

"He called me a *what?*"

"And he made fun of your name. He said Romaine Very was a funny name."

"Why, that turd!" Very bristled, his left knee starting to quake. "That second-rate fucking turd! I'll eat his fucking lunch! I'll—"

"Careful, Lieutenant. Remember your brain waves."

Very stopped short. He forced a sickly sweet smile onto his face. Right away he started the deep breathing thing, in and out, in and out.

"Toxicology findings on Thorvin Gibbs came in," Slawski informed me. "They found a .23 percent blood alcohol level in Gibbs' body at the time of death. More than twice the legal limit. Man was prime-time drunk."

"Too drunk to be conscious?" I asked.

"Gotta figure he'd be dazed at the very least," said Very.

"Did he often drink at ten in the morning?" Slawski asked me.

"He drank when he felt like it. Thor Gibbs did everything when he felt like it."

Clethra returned now with Very's Cream Stout. She'd brought one for me as well. We both thanked her. She sat, sneaking shy looks at Very.

"Was Thor drinking heavily the morning he was murdered?" I asked her.

"Um . . . no. At least, I don't think so. He was planning to take a swim." She looked blankly from me to Very to Slawski. "How come?"

Her question sat there in the air a moment. No one wanted to touch it.

I was about to when Slawski said, "The lieutenant and myself are en route to the Barry Feingold residence in Essex. Munger be doing some questioning there this evening at 7 P.M."

"We thought you might want to tag along, dude," said Very, tasting his stout.

"That's most considerate of you."

Very and Slawski exchanged a look.

"Straight up, dude," Very explained reluctantly, "we bring you along we got a legit reason to be there—you being the man's prime suspect and all. Otherwise . . ."

"Otherwise we don't," Slawski said, between clenched teeth.

"Oh, so that's how it is."

"Whoa!" Clethra was gawking at me, incredulous. *"You're* the prime suspect?"

"What is this, Trooper, a turf thing?" I asked Slawski.

"More of a protocol thing," he answered. "It seems I invited Lieutenant Very out when it should have been Lieutenant Munger's privilege to do so. Least that's how he sees it. Consequently, Very here ain't exactly been invited. And I certainly haven't been."

"No way," said Clethra. "I'm, like, that's so *petty*."

"I heard that," Slawski concurred.

"Can he do it, Lieutenant?" I asked Very.

"Long as it's his investigation he can."

"Well, that settles it then—I'm going with you." I took a drink of my stout. "Care to join us, Clethra?"

She hesitated. "Um . . . no."

I studied her, sensing the first hint of daylight. "You sure?"

"Like, I would *maybe* come, okay?" she admitted, squirming in her chair. "Only, Dwayne's bringing a pizza over at eight. Like, we're gonna hang out. I mean, if it's okay."

"It's okay."

"Who's Dwayne?" Very wanted to know.

"The hired man I told you about," Slawski said.

"We're just friends," Clethra added quickly, for Very's benefit. "I can take care of Lulu if you want," she told me.

"Thanks, only Lulu's coming with us. Her kind of deal." I turned to Slawski. "Unless Klaus will have an ego problem."

"Why should he?" Slawski demanded crossly.

"His pride ought to be severely wounded by about now, don't you think? Frankly, he's done *bupkes* so far. Lulu's carrying him."

Slawski shook his head at Very. "Don't he ever cut this shit out?"

"Not in my experience," Very replied brightly.

"When the time comes, Piffle Man, you'll see what Officer Klaus can do," Slawski warned me, glowering down at Lulu. "And so will she."

"If you say so, Trooper." I got to my feet. "C'mon, amigos. Let's ride."

. . . . .

"That girl's putting up a mighty brave front," commented Very as we tore down Joshua Town Road in Slawski's cruiser. Mr. Serenity was riding in back with Officer Klaus. Lulu was up front between Slawski and me. Klaus she ignored. Or pretended to.

"How so, Lieutenant?" I asked him.

"Check it out, dude," he explained. "Her whole world's collapsed around her, and there she is trying to act like everything's cool. Which it's not. Damned shame, really. Seems like an okay kid. Major set of zoomers, too."

"Why, Lieutenant, if I didn't know you better I'd swear you were hot for her."

"I'm hot for whoever killed Tyler Kampmann and Thorvin Gibbs." He poked me in the shoulder. "Think it coulda been her, dude?"

"Lieutenant, I don't know what to think anymore. You're welcome to stay with us tonight, by the way. We have plenty of room."

"Thanks, dude, only—"

"He's crashing with us," Slawski informed me.

"Us?"

"Klaus and myself."

I tugged at my ear. "Tell me, Trooper, does Klaus sleep with you or does he have his own room?"

Slawski didn't respond.

"Don't tell me he stays in the cruiser all night."

Slawski still didn't respond. Just nodded to himself, pleased. "Uh-huh. You done got that right, Lieutenant."

"Told ya," Very said.

I frowned, perplexed. "Got what right?"

"It *do* be just like street noise," Slawski agreed. "After a while, you don't even hear it no more."

It was completely dark by the time we turned off onto the long, narrow dirt road through the forest to Barry's house. It was not easy going. There were no streetlights, no house lights. The road was bumpy and twisting. Slawski kept the pedal to the floor, his brights on, his huge hands gripping the wheel tightly. We were maybe a quarter mile from the house when we came hard around a curve and there she was—staggering blindly down the middle of the road, flailing her arms, her face and her chest bloodied.

We nearly ran smack into her.

Slawski had to go skidding into the ditch or we would have. A thick growth of forsythia stopped us inches short of the trees. By the time we scrambled out of the car she was facedown in the road, blood pouring out of the wounds to her head and neck and shoulders. They were sharp wounds, deep wounds. And there were so damned many of them. Slawski snapped a command at Klaus, who went crashing off into the brush. Then the trooper radioed for an ambulance, wasting no time. But it was no use.

Baby Ruth Feingold was already dead.

Ten

WE WERE still standing over Ruth in the middle of the road when Klaus came loping back, panting heavily. He was not in what I'd call tip-top shape. But he was well trained. Sat right there at Slawski's heel, gasping for air, while he awaited his next command.

"Attacker must have cleared out already," Slawski concluded, patting him stiffly, like he was a piece of furniture.

Very crouched over Ruth with Slawski's flashlight, examining the wounds. "I'd say some kind of ax made these."

Lulu started yapping at us from the brush about twenty feet away.

"What's she doing on us now?" Slawski muttered irritably. This was him getting competitive.

I borrowed the flashlight and went to investigate. "What would you say to a hatchet, Lieutenant?"

It was a kindling hatchet, maybe fifteen inches long, made of heavy-duty tempered steel. Common make and model. Well used. And covered with blood. Lulu had found it lying in the bushes a few feet off the road.

"Now don't let her be touching it!" cautioned Slawski.

"Don't worry, Trooper. She won't."

He narrowed his eyes at her, then glanced back at Klaus. "Who trained her anyway?" he asked resentfully.

"She's a keen huntress. It's in her blood. Plus she's had a lot of experience." Too damned much.

"Okay, that explains it," said Slawski, nodding. "Klaus is only just out of the academy. A rookie."

"He might pick up a thing or two if she took him under her wing. I can ask her for you, if you'd like."

"I'm warning you, man." Slawski's voice turned low and menacing. "I ain't in the mood for none of your piffle right now."

"I'm sorry, Trooper. Truly I am. Sometimes it's the only way I can deal with it."

"With what?" he demanded.

"With that," I said quietly, glancing back at Ruth. Or what had been Ruth.

"Oh." Slawski hesitated, softening. "Yeah, I be down to that."

We heard a car coming toward us now. Got back onto the road to wave it down. But it wasn't the ambulance. It was a Ford Tempo rental car. Barry and Marco climbed out of it. Both wore lightweight ski jackets and semi-glazed expressions.

"Good evening, gentlemen!" Barry called to us, cheerily and thickly. Until he caught sight of his ex-wife lying there. He let out a yelp—a strangled, awful yelp—then hiccoughed and went stumbling into the darkness to be sick.

Marco Paolo, the former bouncer, stood his ground, his

eyes fixed on her, his rugged features revealing nothing. He did not seem particularly upset. Or surprised.

Slawski had a rain slicker in the trunk of his car. He used it to cover Ruth. "Mr. Paolo, I'm sorry you gentlemen had to encounter the victim in this particular manner," he stated, retreating into cop-speak. "We only recently arrived at the scene ourselves. Emergency medical services personnel are presently en route. I was just about to contact Lieutenant Munger and apprise him of the situation."

"He's here," Marco said.

"He's what?" said Very.

"He's up at the house," Marco said. "Or at least he was a half hour ago. Showed up two seconds after we got here from the city. He was practically here waiting for us."

Barry returned, swiping at his mouth with a hankie, his eyes averted from Ruth. "I told him we had to run out for groceries and things first," he explained hoarsely. "Before the stores closed for the night."

"Kind of early for that, isn't it?" said Very, turning suspicious.

"Not for liquor it isn't, Lieutenant," I informed him. "The stores close at eight in Connecticut." I glanced at Grandfather's Rolex. It was nearly eight now.

"And us without a thing in the house to drink," Barry added. "Quite honestly, the thought of spending an entire evening sober discussing Thor's murder with someone named Chick Munger was simply too horrifying to . . . to . . ." He shuddered. Slowly, his eyes returned to Ruth. "Aw, Ruthie," he moaned. "What did they do to you, Ruthie?"

"Why'd the both of you go?" Very asked Marco.

"We wanted to be alone together for a few minutes, okay?" Marco answered defiantly, placing a meaty arm around his distraught lover. "We stopped off at the Black

Seal for a drink." Again with the Black Seal. "To psych ourselves up for the questioning. This whole thing has been such a drag."

"And getting to be more of one by the hour," I put in.

The ambulance pulled up behind Barry's rental car, followed by a pair of troopers in cruisers. Slawski went over to fill them in. Very and I remained with Barry and Marco.

"How long were you two there?" Very asked Marco.

"Oh, who the fuck knows?" Marco snarled. The anger was always simmering just below the surface with this one. "Ask the bartender there. Go ahead and ask him. Go look in the trunk. There's liquor and groceries in there. Go ahead and fucking *look*. Ask the clerks. They'll remember us. Go on!"

"Christ, *we* didn't do this, Lieutenant," Barry protested. "We had nothing against Ruth. You have to believe me."

"I don't have to do anything, Mr. Feingold," Very pointed out politely.

"Any idea what she was doing out here in the dark?" I asked them.

"No idea," Barry replied.

"None," echoed Marco.

Slawski strode briskly back to us. "They'll take over from here. C'mon, we'll walk the rest of the way."

We pretty much had to—Ruth was blocking the road. Marco grabbed the booze from their trunk to take along and we five started up the road toward the house. Lulu kept her nose to the ground, snarfling vigilantly. Klaus stayed behind in Slawski's cruiser. Possibly the officer needed a nap.

We walked in silence. I was thinking about how solid Barry and Marco's alibi was. And about how solid it wasn't. Because they could have gone out shopping exactly like they said yet still have attacked Ruth *after* they got back. It wouldn't have taken very long to hack her to death. Especially for someone as big and strong as Marco. Especially if Barry helped him. Their "return" just now could have been a complete ruse. Strictly for our benefit.

They could have done it. Sure they could have.

I didn't know what Very and Slawski were thinking, but I suspected they were thinking the same thing.

There were floodlights on outside the house. Munger's unmarked cruiser was parked out front. Barry's bug-eyed Sprite occupied the garage. Very stopped to lay a hand on its bright yellow hood. He gave Slawski one brief shake of his head. The engine was cold. We went inside.

Munger was in the living room slurping from a container of Dunkin' Donuts coffee and talking to Arvin, who was sitting on the sofa wringing his hands. The lead investigator was not at all happy to see me there in the doorway. Or Slawski either. Romaine Very he just sort of sniffed at.

"I guess you'll be the hotshot from New York," he growled.

Mr. Serenity smiled and stuck out his hand.

Munger shook it grudgingly. "Dunno what you hope to accomplish vis-à-vis being here, Very, but you may as well hang around long as you're here. Spot Ruth Feingold on your way in?"

"We did," I affirmed, my eyes on Arvin, who was staring at the expression of utter horror on Barry's face. Neither Barry nor Marco would make eye contact with the kid.

"Where is she?" asked Munger, glancing impatiently at his watch. "We oughta get started."

Slowly, Arvin rose to his feet, teetering slightly. His face was ashen. "She's dead, isn't she?" he whispered.

"Yes, Arvin," I said. "She's dead."

"*What?!*" Munger erupted. "She *can't* be dead! She just went out for a walk! To stretch her l-legs after the l-long car ride . . ." He was starting to sputter, his career, his pension, his life passing before his eyes—one of which, the left, was busy sending out an SOS. "She said she had sciatica," he added miserably.

"When did she go out?" asked Very.

"Geez, I dunno. Few minutes after seven maybe." Munger hung his head and ran his hands through his rather limp hair. "Oh, geez."

"And you, Arvin?" asked Slawski. "Where were you while she was out?"

"Now you just hold it right there, superstar," Munger warned, pointing a trembly finger up at the towering resident trooper. "If there's questions to be asked, I'll ask 'em. This is my investigation."

"And you're doing one hell of a job, Lieutenant," I observed. "One of your prime suspects just got chopped up with a hatchet out there while you were sitting in here drinking coffee."

"Don't push me, Hoag!" he spat angrily.

"Someone ought to," I shot back.

That sent Arvin running out of the room. I heard footsteps on the stairs, going down to the basement.

"Drinks, anyone?" offered Barry, slipping nimbly into the role of urbane host. A bit forced. And more than a bit Noël Cowardish. But it worked for him.

Not that anyone answered him. He motioned to Marco, who went off to the kitchen to fix both of them something stiff.

"Where was Arvin?" Slawski asked stubbornly.

"In his room," Munger answered, reaching for his coffee.

"It's downstairs," said Barry. "I converted the basement into a guest room."

"Is there an outside door down there?" I asked him.

"Of course," he replied. "Why?"

"I'm with you, dude," Very interjected, hopping aboard my train of thought. "The kid could have gone out after his mom and done her and the lieutenant here wouldn't have seen or heard a thing."

"But that's impossible!" cried Barry, his voice cracking with emotion. "Arvin loves Ruth. And she loves—loved him. There was a bond between them. A special bond."

I stiffened. The hair on the back of my neck was standing up all of a sudden, the way it does whenever I hear Jeff Healey's guitar solo on *Confidence Man.* But I wasn't hearing any music right now. No, that's not what was happening. It had just fallen into place for me was what was happening. It had all become clear. Just like that.

But how to prove it? How indeed?

Lulu gazed up at me expectantly, sensing a major breakthrough. I shook my head at her. Timing is everything, which is something she has yet to learn. That and how to do her own tax returns.

"Maybe we should keep an eye on him," said Very, glancing at the hallway. "In case he decides to split or who knows what."

"That boy won't go anywhere," insisted Barry. "He's harmless."

I gave Lulu a brief nod. She went downstairs after him. If his door was open she would keep him company. If his door was closed she would stand guard outside it and start yapping if he went anywhere.

Munger watched her go, then turned his flickering glare on me. "What I want to know," he said harshly, attempting to seize back the offensive, "is where *you* was when it went down."

"With us," Very answered.

"He's been with us for the past two hours," added Slawski.

"Sorry to disappoint you, Lieutenant," I said. "I truly am."

Munger grimaced and climbed dejectedly to his feet. He started to pace the carpet, hands knotted behind his back, his knuckles white, his eye twitching furiously.

Marco returned from the kitchen with two scotches. He handed Barry one and stood there next to him, sipping his own, his face flushed with fever in the bright living room lights. He seemed frightened to me. Genuinely so.

"You didn't hear anything outside?" I asked Munger.

He stopped pacing. "Like what?" he demanded, clearly not enjoying this role reversal.

"A car pulling up, a scream, anything?" Me, I was loving it.

Munger shook his head. "Nah, I had the TV on. That show, *Hard Copy,* is on at half-past seven. Wanted to see if they had anything."

I tugged at my ear. "I get it. So while you were busy watching yourself on the tube Ruth was busy getting herself hacked to death. Nice work, Lieutenant. What's your secret? Or don't you share it with amateurs."

"Who you talking to, huh?!" Munger screamed at me, quivering with rage. "Who the fuck you think you're talking to, punk? *Huh?!*" And then the man, well, the man just plain lost it.

Charged me from halfway across the room and knocked me to the rug with a textbook Pop Warner league tackle. The two of us landed with a thud, him right on top of me, throwing cupcake punches.

I sure was glad Lulu wasn't in the room to see it.

"I'm tired of you pushing me, Hoag!" Munger gasped, his breath sour on my face. "You're pushing me, pushing me, *pushing* me!"

Me, I kept my cool. I just wished someone—anyone—would get him the fuck off me.

Slawski obliged. He lifted Munger up by the scruff of the neck, one-handed, and tossed the lieutenant into a chair like he was an overnight bag. I decided right then I never wanted to find out just how strong Slawski was.

Barry and Marco just stood there with their drinks, transfixed. They reminded me of those mannequins in their apartment.

"Cut the man some slack," the resident trooper ordered me angrily. "He knows his job. Can't help it if this went down on his watch. Could have happened to anyone."

Munger slumped there trying to catch his breath, a curiously pained and bitter expression on his narrow face. Clearly, he was not happy that Slawski was standing up for him. Because this meant that Slawski was a better man than he was, and I don't believe he was prepared to admit that to himself. "Where'd it go down?" he asked after a moment, his voice thin and quiet.

"Down the road," Slawski replied.

"You can't miss it," added Very.

"Fine." He shot me a cold, hard last look. Then he stormed out.

"Whoa, dude," exclaimed Very, shaking his head at me. "I thought *I* didn't like you. But he *really* doesn't like you."

"You've got that all wrong, Lieutenant," I said, straightening my clothing. "The man's crazy about me. He's just having a hard time dealing with his feelings."

"Uh-huh," said Slawski.

"Clethra must be told."

"Not yet."

"But he *has* to notify her of her mother's death, dude," Very said.

"It's my official responsibility to notify her," Slawski said.

"Not yet."

The three of us were choking down cheeseburgers, spiral fries and chocolate shakes at the Hallmark, a venerated local drive-in situated on the Shore Road down near the beach. They made their own ice cream, all kinds of flavors, though I still couldn't get them to make licorice for me. There were picnic tables around back. We were seated at one of them under the floodlights, the marsh grass out in the darkness smelling somewhat yeasty from that day's rain. Munger was still at the murder scene. A trooper in uniform was baby-sitting Barry, Marco and Arvin. Slawski's mission was to notify Clethra. I had persuaded him to stop and talk it over first.

"Well, why the hell not?" he demanded.

"I have my reasons," I said quietly, not liking a single one of them.

Slawski stared at me. "What, you think *she* the one did her?"

"I have my reasons."

"Dude always has his reasons," Very informed him, chewing on a fry. "And they always seem kinda whacked on the surface. It isn't until you trip on 'em awhile, check 'em out from a million different angles, that you realize how totally whacked they really are."

Slawski ate the last bite of his hamburger, dabbing at his mouth with his napkin. He was a dainty eater for such a big man. "If I'm going to be sticking my own individual neck out, then I got to know what those reasons are. What's on your mind?"

"Two things, Trooper. One of them has to do with Lulu."

She immediately sat up, tail thumping eagerly.

"What about her?".

"The way she behaved that day you and I went to Barry's house to tell everyone Thor had been murdered."

Slawski frowned. "How did she behave?"

"The other thing has to do with something an extremely wise old man said to me not long ago."

"Gibbs?" said Very. "What did he say?"

"I may be completely wrong about this," I continued. "And, frankly, I hope I am. But if I'm right, our killer has all but gotten away with three brutal murders. We haven't got much of a chance, not unless we move fast and we move smart. That means we have to have a plan when we show up to notify Clethra. Before we go, Lieutenant, there's something you need to check out from the New York end. Something you can do that I can't. I have to make a couple of phone calls myself. I'd like to make one of them right now." My mouth was getting dry. I took a sip of my shake. "If we stick together we'll have this whole case wrapped up by morning. And Munger will be left hanging in the breeze, saluting his own shadow. You'll be the big hero, Trooper. You and the lieutenant here. What do you say?"

Slawski hesitated, scratching his square chin with a big thumb. His eyes met Very's, then returned to mine. "I say the pay phone's over there by the men's room. And I hope you know what the hell you're doing."

"So do I, Trooper."

The narrow, twisting stretch of Joshua Town Road approaching the farm was blessedly dark and deserted, almost like old times. Almost but not quite. Our timing was good, that was all. The resident press corps had gone tearing off to Essex to cover the hatchet murder of legendary feminist leader Ruth Feingold. Their lucky night.

They didn't know yet just how lucky.

We pulled up in front of the carriage barn next to Dwayne's truck and got out. We were one fewer. We'd dropped Very off at Slawski's house to do his phone work.

Klaus stayed in the cruiser. Klaus always stayed in the cruiser.

They were sitting down by the salt marsh where we'd left her, an oil lantern throwing light on the greasy pizza box and a dozen or more empty beer bottles that lay there in the grass. Lulu made straight for the pizza box in hopes of finding anchovies. And right away there was a flurry of movement in one of the Adirondack chairs—Clethra scrambling up out of Dwayne's lap. She staggered to her feet, eyes bright, face wet and shiny, her clothes rumpled and partly unbuttoned. Dwayne stayed where he was, looking pretty much the same way.

"Evening, Mr. H," he mumbled guiltily, wiping his mouth with the back of his hand. His eyes avoided mine.

"Good evening, Dwayne," I said coolly.

Clethra reached for her cigarettes and lit one, straightening herself. "We were just, like, *talking,*" she whined, going indignant teenager on me. "It's not like we were *doing* anything."

"Ms. Feingold," Slawski spoke up. "I'm here to inform you that your mother is dead."

Clethra froze. "Wha . . . ?!"

"She was murdered earlier this evening on the grounds of your father's residence." Slawski took off his hat and examined the brim. "In a rather brutal fashion, I'm sorry to report."

Clethra's eyes filled with tears. She tried to speak, but no words came out. Just a gurgle.

"Fuckin' A." Dwayne's voice was a hollow gasp. He looked up at her in astonishment, then ducked his head, shaking it. "Fuckin' A," he said softly.

"If you so desire, Ms. Feingold," Slawski offered, "I can transport you there so that you may presently join the immediate family."

"D-Do I have to?" she moaned.

"You may remain here if you so prefer," Slawski assured her. "The choice is entirely your own. I am merely here to inform you of her demise and to offer you any professional courtesies of which you may choose to avail yourself." The resident trooper stayed there a moment, grimly turning his hat in his hands. Then he put it back on his head and said goodnight. He started back up toward his cruiser without looking at me.

Clethra stayed where she was, looking blindly around at the darkness surrounding her, the cigarette between her fingers forgotten. "Like, c-could I be alone for a while?"

"Of course," I said.

Dwayne and I trailed Slawski across the pasture.

"Guess I owe you an apology, Mr. H," he said, tugging at his scraggly goatee.

"Now isn't a good time, Dwayne."

"I remembered what you said—how I shouldn't be bustin' a move on her or nothing. And I wasn't, I swear. We was just chillin' is all. And next thing I know she's all over me. Practically tore my clothes off. I'm only human, y'know?"

"I said now isn't a good time."

"You pissed at me?"

I sighed wearily. "I suppose if I gave it any thought I'd be a little disappointed, but I have a lot on my mind right now."

Slawski was leaning against his cruiser, waiting for me with his arms crossed.

"You'd better run along now, Dwayne," I said, not unkindly.

The kid lingered, pawing uneasily at the gravel with his work boot. "You firing me?"

"No. I'll see you in the morning."

"You got it, Mr. H," he said gratefully. He hopped in

his truck and started it up. The death metal came right on, blaring. He turned it down, waved and took off.

Slawski and I stood there watching his truck head down the drive. Then I heard the phone ring inside. I raced in the kitchen door and answered it.

It was Very. He said one word. He said, "Bingo."

I called Merilee when I got into bed, Lulu snuggling close to me for warmth. The bedroom was chilly in spite of the fire I'd made. A storm had blown in, this one complete with lightning and thunder and cold gusts that shook the dark old house and rattled its windows.

Not that Clethra had noticed one bit of it. She hadn't spoken a word to me the rest of the evening. Just sat there by the marsh smoking cigarette after cigarette and staring numbly out at the darkness. No doubt she would have stayed out there all night in the cold rain if I hadn't fetched her and toweled her off and put her to bed in the chapel.

"Oh, thank God it's you, darling!" Merilee cried when I got through to her. "Pam and I were just sitting here watching the late news when they said—"

"You've heard about Ruth then."

"When will this end, Hoagy?" Merilee wondered, her voice heavy with sorrow.

"Soon, I hope."

She was silent a moment. "You sound funny, darling."

"Funny ha-ha?"

"Funny weird."

"It's this bed."

"What about it?"

"It's awfully cold in here."

"That's because you don't have me there to keep you warm."

"Have I told you recently I'm nuts about you? Both of you?"

"Not in ages and ages," she answered solemnly. "And if by 'both of you' you're referring to Tracy the answer is never. As in not ever. Have you been drinking tequila? You know what that does to you."

"No, I haven't, Merilee."

"What about Lulu?"

"She hasn't been drinking tequila either."

"I meant, sir, how does *she* feel about Tracy?"

"She's accepting the fact that she can't go back, only forward, and that if she'll just give Tracy a chance she'll find her enriching her life, rather than intruding upon it."

"Mighty complex ruminations for a gal with a brain the size of a garbanzo bean," Merilee said tartly. ". . . Hoagy?"

"Yes, Merilee?"

"You're not doing something reckless and foolhardy, are you?"

I took a deep breath and let it out slowly. It seemed to work for Very. "Of course not. Why would you say that?"

"Because I know you, that's why. Are you sure?"

"Positive."

"When can I come home? I miss my garden somethin' arful."

"Tomorrow, Merilee. Just . . ."

"Yes, darling?"

"Just don't make it too early."

"That'll be perfect. They want to talk to me at ten about doing *Gilligan: The Musical.*"

"Oh, no . . ."

"Oh, yes."

"Would you be Ginger or Mary Ann?"

"Actually, they're offering me the title role."

"But—"

"It's a feminist interpretation, darling. I'd be Gilligan. Chita Rivera has already signed to play the Skipper. And they're talking to the Cassidy brothers, David and Shaun, for Ginger and Mary Ann."

"I don't even want to know who's going to play Thurston Howell."

"Sandra Bernhard."

"I told you, I didn't want to know. Merilee, you're not actually considering this, are you?"

"I miss the action, darling," she confessed. "I hate to admit it, but it's the truth. I've been realizing it ever since I've been back here. And a play is ideal. Tracy can be with me all through rehearsal, and then once our run starts I can be home with her all day. Okay, so it's not Sondheim. But—well, it *is* a stretch."

"That's certainly one word for it."

"But what am I dithering on about?" she said, shifting gears. "You don't want to hear about my silly career right now."

"Yes, I do. More than you can possibly imagine. Hurry home, Merilee. I love you."

"I love you, too, darling. Goodnight."

I hung up the phone and stared at it, my heart starting to pound.

Everything was in place. Everyone was ready. Now it was my play. A high-risk play, no question. But the only play. No question there either.

I picked up the phone and dialed the number. When I got the voice I wanted to hear I said: "I love Clethra and Clethra loves me. We've been sleeping together ever since Merilee went to New York. We have sex every night. Incredible sex, the best sex she's ever had. Now that Ruth is gone there's no one who can keep us apart. We're running away in the morning to start a brand-new life together. You'll never see her again. She's mine, do you hear me? She's *mine!*"

Then I slammed down the phone.

And lay there, tensed, watching the patterns of the fire dance on the wall of the darkened room. I lay there and waited, the rain pounding on the roof, the lightning flashing, the wind howling. I thought about Merilee and Tracy. I thought about that last conversation I'd had with Mother out in the parking lot at Exit Meadows. I thought about Father and that creak on the stairs in the night. I thought about Thor and Ruth and that kid Tyler, who got himself strangled in his dorm room for being greedy and stupid. I thought about how I was lying there alone and that I didn't enjoy being alone as much as I used to. I thought about a lot of things. A high-risk play will do that to you. I thought about everything except sleep. Sleep was out of the question. I waited, Lulu snoring softly next to me.

It was nearly one when I heard it.

At first I wasn't really sure I had because of the rain. But I had—the soft crunch of footsteps in the gravel driveway out by the back porch. The kitchen door opening with a squeak. I'd left it unlocked, like we always did. Someone rattling around in the kitchen. Drawers being pulled open, a cupboard door smacking shut. Footsteps. The creak of a floorboard down below in the parlor. Lulu stirred and opened one eye, a growl coming from deep in her throat. I shushed her. Reached down under the bed and hit the on switch, then dove back down under the covers, waiting . . . A creak on the stairs now, footsteps climbing quickly . . . Stopping at the top of the stairs, hesitating, starting down the hall toward me. Arriving outside my bedroom door. Slowly, the door swung open, its hinges squeaking. They could use some WD-40. Every hinge in the house needed some after the summer. I'd have to take care of that when I had a chance . . . One step toward me, the floorboard groaning . . . Another step . . . Nearing the foot of the bed . . . Closer . . . Still closer . . .

Until I sat right up and flicked on the bedside lamp, freezing him there with the kitchen knife clutched tightly in his powerful hand.

"Greetings, Dwayne," I said. "What took you so damned long?"

Eleven

DWAYNE stood there blinking furiously at the light, his tongue flicking at his lips. He was shivering. His clothes were soaked through, his hair dripping wet, the drops plopping softly on the hooked rug at his feet.

"I had to hike through the woods to get here, Mr. H. Didn't want nobody to hear me coming. There's that trooper stationed down by the . . ." He stopped short, his eyes darting around the room in confusion. "She's not here. Where is she?"

"In the chapel, Dwayne," I replied, my own eyes on the knife. So were Lulu's. "That's where she sleeps, generally. She and I aren't running away together, or having incredible sex, or ordinary sex, or any kind of sex at all. I'm afraid I tricked you. Had to. It was the only way I could get you to show your hand." I sat back in the bed and crossed my arms, trying to look relaxed. Which I wasn't. It was a big knife, ideal for chopping vegetables and assorted limbs. It was a sharp knife. I knew this. I'd sharpened it myself. "What were you planning to do when you found us here together? Kill us both?"

Dwayne shook a damp, crumpled cigarette loose from the pack in the pocket of his flannel shirt and managed to light it, tossing the match in the fireplace. "No way, man. Not Clethra. Never Clethra. I love her. More than I've ever loved any girl. More than I ever will. I-I was gonna show her how much. Prove it to her."

"By killing me," I said. "Just as you killed Thor and Tyler and Ruth."

Dwayne fingered his stringy moustache, squinting at me over his cigarette. "By taking what I want, no matter who don't like it. Just like Mr. Gibbs said."

I stared at him. "Christ, Dwayne, is that what this is all about? Thor's teachings?"

"Man is a conqueror," Dwayne recited, his voice hushed and reverent. "If he sees what he wants he must take it. He must be true to himself. No matter what other people think. No matter if they get hurt. No matter if—"

"They get dead?"

"Someone like Clethra," he went on, glancing down at the knife in his hand, "someone so beautiful, so smart, so sweet, she's always gonna belong to somebody else. I didn't have to tell him that. He *knew* it. Just like he knew it's another man's right, another man's *destiny,* to come along and take her away from him. Which is what I tried to tell him, man to man, as someone I-I looked up to, as someone I-I . . ."

A log fell in the fireplace grate. He jumped. All three of us did.

"Go on, Dwayne. Tell me what happened that morning."

He stood there a moment, his eyes narrow and vulpine, his chest rising and falling. "I knew you all were going to

Essex. Clethra told me. She told me he'd be here all alone.
So I came here, like a man, to tell him straight up I loved
her and wanted her to be mine."

"And what did he say when you told him?"

"He laughed at me," Dwayne answered bitterly. "He
fucking laughed in my face."

"He was drunk, wasn't he?"

Dwayne nodded. "Sitting there by the woodpile, nasty
drunk like he was that day at Slim Jim's. Calling me
dickless. Telling me I was just some lousy Lost Boy, and
what right did I have thinking I could ever offer Clethra
anything."

"And what did you say?"

"I said," Dwayne recalled angrily, "I sure as hell could
give her one thing he couldn't—a good straight fucking."

"She'd told you they hadn't had sex?"

He sniffled, swiping at his nose with the back of his
hand. "No, not exactly."

"You overheard it, didn't you?" I suggested. "That night
I came back late from the city, when she was out there
waiting for me on the Land Rover, all sweaty and itchy.
She'd been with you, hadn't she? That's what she was
doing out there. She'd slipped out on Thor to be with you.
And you were there listening that whole time we talked,
weren't you? In the carriage barn. I heard a noise in there,
but I figured it was Sadie stalking a mouse, since Lulu
didn't bark. But she wouldn't bark—not at you. She
knows you."

"That was our second date," Dwayne recalled, a look of
utter rapture on his scarred, stitched face. "Our first was
that night you and Mr. Gibbs went away camping. She
ducked out for some munchies, least that's what she told
Miss Nash. I met her there at the general store. We parked
in the woods. Drank some beer and talked. Just kicking it,
until she had to get back on account of Miss Nash would

think she cracked up the Land Rover or something. All we did was talk, Mr. H. But we just . . . I just . . . Damn, she treated me like a *person,* not like some townie retardo whose old man's in jail. She listened to what I had to say. She really listened. You know what that feels like? When someone that smart, that pretty . . ." He trailed off, shaking his head in awe. "Man, I just *knew* she was the one for me. For life. Have you ever met someone and *known?* Just like that?"

"Yes, Dwayne. I have."

"That second date," he went on, "we made for late, after Mr. Gibbs passed out, which she said he almost always did from drinking so much and being so old."

"I'll have to remember that for the future," I reflected.

"I left my truck down in the woods and hiked up to your place so nobody'd get wise to us—I figured you wouldn't be too happy if you found out. And I *knew* he wouldn't be. We sat out there in the backseat of your Woody, making out like crazy. She was on fire that night, man. And so was I. Our flesh *burned.*"

"I'll never be able to drive that car again," I muttered. "Did the two of you . . . ?"

"We would have if you hadn't pulled up when you did," he assured me. "I had her *naked,* man. Her juices were streaming down my fingers like hot soup."

"I'll never be able to eat hot soup again either."

Lulu, she'd had just about enough of this whole thing. She jumped down to the floor with a huff and started primly for the door.

"Where's she going?" Dwayne's knuckles tightened around the gleaming knife.

"Ask her yourself."

"Tell her to stay!"

"Tell her yourself."

Not necessary. She halted in the doorway, knowing better than to make things any worse, then sidled over to the rocker by the fireplace, where she curled up and eyed him with withering disapproval.

Dwayne tossed his cigarette butt in the fire and lit another, dragging on it deeply. "I was there in the barn listening to you two the whole time, like you said. Heard her tell you how she and Thor had never even done it."

"What exactly had she told you?"

"Just that it was all a mistake, her running off with him. That she was sorry she done it. That he was too old for her. That he was . . ." He trailed off, his eyes on the fire. I thought about making a dive for the knife. I didn't do it, but I thought about it. "When I heard her tell you that, man, that's when I knew it was for real, her and me. Because she *wasn't* his, y'know? He wasn't really possessing her. Me knowing that, well, that's what give me the nerve to tell him about us Sunday morning. I showed up here like I was gonna do some work. Y'know, like it was just an accident us getting to talk. I even pulled a couple of rotten sills, full of rusty nails."

"Which explains why you had your gloves on," I said.

"He laughed at me, Mr. H," Dwayne said angrily. "He laughed in my face, the mean fucking bastard. Called me names. Shoved me. And kept on shoving me. I-I don't like to be pushed, man. I really, really don't like it. So I grabbed the nearest thing . . ."

"The sledge."

"And I popped him with it—two, three times. I-I lost my head. But he drove me to it, man. Brought it on himself. I mean, he was just so completely full of shit. All that stuff he wrote, that stuff he said a man oughta do. And I *believed* him. I thought . . . I thought he *meant* what he said. I thought he *cared*. But he was full of shit, just like everyone else. *Everyone*." He paused, breathing heavily. "I did what he'd said to do, man. And when I did it, when I fucking grabbed for it . . . he fucking *laughed* at me!"

"Why did you Bobbitt him?"

"To make it look like his wife maybe done it," he replied simply. "Idea just came to me."

"Shrewd. Only why toss the shears in the pond but leave the sledge right there for anyone to find?"

Lulu harrumphed indignantly at this. It hadn't been "anyone" who'd found the sledge. It had been her.

"I was gonna hide the shears and the sledge both," Dwayne answered. "Y'know, like bury 'em somewhere maybe. Only I started to freak out about time. Plus there was his body to take care of. I mean, I had to get rid of *him*. I was afraid to cart him away in my truck in broad daylight. Figured I'd get spotted dumping him somewhere. Lot of guys out hunting now, or laying in firewood for winter. So I weighed him down and dumped him in the pond. Figured the water'd be getting deeper from all this rain, and then in a few weeks it'd freeze right over. Be ages before anyone found him." He scratched his head ruefully. "I didn't figure on Lulu taking a swim soon as she got home."

"One never does. Her unpredictability is one of her most endearing traits. In fact, it's her only endearing trait."

She harrumphed at this, too. She was doing a lot of harrumphing. I would pay for this later. If there was a later.

"Still, you were plenty careful, Dwayne. You didn't have to worry about the mud around the edge of the pond. There were a million footprints there, and no reason why your own would set off any alarm bells. You've been working here for weeks. But the driveway was another matter."

He nodded. "It was raining. Just a drizzle really, but the

driveway was wet. And when I started backing out I realized I was leaving a dry patch there in the gravel where my truck had been. Anybody came back soon and saw that dry patch I'd be smoked for sure. All they'd have to do is measure it and they'd know it was my truck—I got custom bumpers. So I jumped out and hosed it down real fast. And then I got the hell out of here."

"Where did you go?"

"Straight home. Told my mom if anyone asked her I was around the house all morning helping her out."

"Did she ask you why?"

Dwayne snorted. "In my family, it's not smart to ask why."

"And you're nothing if not smart, Dwayne," I told him. "You sure fooled me. All along I was wrong. I thought for sure it had to be one of the family. It had to be Ruth. Or Arvin. Or Barry—with or without help from Marco. After all, they were the ones who hated Thor the most. And loved Clethra the most. After all, Thor's killing took place when they were all out here at Barry's place. And when Tyler Kampmann was murdered they were all back in New York. It had to be one of them. It just had to be. Only it wasn't. None of them were involved, except as victims. I was wrong all along," I confessed, tugging at my ear. "And Lulu, it turns out, was right."

She sat up in the rocker, tail thumping expectantly.

"How so?" Dwayne demanded, scowling at her.

"When we got to Barry's house after Thor was murdered she sniffed everyone's shoes, one by one, to see if any of them had traces of our pond mud on them. Marco started acting really panicky—I later found out because he was afraid she'd sniff marijuana on him and get him in trouble with Slawski. But it was mud Lulu was after, and the bottom line was that she discovered none, just as she discovered none on the wheels of their cars. I didn't know what to make of the cars, but with the shoes I figured, okay, the killer had time to change them before we got there. A simple, plausible explanation. And totally wrong. Because the simple truth is that Thor's killer wasn't there at all. Because Thor's killer was you . . . After you told your mom to cover for you you went out and helped your neighbor Billy in his yard. When Billy got the call to come tow Thor's body out of the pond you followed him up here, pretending to be greatly distraught. You even jumped in yourself and hooked up Thor's body to the winch. Pretty weird behavior, considering you'd just put him there."

"It would have been weirder if I hadn't come," he argued. "Working for you folks the way I do and all. Besides, a guilty man would never come right back here and do that. At least, that's how I figured it."

"You figured it right," I acknowledged. "It never occurred to me it could be you. Especially after Tyler got himself strangled in his dorm room at Columbia the next morning. I'd spoken to you myself that very morning. You'd phoned me to say you wouldn't be showing up for work. You thought we'd want to be alone for the day, was what you said. Naturally, I assumed you were at home when you called me. You even yelled out something to your mom, something about how you'd be right with her. Exceedingly clever, Dwayne. Because the truth is you *weren't* at home when you called. You were phoning me from Tyler Kampmann's dorm room, where he lay dead on the floor right next to you after you strangled him. You're smart, Dwayne. Smart enough to throw off suspicion by calling me that way. Smart enough to pretend to be Tyler when his neighbor pounded on the door on his way to a nine o'clock French class. You groaned something to him through the door about you weren't feeling well—which has to be the understatement of the year. And the neighbor bought it. He and Tyler had been out celebrating the night before. And he *assumed* the voice he heard was Tyler's. It didn't occur to him it was someone else's—that wouldn't occur to anyone. In fact, Tyler had already been dead for an hour, which explains the discrepancy between the coroner's estimated time of death and the time when the neighbor said he spoke to him. Must have been real cozy, you and Tyler together there in that tiny room all that time."

"I had no choice," Dwayne insisted. "I couldn't come out until everyone on the floor had gone to breakfast or class or whatever. Couldn't take a chance of someone spotting me." He sniffled. "I read some of his books. He had all kinds. History, art, philosophy . . ."

Lightning crackled across Whalebone Cove. He turned his face to the windows. It was an angry face at that moment. A proud face. I had never seen it proud before. But then, I'd never really known Dwayne before. Not really. I'd thought he was a good kid who'd had some bad breaks. But there was more to Dwayne Gobble than that. A lot more. And none of it was good.

Thunder rumbled, shaking the house down to its stone foundation. The wind and cold rain tore at the casement windows.

"How did you get in the dorm, by the way?"

"By looking like any other student," Dwayne replied, sneering at me. "I'm the right age, I dress right—I just flashed the guard down in the lobby my fucking driver's license, man, and he let me right on through. He didn't give a fuck. Must have been the end of his shift or something. It was early in the morning, not even seven."

"And Tyler let you into his room?"

"He was half asleep. Thought I was one of his friends."

"Smart, Dwayne. Real smart. Me, I was real stupid. I figured Tyler died because of what Clethra had told him about her previous love life. Before she met him, I mean."

Dwayne stiffened, his eyes narrowing to icy slits. "What previous love life?" he demanded, moving closer to me. Him and the big knife both.

"It did occur to me, of course, that the killer might be Clethra herself. I remembered how the phone was back on the hook when I returned from my walk that night she and I were alone together. I'd left it off the hook when I went out. Clearly, she'd used it. Only, who had she called? Had she called Tyler? Had she called Arvin?"

"She called *me.*" Dwayne thumped his chest with a clenched fist. "She called to tell me how bummed she was about everything and to ask me when she'd see me again. She called *me.*" He stood there glowering at me. "*What previous love life?*"

"Oh, that. Something rather damaging, actually, involving Clethra and another guy. She'd made the mistake of telling Tyler about it once, and it was reasonable to assume that if Tyler was willing to peddle her video striptease he'd be more than willing to peddle her deepest, darkest secret. I figured that was why he died—so the secret would die with him. Only, once again, I was wrong."

"What other guy?!" Dwayne raged. "*Who?*"

"That's not important."

"The fuck it's not! I want to know who it is. Tell me, damn it!" His teeth were clamped tightly together now, his jaw tensed. "You just better tell me."

"You want all of her, don't you, Dwayne? Even her past. Well, I'm sorry. It doesn't work that way—no matter how badly you want it to. And, let's face it, you want it plenty badly . . . That same night you overheard Clethra telling me about her and Thor you also heard her tell me who peddled the videotape. You heard all about Tyler— how he was her first boyfriend, how he used to dick her friends behind her back, lie to her—"

"He was a scumbag," Dwayne snarled. "Dragged her

through the mud for money. Shat all over her. And he didn't even fucking *care* about her. Not a lick. I-I couldn't let that happen. I couldn't let him get away with treating Clethra that way. Not Clethra. The scumbag had to pay. Had to."

"So you made him pay."

"That's right," Dwayne affirmed eagerly. He was anxious to tell me about it. He was proud. "I drove into New York in the middle of the night, after Mom went to sleep. I knew where he lived. She told you the name of his dorm. I confronted him, face to face, like a man. Told him I didn't like what he was dealing her, y'know? The scumbag couldn't even figure out what my problem was. He had no regrets. He . . . He deserved to die. He corrupted her. He dirtied her. He *hurt* her." Dwayne was panting, his chest rising and falling as if from a great exertion. "After I did him, I phoned you so you'd think I was home, like you said. Figured as long as you were vouching for me everything would be cool."

"Which, again, was smart of you, Dwayne. But only half smart. Because that was also your one mistake. Damned big one, too. You made a long-distance call, Dwayne. They keep records of those. Lieutenant Very just checked them. Someone used Tyler's phone at 8:41 A.M. the day of his death to call this number. And that someone was you, Dwayne. Had to be you. Because Tyler was already dead."

"I didn't want to call from there," he admitted grudgingly. "But I couldn't leave the room for at least another hour. And you'd be expecting me for work if I didn't call ya. So I took a chance."

"You blew it, Dwayne. You're toast. They're on to you now."

"I could give a fuck," he boasted, tongue flicking at his

lips. "I'm out of here tonight, man. And where I'm headed they'll never, ever find me."

"May I finish my story before you go? Or do you have to run right away?"

He seemed distracted now. For a moment, I thought he hadn't heard me. But then he shuddered and nodded for me to go ahead.

I went ahead. "When I got back from the city this afternoon you and Clethra were working on the barn together, talking over her plans for the future. You gave me the impression she was still pretty undecided about where she'd end up. But that wasn't the case at all, was it? She'd decided precisely what she wanted to do. Go back to Ruth. Back to the life she'd known before this whole crazy thing with Thor went down. She told you she wanted to go home to her mother, didn't she, Dwayne?"

"What she said," he replied testily, "was she needed to get normal for a while."

"Which has to rank as our runner-up for the understatement of the year," I said. "You freaked out when she told you this, didn't you? Because this was goodbye. You were going to lose her. After everything you'd done for her, you were going to lose her to her old life. And you couldn't stand that, could you? No way. A man has to take what he wants, right? Which left you with only one choice—do away with her old life. Erase that mother. Erase that home. Make her yours, all yours. You'd already killed twice for her. It wasn't too hard to kill a third time. You knew when Ruth and the others were going to arrive. Clethra told you. You parked your truck in the woods near Barry's place, hiked to the house and waited out there for your chance at her. All you needed was a minute. Just one minute. Only it didn't look too promising, did it? You must have figured . . . well, what did you figure when you saw Munger pull up?"

280

280 / David Handler

"I figured," he confessed, "no way."

"But then Barry and Marco went out to the store," I continued. "And you got lucky. And Ruth got real, real unlucky. She decided to stretch her legs. You followed her. Followed her and killed her with a hatchet you had in your truck. You murdered her while the detective in charge of the case was sitting right there in the house. That's bold, Dwayne. Mighty bold. You took off in your truck just before we got there. Tidied yourself up. Picked up a pizza, as planned, and hightailed up here to see Clethra. You had pizza and beer with her. You kissed her and you fondled her breasts—all the while knowing you'd hacked her mother to death just minutes before. That's not love, Dwayne. That's just plain sick. At least that's what I told her."

Dwayne frowned at me, perplexed. "You told who?"

"Your mom."

He swallowed. "Wait, you spoke to my mom?" he demanded, his eyes widening. Dumb he wasn't. Brains were never Dwayne Gobble's problem.

"Tonight," I confirmed. "We had a nice talk on the phone. You were right to count on her, Dwayne. As your alibi, I mean. Strongest bond there is, a mother's love for her child. She'd do anything for him. Even lie to protect him if she had to. Not that the truth ever actually occurred to her. Not that she could in a million years think that her own son would coldly and systematically murder three human beings. Like I said, you were right to count on her love. Mothers always protect their young. But what you didn't count on, Dwayne, was how her love could be turned right around on you. I told her what you'd done, Dwayne. I told her we had proof it was you. I told her you were a sick, sick boy. And that you need help. And that if she loved you she'd help us make sure you got that help. She wept for you, Dwayne. Uncontrollably. It was one of the saddest things I've ever heard in my life, the way she wept for you. And then she told me the truth—that you hadn't been helping her around the house when Thor was murdered. That you hadn't been home the morning Tyler died either. She had no idea where you were that morning. Your bed hadn't even been slept in. She was worried about you. She was afraid you were out on the streets of New Haven buying drugs. She didn't know. Poor woman had no idea just how sick you really are."

"God, I wish you'd stop fucking saying that!" Dwayne cried. "I ain't sick! You of all people should know that. You were a friend of his, man. I-I wanted something *better* for myself in this world. I found it. I found *her.* A man takes what he wants when he sees it. I'm taking it, man. So what if people think I done something wrong? That don't make any of you or your stupid laws right. Man is an outlaw. All of our heroes are outlaws. Robin Hood was an outlaw. Zorro was an outlaw. Jesse James was an outlaw. Any man who's true to his wild self, any man who gives a shit about *anything,* is an outlaw. When people are coming after you, pissed off at you, ready to string you up . . . Christ, that's how you know you're doing something right."

"Killing people is not something right, Dwayne," I shot back. "I knew Thor, like you said. And he valued human life. He didn't believe in destroying it. That's not what he was saying. You've got it wrong. All wrong."

Dwayne stared down at the knife in his hand for a moment, then slowly raised his gaze to me. "I'm sorry this had to happen, Mr. H. On account of I respect you. You been decent to me. Didn't ever talk down to me or anything. But you've put yourself between me and Clethra. And I can't allow anyone to do that to me."

"So I've noticed. What happens now?"

"What, you mean after I kill you?"

"If you say so."

Lulu let out a mournful yowl from the rocker. She did care after all.

Dwayne tugged at his goatee, grinning at me. "We take off for Mexico, just we two. Live off the land. Live the life of desperadoes."

"What if she says no?"

"She won't. She just won't. She loves me same as I love her. I know it."

"If you know it then what are you doing here?"

Dwayne furrowed his brow at this. "What's that supposed to mean?"

"I hate to be the one to break it to you, Dwayne, but this isn't how it works when two people are genuinely in love. When someone loves you back then you don't need to kill her current boyfriend, her ex-boyfriend and her mother as a token of your undying affection. None of that happens when there's love, Dwayne. There's trust when there's love. There's commitment. Clethra Feingold played around in the backseat with you for a while, but she doesn't love you. She barely even knows you."

"Man, you are so wrong. She loves me like she's never loved anyone. And she's gonna run off with me and you're gonna be dead and ain't nobody gonna be the wiser."

"Check, dude, I'm down to that. But school me, there's still one thing I can't conceptualize."

It was Detective Lieutenant Romaine Very who said this. I don't generally use words like conceptualize. At least I try not to.

He stood directly behind Dwayne in the bedroom doorway, his gun pointed right between the kid's shoulder-blades. Evidently he'd decided it was time to vacate his post next door in the nursery. The storm had covered the sound of his footsteps.

Lulu snarfled excitedly at the lieutenant. She's always

happy to see Very, especially when he has a loaded gun. I don't possess one, loaded or otherwise, and I think it's a source of great disappointment for her.

"Only one thing, Lieutenant?" I asked him.

"Yo, couldn't you *tell* it was a long-distance call? When he phoned you from New York, I mean."

Dwayne, he just stood there, frozen.

"Not at all," I replied. "It sounded no different than a local call. The connection was perfect."

"Hmm. Wonder who it was."

"Who what was, Lieutenant?"

Dwayne's eyes were darting wildly around the room now, searching for an escape.

"Dig, I'm shopping for a new long-distance company. I dropped my old one on account of first they fucked with my bill, and then they copped a 'tude when I questioned 'em on it. Which is cool. The old me woulda gotten into a big blowout with 'em. New me just chills and goes shopping. Real progress, huh?"

"I'd certainly say so, Lieutenant."

Very turned his attention back to Dwayne, not that it had every really left him. "Drop the knife, putz."

Dwayne clutched it even tighter. "You got nothing on me," he insisted, an ugly sneer crossing his face. "No proof. No nothing."

I reached down under the bed. "Except for this, Dwayne," I informed him, pulling out my tape recorder. It whirred softly, still recording every word we said. "Your full confession, in your own words. If you're real nice to me I'll let you have a copy. You can sell it to one of the tabloid shows to pay for your defense. Not that you've got a prayer."

"Drop it, Gobble." Very nudged him in the spine with the nose of his gun.

But Dwayne had something else in mind.

The windows—the old casements that overlooked the herb garden. And were presently shut tight against the rain.

He dove for them. He dove *through* them, headfirst, shattering the glass and the brittle old wood before he went hurtling out into the wet and windy night and crashed to the ground below, Very firing off two quick shots. One clipped him on the shoulder.

The boxwood hedge that edged the garden broke his fall. He scrambled to his feet, bloodied but unshaken, and made a mad dash for the driveway, still clutching the knife.

He never saw Slawski, who was stationed in the shadows of the carriage barn next to his cruiser. The resident trooper issued a one-word command. And then Klaus went streaking off down the driveway after Dwayne Gobble, a ferocious growl coming from his throat. Slawski hit the cruiser's lights just in time for us to see Klaus leave his feet. That dog flew—and I do mean *flew*—at least twenty feet through the air before he tackled Dwayne hard to the ground, pinning him there like a squirming pancake, his jaws clamped tightly around Dwayne's leg.

It was the single greatest open field tackle I'd ever seen. I just stood there in front of the shattered windows, gaping. Lulu was positively goggle-eyed.

The commotion woke Clethra, who came padding out of the chapel in a flannel shirt and nothing else, wondering what the hell was going on. Slawski told her.

Me, I was still staring. "Well, that settles that, Lieutenant. My last unanswered question."

Very frowned at me. "Which unanswered question's that, dude?"

"I finally found out what Klaus does."

Twelve

THEY KEPT DWAYNE in Lawrence and Memorial Hospital in New London for three days. He was treated there for the gunshot wound to his shoulder as well as several rather nasty dog bites. When he was well enough to be discharged he was arraigned in New London County Court and charged with the murders of Thor Gibbs and Ruth Feingold, not to mention the attempted murder of Stewart Hoag, onetime literary luminary. He would be tried separately in Manhattan for the murder of Tyler Kampmann.

Naturally, the press was all over it. They were especially hot for the real inside story of how Dwayne was brought down. Hard to blame them, considering that the man who'd been spearheading the investigation, Lieutenant Chick Munger of the Connecticut State Police Major Crime Squad, was home in bed with his wife at the time of the arrest. And was a bit fuzzy himself on the details. So, for the record, here's the real inside story. And remember, you read it here first:

Detective Lieutenant Romaine Very of the New York Police Department happened to be at the scene of the attempted murder because he was my house guest for the night. Very heard a commotion in my bedroom. Thinking that perhaps it was a break-in, he approached the scene with his firearm drawn and attempted to apprehend the suspect. Tyrone "Cole" Slawski, Lyme's resident trooper, was cruising down Joshua Town Road on routine patrol when he heard shots being fired. Slawski immediately rushed to the scene and, with the assistance of a member of the state police's K-9 corps, was able to subdue the suspect and take him into custody.

Slawski got most of the credit for Dwayne's arrest, since it went down on his home turf—although there was still plenty of ink left over for Klaus, who was the subject of many glowing feature articles. Klaus really bogarted the pub, if you want to know the truth. Lulu was livid. I had to sit her down and explain to her how the deal this time was that we weren't getting any credit. A concept she fully understands, having been through the ghost wars with me many times before. But she was still pissed.

As for Dwayne's tape-recorded confession—portions of which the Connecticut State Police soon released to the press—that was simply a case of quick thinking on my part. Professional writers often keep a small tape player by their bed for recording the many wise, deep thoughts that occur to them in the night. I had simply managed to flick mine on without Dwayne noticing. And just in case you're wondering . . . the answer is no, I don't usually keep a tape recorder by the bed. I don't need one, being neither wise nor deep. But the press bought it. In fact, they bought the whole package. Had no reason not to. It made good copy.

Dwayne Gobble was front-page news all over the world for weeks to come, a mega-celebrity whose scarred face graced the covers of *Time, Newsweek, People, The National Enquirer, The Star* and *Rolling Stone* all in the very same week, a rare sweep previously credited only to Madonna, Jacko and the Juice. The verb "to Gobble" soon supplanted "to Bobbitt" as common vernacular for castration. Inevitably, the jokes started. They always do. They were bad jokes. They always are. Like: What did Jeffrey Dahmer say to Dwayne Gobble? Answer: "You gonna eat that?" There were many more, but one is my limit. Someone's putting out a quickie paperback joke book if you want to read the rest.

Everyone kept waiting for Dwayne to apologize for what he'd done. He wouldn't. He insisted that he'd simply done what a man, any man, is meant to do. His court-appointed attorney was leaning toward an insanity plea, figuring that a man, any man, who kills three people and isn't sorry has to be insane. Psychobabble filled the talk-radio airwaves day and night; everyone so desperate to *understand* Dwayne. But there wasn't much to understand. He was one of Thor's Lost Boys, a fatherless mutant who had no sense of right and wrong, no sense of who he was, and nothing to believe in. Nothing but a hunger deep down inside. A hunger that happened to fixate on Clethra Feingold.

Thor was right—we don't know how to make men anymore. We have way too many Lost Boys like Dwayne in our midst. And we're producing more and more of them every single day. Soon they will be old enough to inherit the world. It will all be theirs. I think about that a lot in the night. I won't be around to witness it, I hope. But Tracy will be. That's why I think about it.

Naturally, the one person who didn't swallow our version of how we nailed him was Chick Munger. The lieutenant was positive we three had conspired to bone him out of his collar. For some strange reason, he decided to blame me most of all. But for some even stranger reason, he decided to be big about it.

"Wanna have a word with you, Hoag," Munger growled after he and his crew had wrapped things up that rainy night. Dwayne was en route to the hospital, Slawski sticking with him. "Something needs saying."

I was slumped at the kitchen table in my silk target-dot dressing gown, drinking a Macallan. Very was sitting there drinking one with me. Munger kept glancing suspiciously back and forth between us, as if he thought one of us was making funny faces at him behind his back.

"Go ahead and say it, Lieutenant Munger," I said to him.

"I know I gave you a pretty hard time," he admitted. "You went and gave me a hard time right back. Far as I'm concerned, we're even. What I'm saying is . . . why don't we forget all about it, huh? Main thing is we got to the bottom of it."

I tugged at my ear. "Yes, we certainly did."

Munger stuck out his hand. "No hard feelings?"

I stared up at it. "Your hand, Lieutenant, is extremely dirty. I'd appreciate it if you'd get it out of my face."

He turned bright red. Stood there a moment, sputtering with rage, then stormed out, slamming the kitchen door behind him.

Very sipped his scotch, shaking his head. "You never change, dude."

"Why, thank you, Lieutenant."

"I didn't mean it as a compliment."

"That doesn't mean I can't take it as one."

"School me, dude. Why you always got to piss off authority figures?"

"Everyone ought to have something they truly enjoy

doing in life." I refilled our glasses. "And you, Lieutenant?"

"What about me?"

"How are your brain waves?"

"Way cool," he replied, with that blissful, creepy smile of his. "I'm digging the life out here. It's real peaceful."

"This is your idea of peaceful?"

"You may not get rid of me so fast," he confided, beaming at me from across the table. "Slawski's invited me to crash at his place for a few days. A good guy, Slawski. Major sense of humor."

I frowned. "Are we talking about the same Slawski?"

"He's one funny dude."

"*Our* Slawski?"

Very nodded. "Only reason you haven't seen that side of him is that you intimidate him."

"I do?"

"What he said."

"I can't imagine why."

"Just between you and me, dude," said Very, draining his scotch, "I can't either."

A big memorial service for Ruth Feingold was held a few days later in New York City at Lincoln Center's Avery Fisher Hall. Several hundred people showed up, among them a who's who of American feminism, past and present, as well as one vice president, two senators, the governor, the mayor, four former mayors, six congressmen and a partridge in a pear tree. Kim Basinger sent that. She was there. Barbra Streisand was there. Jane Fonda and Ted Turner were there. So were Paul Newman and Joanne Woodward, Phil Donahue and Marlo Thomas, Mike Nichols and Diane Sawyer, John-John Kennedy, Barbara Wawa, Beverly Sills, Ralph Nader and supermodel Naomi Campbell, who wore a frilly baby-doll dress, spiked heels and no stockings. I was there with Merilee. Clethra was there with Arvin, the newest and saddest of the Lost Boys. Barry was there with Marco. Both wore sunglasses. A lot of people got up and made speeches about what Ruth had meant to the women's movement over the past thirty years and to them personally. Some were funny. Some were sad. Joan Baez sang *Amazing Grace*. Everyone cried. Everyone except for Arvin, who sat there stoically throughout. He still would not cry.

Afterward, we gathered up Tracy and headed back out to the country with the family for yet another memorial service. This one for Thor, who had been cremated. We drove out to Griswold Point together and scattered his ashes in Long Island Sound.

Merilee and I held hands as we walked back along the beach toward our car. She looked uncommonly radiant that day, her cheeks flushed from the brisk sea air, her long, golden hair shimmering. Tracy bobbed happily along in her kangaroo pouch, her knit cap set jauntily on her abnormally large head. Lulu chased seagulls.

Clethra caught up with us. She was still awed and more than a little shaken by what had happened. "I'm, like, you know what I keep thinking?" she said, her voice rising over the surf. "He *killed* for me. That's just so extreme. I'm, like, it's heavy metal love, y'know? People fantasize about it, but he actually *did* it. And all because he loved me."

"How did you feel about him?" Merilee asked her.

Clethra shrugged her shoulders in her leather jacket. "I thought he was cute."

There it was. Clethra Feingold's epitaph for the entire awful episode—she thought he was cute. God, she was so young. And to think she'd unwittingly set off a killing spree that had left three people dead and more than a few permanently scarred, herself included. What a burden to have to carry around. I sure wouldn't want to.

"It's not your fault, you know," I said to her. "You didn't have anything to do with what Dwayne did."

She walked in silence a moment, her mouth scrunched tightly shut. "I know I didn't. But I also *did,* somehow. Because he did it for *me.* And that's . . . it's just such a weird thing to think about. Because, like, what if I'd just blown him off from day one? What if I hadn't let him kiss me that night in the car? What if I'd just . . . ?" She stopped short, her words choking with emotion. "Thor and Mom and Tyler might still be alive. I mean, that's just so weird, y'know?"

"Yes." I put my arm around her. "I'm afraid I do."

"I'm worried about Arvy," she said, lowering her voice. "He's like this brain-snatched humanoid zombie. He won't even, like, react."

I looked over my shoulder at him. He was plowing along listlessly in the sand, hands in his pockets, his eyes hollow and remote.

"Will you talk to him for me? Like, man to man?"

I said I'd be happy to.

She thanked me and fell back alongside him, holding her hand out to him the way one would to a stray cat. He took it, slowly and shyly, and brother and sister walked along together, hand in hand.

"You know, darling," Merilee observed, "you were right."

"What about?"

"It *was* a love story."

"That's true, it was. But I'm afraid that's the only thing I was right about."

Her eyes flickered at me. "You blame yourself a little, don't you?"

"I blame myself a lot, Merilee. If it hadn't been for me, Dwayne and Clethra would never have come in contact with each other. I'm the link. I brought the two of them together."

"Now you're talking horseradish, mister. If Clethra's not to blame, then you're not to blame either."

I left that one alone. "Well, at least Thor got his way."

"Oh?" She arched an eyebrow at me.

"He told me I needed to get out of my comfort zone," I replied. "I'd say this qualified, wouldn't you?"

We all went back to the farm after that and drank a great deal of wine and grilled a few chickens marinated in fresh rosemary, shallots and lemon juice. Barry made his potato salad, which was well above average. He was in an uncommonly bubbly mood that day. Relief, mostly. Marco's fever had broken. The bug that he'd been fighting had cleared out, and he felt fine—for now, anyway.

Marco was much better company himself as a consequence. Not nearly so combustible. He even made a special point of admiring the house. That earned him the grand tour.

"Hoagy, I'm sorry I've been behaving like such a shit," he apologized softly when I was pointing out Josiah Whitcomb's paneling in the front parlor. "I've had a lot of scary, awful things on my mind."

"Not to worry, Marco. We all have."

Our new handyman was busy upstairs in the master bedroom repairing the windows Dwayne had shattered when he made his dive for freedom. It was painstaking work, but he was a skilled and patient craftsman. We'd hired Kirk, actually, that kid Thor provoked into the fight at Slim Jim's. Kirk needed the work and he absolutely swore to me that his days of smoking illy were behind him —largely because his girlfriend, Jennifer, absolutely swore to him that she'd drop him otherwise. Fortunately, he showed zero interest in Clethra. And Clethra wasn't interested in him.

No, it was Romaine Very whom she was interested in. He and Resident Trooper Slawski, the buddies, came by and hung for a while. Clethra latched right onto the lieutenant. The two of them sat together and talked and talked. She seemed to be doing most of the talking. He seemed to be ill at ease. Shy, even. After a while Clethra convinced him to take a walk in the woods with her. They were gone a long time.

Slawski was out of uniform for the first time since I'd met him. The trooper looked much younger in jeans and a sweatshirt, though still most imposing. I brought a beer to him out in the pasture, where he was tossing sticks for Klaus, who was prancing and frolicking like an ebullient pup. Quite some personality change. Lulu watched him from between my legs, most suspicious of this new development.

"What's gotten into your partner, Trooper?" I wondered, as Klaus arfed at him playfully. "A testosterone rush from all of that pub?"

"Nothing like that," Slawski replied gruffly. "He's off duty, that's all. Likes to unwind just like any other officer."

Slawski wound up and fired a stick high and deep across the pasture. He threw it so far I could barely see it come down. But Klaus was already there waiting for it when it did. Grabbed it in his mouth and came streaking back with it, dropping it at Slawski's enormous feet.

"He's very good," I observed.

Slawski shot me a look.

"I'm serious, Trooper. He really showed me something that night he took down Dwayne. Lulu couldn't have done that."

"Well, he's a professional," Slawski said modestly.

"Let that be a lesson to you," I said to Lulu.

She snuffled at Klaus most beguilingly and offered him

various parts of her anatomy to sniff. He obliged, what with being off duty and, like the trooper said, raring to unwind just like any other officer. I don't know what will happen between them. I can't, somehow, see her getting mixed up with a cop. Especially a rookie. But stranger things have happened. And will continue to happen. This much I am sure of.

Slawski drank his beer down thirstily and let out a sigh of pure pleasure. He examined the label carefully for future reference. It was a Double Diamond.

"How about another one?"

"I'm down to that," he agreed.

We started back toward the house together, leaving our partners to their . . . whatever.

"Very tells me you've got quite some sense of humor."

Slawski shrugged. "You may not think so, being more inclined toward the art of witty repartee."

"You must have me confused with someone else."

"Myself, I tend toward the humor of deconstruction. My own idols are Beckett and Ionesco and possibly Mr. Joe Orton." He cleared his throat nervously. "Still, if you wouldn't mind, I'd like to show you some of my material sometime."

"Your material?"

"I write plays in my spare time," he said, smoothing his high-top fade with his hand. "Just my own way of kicking it, recreationally speaking. I've authored three full-length plays and several one-acts. But I haven't . . . what I mean is, I've never shown them to anyone. And I could use some intelligent feedback."

"If that's the case, then why show them to me?"

"See? That's what I'm talkin' about," he said, flashing a rare smile at me. I guess Klaus wasn't the only one who loosened up off duty.

"I'd be happy to look at your stuff, Trooper," I assured

him. "But Merilee's the one you should really talk to." The lady in question was sitting on a blanket under an apple tree with Marco, the two of them busy watching Tracy try to sit up.

"Get outta here, man!" Slawski exclaimed, awestruck. "Think *she'd* actually read my material?"

"Of course she would. She's looking for a play right now, as it happens. And, believe me, if you show any promise at all you may save her from a fate worse than death." I fetched him a Double Diamond out of the cooler I'd brought out. "Although I'd sure hate to think we might lose you to the Great White Way."

"Not in this particular lifetime," he shot back, with a huge guffaw. "A word of advice, by the way."

"What's that, Trooper?"

He opened his beer and took a gulp. "Don't ever get yourself mixed up in another major crime around these here parts."

"Not that I intend to, but why not?"

"Munger." He said it like it was a dirty word.

"What about him?"

"He wants to bury you."

I patted Slawski on his broad back. "Trooper, I can't tell you how glad I am to hear that."

Arvin was sitting off by himself down near the water, wringing his hands and gazing mournfully out at nowhere.

I sat and gazed out at it with him. "You okay, pal?" I asked, after a time.

"Uh-huh."

"Do you remember when I told you about how it was okay to cry?"

"Uh-huh."

"Well, it's also okay when someone asks you if you're okay to say you're not okay," I said. "Okay?"

He hung his head sullenly. "Okay."

"See, it's bad to hold everything in. You have to vent from time to time. Otherwise you'll explode."

"You mean like Dwayne?" he asked. His voice was husky.

"I mean like Dwayne."

"It's just that . . ." He glanced up at me, then back down at his hands. "None of it . . ."

"None of it what, Arvin?"

"W-What happened," he stammered. "None of it makes any sense. I mean, it's not *fair!*"

"I know it's not," I conceded. "Life's supposed to be. That's what they tell us when we're kids—that it really and truly is. But it really and truly isn't, Arvin, and I'm not going to shit you, because you're not a kid anymore. I'm sorry you had to find it out. It's the hardest lesson there is in life. And there's no turning back once you learn it. All I can tell you is I've been a lot better off since I've accepted that everything isn't going to be all right. It makes me appreciate my life during those rare, blessed moments when it somehow is." I unhooked Thor's clunky bracelet from my wrist and held it out to him. "This was your dad's. It was mine for a while. Now it's yours."

He stared at it blankly. "Why?"

"It's a guy thing."

I helped him on with it. The heavy bracelet hung loose from his skinny wrist. He stared at it a moment. Then suddenly his face got all scrunchy and his eyes filled up and just like that he let go. Wrenching sobs that came from deep down inside, tears that streamed down his pimply cheeks by the gallon. He cried for his father. He cried for his mother. He cried for himself and the miserable mess his life had become. He cried and he cried. It all came out. At long last, it came out.

Later, after we had eaten, we gathered for an extended family council meeting, al fresco. Clethra did most of the talking early on, seated there cross-legged on a blanket next to her brother.

"I have, like, a major thing to tell everyone," she announced, speaking with newfound resolve. "I've decided I'm not gonna do that stupid book, okay? Like, I don't wanna write it. I don't wanna make speeches. I don't wanna go on talk shows. That's just not me, okay? I mean, I've been as famous as anyone could ever be. And I don't wanna be famous anymore. I wanna live more like you do, Hoagy."

"Careful. You may get what you wish for."

"I mean it," she said vehemently.

"I know you do."

"Can it be done?" she asked me. "Can I tell them I've changed my mind?"

"All it takes is one fax." Especially since they still hadn't paid her so much as a dime. "Of course, they'll be terribly disappointed."

"How about you? Will you be disappointed?"

"I'll live," I told her. What I didn't tell her was that I had already been approached about helping Dwayne tell *his* story—three publishers were still bidding hard for it. Seven figure advance, easy. I had said no because of the obvious conflict. Now I could say yes. I could if I wanted to, that is. But I didn't. "What will you do instead?" I asked her.

"Apply to Barnard for late enrollment," she answered. "I've only missed a few weeks of classes, and I've got, like, a pretty good excuse. I'll try to get into a dorm. If I can't, Barry said I can crash at their place until space opens up."

"We've room to spare," Barry added cheerily. "And I am, after all, her father."

I found myself gazing at Arvin, the odd boy out. Because Barry was not, after all, his father. Thor's son was staring down at the blanket, his Adam's apple jumping.

Barry followed my gaze. "You're part of our family, too, Arvy," he added quickly. "I want you to know that. Marco and I very much want you with us. As long as we have a home, you have a home. Count on that. Now in a couple of years . . ." Briefly, his features darkened, his eyes avoiding mine. ". . . when Clethra turns twenty-one, she'll be named your legal guardian. Until that time, I would be honored to serve in that capacity."

Arvin nodded glumly and mouthed the word "thanks." Although no sound came out.

"And if you ever need a place to hide out, Arvin," Merilee spoke up, "you're always welcome here. For as long as you like."

He brightened. Not much, but a little. "Really?"

"Really," Merilee assured him. "You, too, Clethra. Anytime you feel like coming. You don't even have to call us. Just show up."

"Although," I pointed out, "we do charge seventy-five dollars a night per person. And food is extra."

Arvin snickered. Possibly there was hope for him.

"While we're on the subject of money," Barry went on, "both of you kids will have some of your own when the estates are settled. Until then, I'll be able to swing your tuitions at Barnard and Dalton soon as I sell the house out here. I can't . . ." He faltered, growing emotional. "I can't live in it anymore. Not after what happened there to Ruthie. Have to sell. And there's my Sprite as well, which should fetch enough quick cash to tide us over. Still interested, Hoagy?"

"I am. And in Thor's motorcycle, too."

"You will *not* get a motorcycle, mister," Merilee said crisply.

"I'll get a helmet."

"I don't care. I will not spend my days and nights wondering if you're smeared across the pavement somewhere."

I grinned at her. "We'll talk," I said.

"We most certainly will *not* talk."

Lulu let out a moan of consternation. She hates it when we disagree. Plus she was holding out for one with a sidecar for her.

"We'll get through this," Barry said, as much to himself as to the kids. "We'll be fine. Isn't that right, Hoagy? Won't we be fine?"

"Yes, Barry. We will all be fine."

He was sitting out by the first tee in his wheelchair with a blanket thrown over his legs. I couldn't tell if he was watching the players out on the course of if he could even tell there were players out on the course. He was just sitting there, the breeze rippling his thin white hair. His nurse sat next to him on a bench.

"Mother is attending a lecture on primroses in the main hall," she informed me with abundant good cheer. "Shall we head back inside? It's getting rather chilly."

"I'll take over from here," I growled, seizing the wheelchair from her.

She flared her nostrils at me and went marching off toward the main hall. I don't predict she and I will be close.

I sat. He didn't seem to notice me there. "Brought you a present, Father," I said, laying it in his lap. "My way of saying thanks."

After a long, long while he glanced down at it. It was a dark chocolate pecan turtle from the Chocolate Shell in Old Lyme. His favorite candy in the world. He gazed at it fondly and reached for it, or tried, but his hand just sort of flopped hopelessly around in his lap before it lay still again. A pained expression creased his long, narrow face.

"Here, let me." I broke off a piece and fed it to him.

He let it sit there in his mouth for a moment so the

caramel would melt and he could chew it. "For w-what, Bucky?" he wondered, after he'd swallowed it. "Thanks . . . f-for what?"

"You cracked the case. Helped me figure out who killed my friend. You're still a pretty shrewd article, you know."

" . . . Bucky?"

"Yes, Father?"

"I was n-never a shrewd article. I was . . . I-I was conventional."

"I wish you wouldn't talk about yourself in the past tense," I said crossly. "Besides, there's nothing wrong with being conventional."

"It's . . . everything you despise. You t-told me that once."

"That doesn't make it wrong. Just means it's not for me."

He narrowed his blue eyes at me. I had to keep reminding myself he couldn't see well out of them. "You've . . . softened some, haven't y-you?"

"No chance. Not me." I fed him some more of his turtle. "Have you decided whether or not to roll over that CD?"

He gaped at me, bewildered. "Which . . . CD?"

"The one you were trying to decide whether or not to roll over."

"Bunch of . . . gibberish," he grumbled. "Man h-has to know Latin to—"

"I can handle it for you, if you'd like. I'll sit down with Gene next time I'm in town, go over your whole portfolio with him. What do you say?"

He chewed on his turtle, saying nothing.

"Father?" I pressed.

"You've . . . got y-your own life and your . . . own worries."

"I've got no worries. At least none that matter to me as much as you and Mother do."

"I c-can manage," he insisted stubbornly. "I'll . . . take care of it."

"No, you can't," I insisted, giving him stubborn right back. That's one of the things I'm best at. "I'll do it. And I don't want any goddamned argument from you, either. I want to do this for you. You will let me do this for you. Is that understood?"

He made a face, as if the matter were way too unimportant to merit further discussion. He was silent after that, his breathing weak and unsteady, the sound of it much like the sound of someone crumpling very dry tissue paper.

The breeze picked up to a gust and blew his blanket away from his legs. I straightened it for him and asked him if he was getting too cold, but he didn't answer. He'd fallen asleep. I pushed him back to their apartment, his head lolling slightly over to one side. It was very warm in there and reeked of that same, sickly-sweet smell he reeked of. Mother was still off at her garden club lecture.

I positioned him in front of the TV set and sat on the sofa. "Father?"

He stirred slightly, looking around. He didn't seem to know where he was.

"Father, do you remember a long time ago when you used to come downstairs in the middle of the night for a glass of milk?"

He didn't respond.

"Do you, Father?"

He stared at me a long time before he spoke. "Where's . . . your p-pal Stink, Bucky?" he said, grinning at me with his horsy teeth. "He still . . . out there t-trying to tie those f-firecrackers to . . . old man MacGregor's cat?"

I sighed inwardly. "Yes, Father. Stink's still out there."

"Well, tell him to c-come on in. Mother will . . . m-make him some g-good hot cocoa. Getting awful c-cold out. Feels like . . . winter."

"You're absolutely right, Father. It's beginning to feel a lot like winter."

It was just past four in the morning when Tracy wanted to be changed. Merilee started to stir. I told her to go back to sleep and got up and took care of it myself. I was awake anyway.

Afterward, I carried Tracy downstairs and threw a log on the coals in the front parlor fireplace. Then I poured myself a Macallan and sat there on the sofa with Tracy in my lap and Lulu on my feet. She was giving me that look again—Tracy, I mean—the one where she was waiting for me to explain myself to her. I didn't know how to. But for the very first time I felt strongly that I wanted to try. So I did something that night I had never done with her before.

I softly closed the door to the hallway and opened the corner cupboard, the one we hid the television in. One of the local stations in New London had the genius to schedule *The Pre-Dawn Moronathon* every morning from four until six—two solid hours of the Stooges. If Tracy wanted to understand me, I could think of no better or healthier way to start her out than this way.

We came in on the one where they're locked in a haunted house, which I realize isn't too specific since they were almost always locked in a haunted house. I took her hand and pointed so she'd know which one was Larry, which was Moe and which was Curly. She took it from there all by herself. And believe me, it didn't take her long. Not with this man's blood coursing through her veins. She was giggling in less than a minute. Squealing with delight in just over two.

God, I was proud.

And pumped beyond belief. Because here, at last, was something we could share, just we two. And I do mean we *two*. Merilee would not approve. In fact, she'd kill me if she ever found out I was polluting Tracy's brain this way. But, hey, she could raise Tracy her way, I'd raise her mine. What a feast lay in wait for her—Daffy Duck, the Roadrunner, Laurel and Hardy . . .

Mitchum I'd save for when she was in the Terrible Twos.

My daughter and I watched a solid hour of the Stooges together, Lulu curled up on my feet with her tail thumping. Not only because she's a big fan herself but because she, too, had started to figure out just how much fun it might be having Tracy around. I guess I had to realize it myself before she could. We have tremendous control over those around us, whether we know it or not, whether we want it or not. That's one thing I learned from this entire experience with Thor.

We sat there together in the pre-dawn darkness, Tracy engrossed in Larry, Moe and Curly, me still wondering about Thor. Why he'd run off with Clethra. Why he'd chosen to show up at my door that night. Thorvin Alston Gibbs wasn't perfect. But he was my friend. In life, he had given me the courage to believe in myself. In death, he had given me something even more precious.

In the morning I wrote.

Sometimes as I sleep I hear a creak on the stairs. For a moment I think it is my father on his way down to the kitchen for a glass of milk in the night, and that I am in my own room, snug in my narrow bed. Briefly, this comforts me. But then I awaken, and realize that it is my own house that is creaking, from the wind, and that I am in the master bedroom. She sleeps next to me, secure in the belief that I know what I'm doing. I don't know what I'm doing.

He never did either. But he was exceptionally good at convincing others that he did—so that they might sleep soundly in the night. This was, perhaps, the one thing he was best at in life. This was, for him and others like him in the middle of the American century, what it meant to be a man.

Quietly, I slip out of bed and go downstairs and pour myself a glass of milk. I check to see that the doors are locked, that the furnace runs smoothly, that the grounds outside my kitchen window are secure in the moonlight. I cherish these moments alone in the night, when my family sleeps. It is my favorite time. It is my favorite thing.

It's a guy thing.